KYRIE WANG

THE THIEF'S
KEEPER

AN ENEMY'S KEEPER PREQUEL

The Thief's Keeper (An Enemy's Keeper Prequel)

Copyright © 2024 by Kyrie Wang

All rights reserved. No part of this publication may be reproduced, distributed, or transmitted without the prior written permission of the author, except in the case of brief quotations embodied in critical reviews. Please do not encourage or participate in piracy of copyrighted material. Thank you for respecting the hard work of this author.

For permission requests, write to the author, addressed "Permissions Request," at author@kyriewang.com

ISBN: 978-1-7389644-4-4 (Paperback)
ISBN: 978-1-7389644-3-7 (Electronic Book)

Any references to historical events, real people, or real places are used fictitiously. Names, characters, and places are products of the author's imagination.

Editor: Allison D. Reid

Cover design: GetCovers.com

Cover art: Natalia Sorokina and Sen Li
Interior artwork: Kyrie Wang and Sen Li
Map: Kyrie Wang and Sen Li

Silver Dreams Publishing

For the author's artwork, music, and more, please visit KyrieWang.com

A Note to My Readers

The Thief's Keeper (An Enemy's Keeper Prequel) is a **no-magic historical fantasy** that takes place in a world that's almost 11th-century Europe, but not quite.

I've woven in elements from other eras, including:

- Celtic tribes thriving beyond their historical timeframe

- Advanced shipbuilding (hulled vessels and hammocks, ahead of their time)

- An effective scurvy treatment unknown to medieval Europe.

This prequel lays the groundwork for a saga where history takes a different turn. In later books, the last Vikings will discover gunpowder and grenades. This is an intentional departure from recorded history.

Historical purists may find these liberties challenging, but readers seeking heart-pounding adventure, wholesome romance, and boldly reimagined worlds will find much to love. Welcome to the journey!

Receive a free ebook of ***The Thief's Keeper*** *(An Enemy's Keeper Prequel)* when you subscribe to my newsletter!
KyrieWang.com/EK

****

Bonus: A free medieval fantasy coloring book and a graphic novel, The First Dance (An Illustrated Epilogue of The Thief's Keeper) Once a month, I send a newsletter with book giveaways, raffle prizes, new character art, historical tidbits, and more!

Dedication

In memory of John Zwaagstra
Friend, father, and musician
Most of all, he loved and was loved in return.

"Kindness is a language the dumb can speak and the deaf can hear and understand."

—— Christian Nestell Bovee

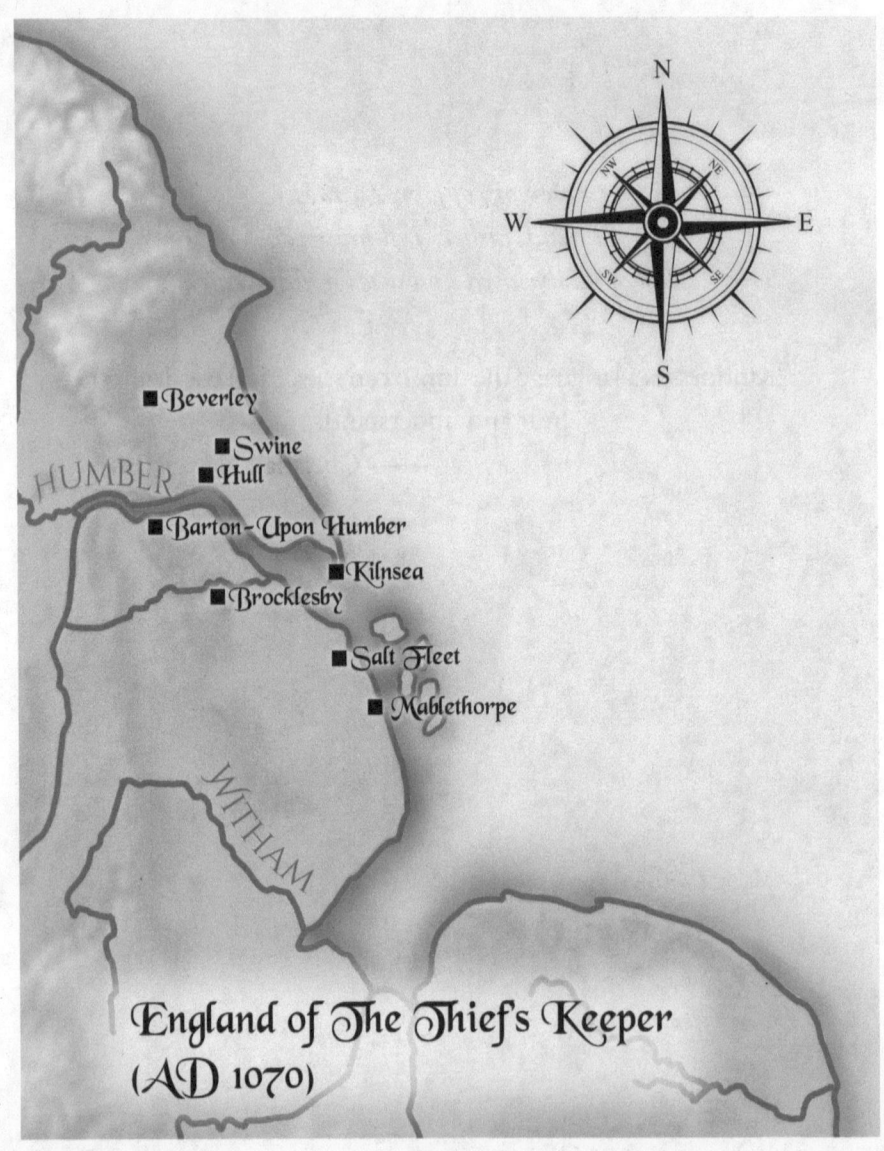

Chapter 1

AD 1070, England
 Four years after the Norman Conquest

Aelfric

Master Cuthbert Staddon proved not to be dead as Aelfric had hoped. The balding merchant threw open the church doors, letting in a blast of cold air. It had only been two weeks since Aelfric and the other thralls had escaped.

"Aelfric!"

Aelfric gulped. He had been playing his recorder inside to collect alms, but the show was over. Swinging his knapsack over his shoulder, he bolted for the church's back door as Cuthbert shoved through the sanctuary seekers. The shadows and lights from the parchment windows flickered over Aelfric like a hundred eyes. He pushed open the rear door and leaped into the sunlight of Mablethorpe's port.

Peasants and carts milled through the cobblestone streets. Aelfric gritted his teeth and darted in between them.

Why was he still thinking of the man who used to beat his grandmother as "master?" From now on, Cuthbert was only Cuthbert.

The Englishman hadn't returned to his carpentry workshop for three months. All his thralls had assumed the Norman army had killed him while crushing an English revolt, but so much for those hopes. Cuthbert Staddon was back to hunt down the escapees.

"Stop that boy!" Cuthbert shouted behind Aelfric. "He's a runaway!"

Aelfric wanted to slap himself. He shouldn't have embellished his music with trills even those he hated would recognize. Cuthbert couldn't see well, but he must've heard the lively music from the docks.

The man continued to yell on the open streets. No one had grabbed Aelfric—yet. He turned left at a pungent spice booth, his worn leather shoes sliding down the muddy slope. Pebbles jammed into the hole in his right sole until he hit the slimy wooden planks of the docks.

His toes curled against the irritating pebbles as he hobbled past fishing boats and ferries, all moored to the pier. These vessels were too barren to hide on, but the square-sailed cogs further ahead were cluttered enough for him to sneak on board. Aelfric kicked the pebbles out of his shoe and kept running.

He'd never reach the first cog.

Cuthbert's oldest son, Edgar Staddon, emerged from a ferryboat. His wavy hair blew about his shoulders as he squinted in the blinding sunlight.

"Grab that boy!" Cuthbert hollered. "He's the thrall!"

Edgar's eyes widened with recognition, and Aelfric yelped. He swerved right and dodged Edgar's burly arms just in time.

Stomping over the wooden dock, Aelfric returned to the bustling dirt road parallel to the waterfront.

The two Staddons continued to shout for his capture. Aelfric pulled up the large hood of his cloak to hide more of his face. As he pushed through the streets, merchants grunted and milkmaids spilled their milk. Chickens screeched and flapped their wings on either side of his pounding feet. Thankfully, no one had joined the Staddons in their wild pursuit, at least not yet.

All the escapees had stolen tools or money from Cuthbert's workshop as they'd fled, but Aelfric had focused on running and hadn't swiped anything. Now, he regretted it. For all the trouble he was going through, he should've at least gotten rich!

His calves burning, Aelfric dashed toward a flock of sheep roaming down an adjacent street. He wove between the ambling animals, his elbows bumping into wool on either side. Bleating erupted in his ears. The disturbed beasts rammed into each other to avoid him. At the rear of the flock, the shepherd waved his staff.

"You, boy! Get out!"

But joining a sheep stampede was a great way to get around.

Aelfric shoved toward the front, following the lambs who darted between the larger sheep. He coughed from the dust kicked up by a hundred hooves as they squeezed between taverns and workshops. A glance behind confirmed neither Cuthbert nor his son had the agility to follow. The flock trotted into a section of the town dotted with blackened homes and collapsed straw roofs. Charred wood and clay shards littered the ground, and the stench of rotten waste lingered in the air.

Aelfric darted around the sharp debris as he followed the sheep into the wasteland. The memory of Cuthbert's workshop burning in Hull flashed in his mind, and a chill rattled him back to the present.

One building remained standing up ahead by the main road—a smokehouse built of stone. A ragged defect in its conical roof revealed a dark interior with no joints of meat suspended for smoking. Abandoned? The door was shut, but there was a hole along the wall's lower edge, like a vigilant eye watching the burned buildings. Someone had removed a stone from that area.

Aelfric's ears swelled from the loud bleating. The hole along the building's foundation enticed him with its darkness and silence. Further ahead on a hill rose the marketplace and its display of colorful tapestries. Aelfric prayed the Staddons would storm into that crowded area and never find him.

The flock began to scatter without buildings on either side to guide them. A sea of sheep divided on either side of the smokehouse, and Aelfric dashed for the opening in the wall.

Falling to his hands and knees, he poked his head through the hole rimmed by stone and dirt. The dank scent of earth filled his nostrils, and the bleating and screaming outside grew muffled.

Space was tight. His fingernails filled with dirt as he clawed and wriggled forward. For once, he was glad to be small for a fourteen-year-old boy. His shoulders squeezed out of the opening, and the rest of him slid through like a fish.

Never mind that the jagged edge of mortar and stone had scraped the length of his back. Aelfric lay on his belly, his chest heaving with triumph. Neither Cuthbert nor his son could squeeze through that. His eyes watered from the dirt cloud of the stampede outside, and he wiped them as he sat up. Now, he had to secure the smokehouse's door if it wasn't already locked.

But as his eyes refocused in the dimness, he froze. A pair of scissors floated not far from his head. Its sharp end pointed at his face.

He wasn't alone. It took all of his self-control not to scream.

But the scissor bearer was a youngster about his age, not some brute ready to bash in his head. Aelfric studied her ragged, slender frame and took a steadying breath. He could handle a girl. She stood glaring at him, but the tremor in her hand gave away her fear.

Aelfric eyed her scissors and put up his hands. "Don't hurt me. I have no weapons. Please, just let me stay a while."

He wasn't about to admit he possessed an eating knife.

Her eyes seemed to dart to the side of his neck, and Aelfric stiffened. The trip through the hole had flung the hood off his head, exposing the beefy whip's lash Cuthbert had left running from his earlobe to his shoulder blade. Who would be whipped like that, other than a thrall or criminal? Aelfric slapped his hand over the telltale mark, but it was too late.

The girl narrowed her eyes. "Who are you?"

The answer came soon enough.

"Aelfric, you flea-bitten churl!" Cuthbert thundered from outside. "I'm going to smack you with a hot iron!"

The menacing merchant must've caught up with his son, Edgar. Aelfric had seen other runaways get pinned down and branded on their torsos as punishment. It was another reason he had to avoid capture at all costs. He stared at the girl pleadingly and licked his lips, keeping his hands up.

"I'll pay you a lot if you keep me a secret," he stammered.

He dared to scoot backward and distance himself from her scissors. His back soon slid up the frigid stone wall, as the rounded smokehouse was

CHAPTER 1

only wide enough for two men to lie end-to-end. Maybe it was because his eyes were watering, but her scowl softened. Her weapon, however, remained raised. Outside, the sheep's bleating rose to a crescendo and died down as Aelfric's heart drummed a double rhythm.

Had the Staddons missed his hiding spot after all?

Even if they had passed, this girl could burst outside and declare his presence. Cuthbert would likely pay her handsomely in return. Could Aelfric tackle her if she ran for the door? He had always avoided picking fights with the other thralls, and now he might have to hurt a girl. Chills rained down his chest.

To his amazement, what sounded like a toddler babbled behind the girl. The girl flinched, the tattered hem of her gown brushing over her shoes. She straightened again and adjusted the grip on her scissors.

"Hide behind those." She pointed at two barrels standing against the wall to her left. Both barrels had a stack of gowns on top in various stages of being cut to pieces.

Aelfric scrambled to his feet and side-stepped toward the barrels, always facing the girl and raising his hands. She watched him with a blank expression, her face dim in the meager light coming through the hole above them. As he circled partway around her, the sight of a child lying on a small hay mattress came into view. Blankets wrapped around his little body, and tendrils of wavy blond hair peeked from beneath his sackcloth hat. He sat up and rubbed his eyes. Unlike the scrawny girl, this child's cheeks were ruddy and full.

What were the two of them doing in an abandoned smokehouse? Not that it was time to ask. Aelfric pressed his lips together and scurried into the dark space between the barrels and the stone walls.

He had just sat and hugged his knees when someone pounded on the door. Aelfric stiffened all over.

His life was at the mercy of a stranger. Crawling into the smokehouse had been a mistake, but he couldn't have known someone was inside. He stared at the hole he had just crawled through. If he dared to crawl back out, Cuthbert and Edgar might hear his movements and yank him out themselves.

From the slit between the two barrels, he watched the girl sit by the toddler and hold a corner of a blanket to the child's mouth. The toddler chewed silently on the cloth.

The banging on the door grew louder. Aelfric's head gave a dizzying spin, and he wiped his sweaty hands on his thighs. Whoever the girl was, she kept him in her peripheral view and embraced the younger child in her lap. Her face was blank.

"Father," Edgar panted from outside. "The tanner said he saw a boy, black hair like Aelfric, running that way."

"Howling fiends," Cuthbert grumbled. "I'll find him if it's the last thing I do. That maggot stole all my tools!"

The other thralls in Hull had stolen Cuthbert's tools, not him. Aelfric curled his upper lip. Those two dozen men had also beaten up merchants, thrown one down a well, and sailed away on a stolen cog ship. Aelfric had been too horrified to participate in the violence, and the others had departed for Scotland without him. Aelfric had been left behind to bear the blame for their theft.

Outside, Cuthbert and Edgar muttered some more before their footsteps departed.

Aelfric sighed and lowered his forehead to his bent knees. That had been close. But with Cuthbert Staddon still alive, he would need to leave England by ship as soon as possible. It was too bad, because he had made a handsome profit as a piper. In three weeks, he had earned enough to sail for Scotland but had stayed in Mablethorpe to earn more during Easter.

He could no longer stay. The ships leaving for Scotland sailed again tomorrow, Monday. Could he avoid detection until then?

Aelfric rubbed his eyes. Everything outside had fallen silent.

He crawled from behind the barrels, shivering with cold sweat, and stared at the girl. She didn't wear a head covering like other peasant women, and her messy brown hair fell to her shoulders. Aelfric had never seen anyone scragglier looking. His stomach twisted at the thought of being trapped with her for hours.

She turned to face him fully.

"You're a runaway?" She smiled.

As if this was something to ask casually. Aelfric's lips twitched. "I'm not a runaway. I'm...that man has a grudge against me."

"Oh, I see." She raised an eyebrow and extended an upturned hand. "Payment for keeping you a secret?"

Aelfric hung his head, still panting. He reached into a belt pouch and fingered the quarter pennies inside. Most had come from hours of playing at the harbor and charming the merchants as they'd returned from sea. Or rather, charming their wives.

He needed thirty pennies for a fare to Scotland, and he had counted thirty-three that morning. Chewing on his lip, Aelfric eyed the starved girl with sunken eyes and decided to be generous. He carefully withdrew the only whole penny he had—a full day's worth of wages for youngsters their size.

Her face lit up. She snatched the coin from his hand. The toddler in her arms squealed and tried to grab the shiny object, but she dodged him and pocketed the penny.

"Another penny if you want to stay here." She grinned.

Aelfric's eyes rounded. He crossed his arms and widened his stance. "I don't have much. And I don't want to stay."

But could he safely leave the smokehouse right now? The whole harbor had heard their beloved piper was a runway thrall, and he'd have to hide in broad daylight. Aelfric's breath hitched. His eyes fell on the girl's cut-up gowns piled over the two barrels.

Inspiration struck.

"I...uh...want to buy a headscarf and a dress," he said. "Got any that fit me?"

She giggled, the sound annoyingly cheerful. "What are you going to do? Wear a dress?"

"Shhh! Just give me the clothes."

He reached into his belt pocket again, intending to pick out two quarter pennies, but his jittery fingers hooked onto the pouch and inverted it as he withdrew. Out came a downpour of quarter and half pennies, tinkling softly as they fell like shiny raindrops.

Aelfric gasped. So did the girl. He had just displayed a month's worth of wages, all painstakingly saved for the ship's fare, a pair of new shoes, and any emergency needs. So much for saying he didn't have much.

With fire dancing on his scalp, Aelfric fell to his knees and rasped the coins back into his hands. He glared at the girl in case she should try to swipe a few, but she only sat with the toddler on her lap and a bewildered stare on her face.

Finally, she picked up a mitten from a pile by the toddler's mattress. Pulling at the seams, she displayed her neat stitches. Her voice changed to one of pleading.

"Is your family looking for anyone to mend clothing? I work quickly and—"

"I have no family."

Aelfric tossed the last of his money into his belt pouch as a lump settled in his throat. Cuthbert had sold his father, mother, and sister to another merchant in Durham two years ago. He never saw them again.

"What happened to them?" she asked.

"They're dead."

Normans had ransacked Durham last winter, killing his loved ones. Had his family been free and wealthy, they would've escaped the deadly rebellion by ship and survived. Aelfric wanted to earn the freedom and prosperity they'd never had or die trying.

The girl lowered her eyes. She said something apologetic that Aelfric didn't register.

"I want to buy a gown and headscarf," he repeated, his voice foggy. He turned to flip through the girl's piles of clothing.

Pulling out several dresses, he threw them open to assess their lengths. The soft wool unrolled over his feet. Their yellow and pink hems, embroidered with roses, were quite a pretty sight. But what was this? All the gowns had squares or rectangles cut out of them. Perfectly fine clothing, destroyed.

He glowered at the girl. "Why are you carving these up?"

She blinked several times before sliding the toddler off her lap. Standing, she approached him and withdrew one gown at the bottom of one heap.

CHAPTER 1

"You should fit in this one. But this is fine wool, high quality." She stroked the blue cloth, her eyes gleaming in the tangential light. "And if you want hair covering to complete the outfit, I'll charge you another penny."

She hadn't answered his question, and paying another penny was out of the question. Aelfric gritted his teeth at the way she cocked her head.

"Well?" she asked. "Do you want it or not?"

He needed a dress. Disguising himself as a girl was a better solution than hiding in this smokehouse. After all, he had to exit at some point if he was to board a ship.

The toddler sitting on the ground smiled at him, and Aelfric swallowed his frustration.

"Let me try on the gown first," he grumbled.

Chapter 2

Aelfric

AELFRIC SHED HIS CLOAK and unclasped his belt. He pulled off his woolen tunic and his linen undershirt, whose collars were too high and would show above the dress's neckline. When he reached for the garment in her hands, the way she seemed to stare at his torso made him tense. He narrowed his eyes and turned aside.

Had she never seen a boy get changed before?

Her brows tightened with sympathy, and Aelfric remembered how his ribs were knobbly from past fractures. Like his father, he had shirked some of Cuthbert's rules and had snuck off for one extra privy break per day until he was caught. Cuthbert had thrown him down and kicked him repeatedly.

This had happened last year, and Aelfric didn't think about it anymore. He sighed and threw the gown over his head. The fabric was scratchy, and the hem fell far enough to cover his toes. It was too long, but he'd have to manage.

The girl offered him a beige headscarf. "This was mine, but you can buy it."

Aelfric pinched the scarf and brought it to his nose. It smelled like thyme, but should he wear something that had touched her hair?

He was still thinking when the girl continued, "I also lost my family in the burning north of York. My father tried to escape with my brothers and me, but it was very cold, and everything had burned down. There was no food left."

"Da." The toddler on the ground smiled.

It wasn't the first time Aelfric had heard a story like hers. Famine would explain why she looked like a skeleton with skin slapped back on, but he wasn't here to commiserate. Aelfric finally unfurled the headscarf over his hair. He needed to leave before she figured out he was a runaway.

The fear of being caught squeezed his chest. Cuthbert would surely whip him and brand him on the face. Aelfric tried to drape the headscarf the way he had seen the women do, but he wound it too tightly around his throat. Soon, he was wheezing.

The girl snickered. She reached for the offending cloth and unraveled it. With swift waves of her arm, she draped it back over his head and shoulders and arranged it with a few tugs.

"You look convincing, but don't talk. You've got a boy's voice, obviously." She stood back and held out her hand. "Another penny, please."

His shoulders rigid, Aelfric lowered himself to retrieve two half pennies from his belt pouch.

"My name is Aliwyn, by the way," she said. "And this wee'un is Godwin."

What a pompous name for a tiny tot. And what was the boy doing here, with the likes of her? They didn't look like siblings.

Aelfric avoided looking at Aliwyn as he stood. Before he tossed the coins into her cupped hand, he noticed red streaks beneath her cracked fingernails. It looked like she was bleeding, but who bleeds in straight lines underneath their nails? As he searched, red pinpricks appeared under her eyes and over her collarbones. The longer he stared, the more red dots he found.

He gulped. Invisible insects began crawling down his back. Maybe she was ill and being isolated in this smokehouse, and he had just touched her.

"I'm leaving." He stepped back but held her gaze. "You can forget you saw me. Please."

Her pale blue eyes followed his every move. "Shouldn't you hide here for a while? Listen...that man is asking others to look for you."

Aelfric hesitated, and Cuthbert's voice from outside rose to the forefront of his attention. The man seemed to be describing Aelfric to onlookers—black hair, brown tunic, tall to here, whip mark on his neck...

Aelfric clenched his fists. He could no longer play music in Mablethorpe, an activity he loved infinitely more than chopping wood in the snow or hammering together furniture for rich people. Now that he was out of work, he had to keep every penny.

"I'm not paying you to stay," he muttered. "So I'm leaving."

He could be captured at any moment if he didn't flee the town...in a dress. Panic flared again. Aelfric picked up his belt and looped it around his waist, always wary of how Aliwyn stared. He plucked his recorder from a belt pouch and stroked the smooth wood with a quivering thumb.

His father had carved the recorder himself. Aelfric carried it protruding from his drawstring pouch, but now he had to hide it. Grimacing, he shoved it to the bottom of another satchel. His fingers plunged into the iridescent clamshells his father had gifted him when he'd turned eight.

Aelfric's eyes stung. He bunched his discarded tunic and undershirt into a ball and stuffed it into his knapsack. Aliwyn approached him with a bouncing toddler in her arms.

"So you were the musician playing outside?" she asked. "Your hood always hid your face, but I've wanted to meet you. You're so talented."

And so stupid. Aelfric tied his cloak back over his shoulders and picked up his knapsack. He wiped his eyes and shuffled for the door, but two steps later, his toes caught on the dress's hem, and he went flying.

Yelping, he smacked face down onto the ground. The impact sent a shock from his ribs around to his spine.

Aliwyn made a hissing sound through her teeth. "Be careful. Hold up the gown when you walk."

Aelfric groaned as he sat up. He wiped dirt and straw from his cheeks.

"Da." Godwin kicked playfully against Aliwyn's waist.

This was the strangest day Aelfric remembered living. His face hot enough to grill a fish, he stood and swung his knapsack over his shoulder. He hiked up the disastrous gown and stepped toward the door.

"Goodbye."

CHAPTER 2

The door featured a fancy lock that could be secured from outside and inside, but guilt wormed into his heart when he clutched the frigid metal latch.

This girl needed help. Perhaps the priest had not treated her yet, especially if the rash was new and spreading in areas she couldn't easily see. Like her own neck. Did she know how horrible she looked?

Aelfric halted and looked behind him. Aliwyn had set Godwin down, and the child tottered around as she gathered the gowns he had flung on the ground. Folding them on her knee, she stood again to lay her gowns on a barrel. Their sullen gazes met. Aelfric blinked first.

"Uh…you…have you sought treatment—"

Before he could finish, what sounded like a key clicked into the door's lock from the outside. Aelfric jolted and almost dove onto the ground.

The door swung open with an earsplitting creak.

"You heard yelling in here, you say?" said a man.

All thanks to Aelfric tripping over his clothes. He didn't wait to see who it was. Grabbing a fistful of his dress, he darted for the hole in the stone wall. Aliwyn spun around and caught his arm. He almost pulled her against him with his momentum, but she held on.

"Good day, sirs," she said in a shrill voice. "What brings you here to see me and my cousin?"

Chapter 3

Aelfric

Aliwyn's grip was painful on his upper arms as footsteps shuffled into the smokehouse. Aelfric turned around with stars washing before his vision. Three men stood in the backdrop of daylight streaming through the doorway—Cuthbert, Edgar, and a dark-haired man Aelfric recognized as the town's constable, Wulfstan. Had Aelfric crawled into the hole, they would've seen his suspicious behavior and dragged him out by his feet.

All three men stared at Aliwyn, a drooling Godwin, and finally at him with their faces red from exertion. No one pounced on Aelfric. With the dress, the headscarf, and plenty of dirt to mask his features, his disguise appeared to be working. Thank Heavens Edgar didn't live with his father and only visited twice a year.

All the same, chills ran up and down Aelfric's spine.

"We're looking for a runaway thrall boy." Cuthbert wiped his greasy brow. He frowned at Aliwyn. "Why didn't you answer the door when we first knocked?"

"We were sleeping," she said. "What does the runaway look like?"

"He's a bit taller than you and has black hair," Edgar paced the room, hands at his hips. As he described Aelfric's original clothing, Aelfric wanted to melt into a pile of mud. Should he dive for the hole and forfeit his disguise, or stay put and trust a girl he'd just met?

Aliwyn didn't let go of his arm. "I didn't see anyone matching that description. I've been staying here with the door shut, but my family comes to see me."

CHAPTER 3

"I've never seen her before." The constable pointed at Aelfric.

"Oh, that's my cousin Ardith. She's visiting Mablethorpe for Easter. She's mute and a bit strange."

Strange? Aelfric's shoulders bunched up under his ears, but the rest of him wobbled like eel jelly. Wulfstan had smiled at Aelfric while he'd played music by the waterfront, but there was nothing merry about the constable now.

The three men squinted at Aelfric's filthy face. He tried not to glare at Cuthbert, whose beady little eyes had turned cloudy a few years back. His vision was hazy now, thanks to what Aelfric would call Providence. One by one, the men inspected the room while Godwin circled their feet. The place was barren except for two barrels, firewood, dresses, and a mattress.

Wulfstan fingered the clothing stacked on the barrels and turned to Aliwyn with his lips hardened. "How did you acquire so many articles of clothing?"

Aliwyn's fingers clawed into Aelfric's flesh, and he winced.

"I'm repairing them and washing them for a fee," she answered. "In fact, we were about to leave and wash them all."

Aelfric's breath rasped in his throat. That sounded like a lie, but he had a colorful history to cover up himself. Aliwyn gave him a foreboding look and pulled him toward the barrels. His stiff legs stumbled to follow. Together, they swept up the clothes and deposited them into a large sack folded at the bottom of the pile.

Aliwyn picked up Godwin, who babbled over her shoulder. Aelfric swung his knapsack over his shoulder. He followed her outside with one hand lifting his gown and the other arm bracing the bag of clothes. The sunlight outside was blinding, and the bitter smell of ashes irritated his nose. Cuthbert and the others stood outside with their arms crossed.

The constable shook his head as she passed by.

"Your curse has not been lifted," he said.

Aliwyn's voice faltered for the first time. She stroked Godwin's blond curls. "I do pray and fast the way Father Norbert told me to, sir. Thanks for lending me spare keys so I could stay here."

The wind chilled Aelfric's sweaty hairline. Of all the people he could've run into, it was a cursed girl who was likely a thief and had been told to fast and repent. But who did he expect to find in an abandoned building—a princess?

He had outsmarted the Staddons for now, but their gazes seemed to follow him as he departed alongside Aliwyn. He tried to calm himself as his feet squished in the mud between the burned buildings. Follow Aliwyn and wash clothes? He could do that.

They approached the forested incline leading to a pond. The sun filtered through the trees, dappling the wildflowers and bushes below in speckles of light. A woman with her basket of washed linens and two skipping children passed them, and Aelfric dared to look back at the smokehouse.

The Staddons had gathered several town militiamen. Cuthbert said something about guarding the town gates and promising a reward for every thrall captured. Maybe the Staddons believed spotting Aelfric meant the other thralls were also close by, but they were wrong. The men who had left Aelfric behind must be in Scotland by now. Those slimy cretins.

Aelfric couldn't risk leaving Mablethorpe tonight if the town militia questioned everyone who approached the gates. He could change his clothes, but not his voice. Tomorrow, he'd have to board a ship as a mute girl. What a fun voyage that would be.

His shoulders slumping, Aelfric stepped on his gown again and almost fell onto Aliwyn as she carried the toddler. They exchanged tense glances but kept plodding up the hill. The sight of her stoic profile soon made him worry about something else. She could easily turn around, betray him, and be awarded the pennies she desperately wanted. What was keeping her from doing just that, anyway?

He swallowed. Whatever the reason, he was grateful and should try to be friendlier.

"Thanks for covering for me," he whispered, leaning closer to her.

She smiled. "You're welcome, Ardith."

The pinprick rash on her neck flashed blood red in the daylight. Aelfric gulped and jerked away. With so much happening, he had already forgotten she was cursed—whatever that meant. He couldn't tell if someone was spiritually cursed, or diseased with something contagious, or both. No priest ever gave him a straightforward answer.

What if he caught her rash?

Her frown fixed ahead, Aliwyn tightened her arms around Godwin. "I've taken care of this boy for a month, and he's still healthy. And you see that no one else in town is ill with what I have. I've been isolated before, but I'm not getting better."

Aelfric had not seen anyone with the same rash, but he distanced himself from her. The further they went, the more people they passed walking up and down the dirt path flanked by dense bushes.

No one stopped to stare at him in a girl's outfit. His disguise had fooled everyone so far, but he couldn't risk returning to the church sanctuary where Cuthbert had first stormed in. The safest place to stay tonight was with Aliwyn in the smokehouse. After all, he was supposedly her cousin and was visiting for Easter.

Itchy all over, Aelfric clawed at his scalp. He had to spend one night with this girl, even if his stomach turned at the sight of her. What would he do if she kept pestering him for money? Somehow, he'd have to keep her quiet without giving her another coin.

When Aelfric, Aliwyn, and Godwin were halfway up the hill, the road forked under the shade of tender spring leaves. A silver stream trickled along the pathway branching to the right, and several women knelt along its banks to launder their clothing on wooden washboards.

Panting, Aliwyn observed the women but made no move to join them. She halted with Godwin clutched in her arms.

"Can we rest for a while?" she asked.

With her skin flushed, the rash spreading over her neck had deepened in color. Aelfric averted his eyes and nodded.

He beckoned her to turn left, where a meadow with tiny purple flowers overlooked the docks. Aliwyn swayed for a moment before taking a step, and Aelfric almost shot his arms out to steady her. He should've offered to carry Godwin for part of the way, but it hadn't crossed his mind.

Aliwyn walked past him before he could speak, and he followed.

He lowered his knapsack to the ground. The three of them sat cross-legged in the clearing, with Godwin happily pulling up grass and tossing the blades over his head. Sunlight cascaded down and warmed Aelfric's back as he watched the main path for any sign of trouble. Women and children walked by, their arms loaded with laundry. No one seemed to suspect him, and a sprinkling of relief soothed his body.

The calls of water birds echoed in the distance. Aliwyn sipped from her water costrel and gave Godwin a biscuit, which the boy took and gnawed. She smiled at Aelfric with water wetting her cracked lips, and he mustered a grin back. He had to keep her compliant without paying her until tomorrow morning, when he'd set sail.

Trying to win her favor came with a problem—he had rarely talked to girls his age for the sake of talking. Friendship between people of opposite genders was prohibited in Cuthbert's workshop, and marriages were arranged. If he spoke to Aliwyn the way he had spoken to men, would it cause problems?

"I adore your music." Aliwyn's eyes were bright. "I listened for it every day when I passed the church, and your version of *Kyrie Eleison* is my favorite. Who taught you to play?"

Aelfric looked around to ensure they were alone before whispering back, "My father did."

When he'd turned seven, Aelfric's father had carved him a recorder so he could express himself when words wouldn't do. The sound of his father's voice in his memories made Aelfric shudder. Despite the man's strong faith, no miracle had saved him or his wife and daughter.

"He was a great teacher." Aliwyn's gaze softened. She turned to Godwin and stroked the boy's ear. "Godwin misses his Da. I want to return him to his parents, but I don't have the money to travel."

If she was telling the truth, this would explain why she kept a child who looked nothing like her. Nonetheless, her story sounded suspicious, and Aelfric narrowed his eyes. He had heard of women kidnapping children to help them appear more pitiful while they begged for money—and this girl wanted money.

"How did Godwin get separated from his family?" he asked.

"They were fleeing from the Normans. Godwin and his nurse lost their way in the chaos. I found her in Mablethorpe about a month ago. She was very kind to me. We became friends, but she passed away from an arrow wound." Her face crumpled, and Aliwyn locked an arm around her stomach. "Before she died, she asked me to take Godwin to Beverley Minster for Easter. His family had decided to meet there if they ever separated. I promised her I'd bring him."

Aelfric raised an eyebrow. "You must be getting a reward? How many pennies?"

"I wasn't promised any money, but if his family accepts me as his new nurse, I'll be happy." Aliwyn smiled.

She was a fool. Who would take on such a task for free? And her quest to find two people amongst hundreds streaming in and out of the famous Beverley Minster sounded ridiculous.

"How do you know his parents aren't dead?" Aelfric asked.

"I just know."

"Just…know?"

"It doesn't hurt to try."

Maybe it didn't hurt, but it would cost time and money. Traveling to Beverley took a few days and required funds for a ferry to cross the River Humber. She should be resting, given how skinny she looked.

Godwin had tossed up enough torn grass to cover his blond hair, and Aelfric frowned. Aliwyn's commitment to some dying nurse was too good to be true. She was trying to wring more money out of him.

"Why can't the priest take this boy home?" he challenged.

"That Cuthbert Staddon and his son Edgar came to church two weeks ago and bought all the children with no guardians."

Aelfric gawked. "He bought them?"

"Father Norbert allowed it. He said he didn't have the food to feed so many children." Her brows furrowed. "And, of course, Father Norbert made a profit from the sale. Both he and Cuthbert are horrible. They tore siblings apart to sell as thralls. There was so much crying outside the church that day."

Aelfric's mouth turned sour. Cuthbert had split up his own family without a second thought, and his chest spasmed with a shock of heat.

"That should be illegal," he stammered. "You can't force orphans out of a church. Even criminals can seek sanctuary for forty days. The constable should've arrested Cuthbert and the priest."

"Wulfstan tried to stop the sale but couldn't arrest anyone. The town charter gives merchants permission to run business as they please. You know that, don't you?"

Aelfric kept his mouth shut because he didn't know. All he had ever followed were the rules in Cuthbert's workshop.

"I don't trust Godwin with anyone else," Aliwyn said. "And I also want to protect you from Cuthbert and that awful priest."

Protect? Since Cuthbert had isolated Aelfric from his family, he had always protected himself. Aliwyn may have lied on his behalf, but that didn't feel like...protection. Sorrow wrinkled Aliwyn's forehead as he scowled at her.

Aelfric cleared his throat. "T-thank you for your help."

"You want to leave this place, don't you?" Her speech quickened. "Do you want to come with me to Beverley? Together, we have enough money for the ferry and a carriage ride."

Not only was Beverley in the same direction as Hull, a place he'd just escaped from, but he didn't want to stay in England. The English had captured his parents from Scotland as plunder following a battle in Dunsinane. Aelfric had been born in England but felt called back to Scotland.

"No thanks," he said. "I have other plans."

Her expression sank, and Aelfric's tongue lay thick in his mouth. The thralls he once spoke to would've just grunted and moved on.

"I just met you," he stammered. "It's a lot to ask of me, to go somewhere with you."

"I suppose so." She picked blades of grass off Godwin's head. "What else do you want to know about me?"

Nothing? A growl rumbled in his throat.

"I had three brothers and a father who died recently. My Mum died when I was younger." Her voice faltered. "I like to sing and spear fish. My best friend was Brona. People in my village praised me for how fast I can sew—"

Aelfric waved his hand. "I don't need to hear the story of your life. I already said I'm not going to Beverley."

"But Easter is coming, and I must be at Beverley by then."

When she looked at him again, the desperation on her face made his stomach twist.

"You don't have to come," she said. "But can you please buy some mittens? I have some in my belt pouch. I sewed them myself. A quarter penny for the pair."

"No, thanks."

"They're very nice ones. I embroidered clovers—"

"I don't need any!"

She sucked in her lower lip. "If you just give me two more pennies, I'll have enough money to take Godwin to Beverley."

She expected him to give her two days' worth of wages? Aelfric wanted to pull out his hair but drummed his fingers on his thigh instead. If he simply refused to give her pennies, she could be angry enough to run downhill and call on the town militia.

"Let me think about it," he muttered.

"No, you won't think about it."

He shuffled in his seat. "I said—"

"The look on your face is obvious. You don't believe anything I just said."

Her nostrils flared, and she looked as though she might threaten him with scissors again.

A dull ache started at the back of Aelfric's head. "I need everything I own to go where I'm going."

"Where are you going that costs that much? Another country?"

"I don't have to tell you that. Have you tried begging for money?"

"Of course I have. People spat on me and ignored me."

"Then you should beg in another town."

"Two pennies, Aelfric." She wrung her hands in her lap. "Don't you think I can make that money by turning you in? But I told you I won't, and now you don't care."

"It's not that I don't care, but I'm paying for a long voyage tomorrow. A-and I need to buy new shoes. And also…"

"What?"

He threw up his hands. "I can't be sure of anything you just said! You could've kidnapped Godwin, and I wouldn't know."

"Kidnapped?"

Her cry was so piercing that Aelfric flinched and spun around. Women slowed their walk along the dirt path and stared back. Godwin sat on the grass, covering a biscuit in drool and not appearing distressed or kidnapped. The onlookers moved on.

"How could you accuse me of such a thing?" Aliwyn asked between her teeth.

"I'm not accusing. I'm saying it's possible."

Her eyes filled, and Aelfric clamped his mouth shut before he could do more damage.

"I did everything I could to keep this little boy safe and happy," she whispered. "He is the reason I get up every day. But you go on calling me what you want. Call me cursed and ugly and all those hurtful things others have called me. Now I'm…I'm a child abductor."

She pulled Godwin to standing and snatched the bag of clothes by Aelfric's side. Hoisting it over her shoulder, she stood and took Godwin's hand.

Aelfric scrambled to stand and spread his arms to block her way. "Where are you going?"

"Why do you care?"

"Because…"

"I already told you I won't tattle on you. Or won't you believe that, either?" She glowered at him. "Get out of my way, or I'll start screaming about who you really are."

Aelfric almost lunged to tackle her to the ground, but that would surely ruin his disguise. She led Godwin past his outstretched arms with her shoulders squared. All the curse words he'd ever learned thundered in his head.

No, he didn't know how to talk to girls, or maybe just this particularly obnoxious one.

The seriousness of his predicament startled Aelfric back to his senses. He didn't trust Aliwyn to keep his identity a secret, and she had just left. The thought of grabbing her, tying her up, and locking her in the smokehouse flashed through his mind. His stomach roiled in response. He couldn't do that to her.

Could he apologize, or was it too late? Picking up his dress, Aelfric hurried down the dirt slope after Aliwyn.

Chapter 4

Aelfric

Aelfric turned heads as he sprinted downhill. His head covering loosened, and he slowed down to adjust the wretched thing. This delayed him until Aliwyn was far ahead. She turned to glare at him a few times but never stopped walking.

He couldn't shout her name and expose his voice with so many people walking on the hill, and his breath scorched his throat.

With daylight fading, Aliwyn entered the smokehouse with Godwin and slammed the door. Aelfric could only stand outside with his pulse drumming in his ears. He raised his hand to knock, but even if she opened the door, he couldn't risk talking and revealing his voice.

Godwin babbled inside while Aliwyn spoke in an undiscernible voice. Aelfric wanted to burst. All he could do was guard her door and ensure she didn't get out.

For the rest of the afternoon, he sat behind the smokehouse, nursing his rumbling stomach and watching the passersby along the harbor. Thankfully, he was one peasant amongst hundreds in Mablethorpe. No one seemed to notice him except the man who sold hot cross buns on a wooden board suspended from his shoulders.

Aelfric waved him over and bought six. He was wolfing down the fourth soft and sweet bun when Father Norbert and the two Staddons strolled into view on the main road.

Aelfric gagged. He scooted along the smokehouse's circular wall, stopping beside the hole and keeping out of their sight. His feet dragged like

CHAPTER 4

bricks as he crawled back to peer at them. The men didn't look his way, but they guffawed and cackled with enough force to be heard across the distance. With jittery hands, Aelfric stuffed the remaining buns into the belt pouch where he kept his father's clamshells. He rose on one knee, ready to bolt if Aliwyn threw open the door and declared his presence.

She didn't.

By the way the priest and the Staddons interacted, Aliwyn's story that they had worked together appeared true. The large wooden cross hanging from Father Norbert's neck made Aelfric's upper lip curl. One day, the priest would face divine judgment. Aelfric couldn't wait to sail away and never see him again.

When darkness fell and the roads became deserted, he knocked on the smokehouse door. Aliwyn didn't answer. Aelfric kicked all the pebbles in sight with fire in his veins. It was just as well. He wasn't sure what he'd say to her, anyway. If she didn't leave the smokehouse to betray him, that was good enough.

Aelfric dragged over pieces of collapsed, thatched roofs from adjacent buildings and made himself a lean-to facing the smokehouse door. He constructed a fire pit, tossed in stones to warm them, and gathered moss and leaves to create a makeshift mattress. When the rocks were hot, he tucked them underneath his bed. The blanket from his knapsack offered some comfort as he wrapped it around his shoulders.

Other than the flickering flames, nothing moved. Aelfric sat on his mattress under the lean-to. Yawning became his favorite activity.

He stared at Aliwyn's door, but his eyelids kept sticking together. *Drat it all.* How was he going to stay up all night?

Maybe a cold drink would wake him up. Aelfric approached the nearby well and drew up a bucket of water. He submerged his costrel with shivers running up his arm. The thrall master he had heard splashing deep within Hull's well seemed to scream again in his memories.

Royd was the man's name. He had been Cuthbert's best friend. The other runaways had snapped his arm and thrown him in the night they'd escaped. He had been a cruel old man, but also frail and in agony as he pleaded for Aelfric's help. Maybe he was dead now.

Aelfric nearly slapped himself. Why did he still blame himself for not helping Royd? For all the thralls that man had beaten over the years, didn't he deserve to suffer? Aelfric had been on the run from Cuthbert, and there had been no time to save anyone.

Sighing, he trudged back to his lean-to and looked at the sky. Glowing clouds drifted past a half-moon, and wispy smoke rose from the hole in the smokehouse's roof. The smoke from his fire pit mingled with Aliwyn's in the darkening sky sprinkled with stars. She still hadn't betrayed him, and he had been so certain she would.

Aelfric had rarely been alone in Hull. His scalp prickled as he eyed the surrounding shadows cast by the flames. This area of town had burned down when the lord's oven caught on fire. Every breath he took smelled of ashes, and whiffs of horse urine punctuated the stench.

What a lovely place to spend the night.

He always slept with his coins in a pouch flush against his breastbone for fear of theft. Had the pouch been bigger, he would've placed his recorder and his father's seashells inside as well. Out here, he'd have to be extra wary of robbers.

Aelfric squashed a surge of fear. There was nothing wrong with being alone.

Godwin sniveled inside, and Aliwyn sang the lyrics to the songs Aelfric had once played. She improvised variations to his music. Her voice flowed like warm honey, but the melody only aggravated the ache in his ribs. She must've been a keen listener to memorize so many of his songs.

If Aliwyn had hoped to meet him one day, she must be sorely disappointed.

He hadn't meant to hurt her feelings or make her mad. Hopefully, she'd make her two pennies selling mittens in the next few days and travel to Beverley for Easter.

Chances were she wouldn't. Did Aelfric need to cling onto his pennies for new shoes when he'd barely walk on the ship? But he had earned his money through hard work and deserved to reap the benefits.

He didn't know what to do. The endless thinking made him thump his knee with his fist. Aelfric drank and wiped his face with water to stay alert, but he soon shivered from the cold. He lay down and curled up on his mattress. The stones underneath warmed his side. Across from him, sparks from the fire soared with the waves of heat and darkened as they rose into the night.

If his father had met Aliwyn, what would he have done? His father had always been generous, helping those in need and mediating disputes within the thrall compound. Everything deteriorated after Cuthbert sold him.

Aelfric knew what Da would've done had he been alive, and his eyes drooped shut. A moment later, he was asleep.

Aliwyn

Several hours into the loud snoring, Aliwyn opened the door a sliver. She slipped out while gripping her scissors. The morning air greeted her with an invigorating chill, and seagulls coasted in a sky streaked with golden clouds.

The same youngster who had accused her of kidnapping Godwin now slept like a noisy nuisance in front of her door. So he didn't want her to leave and reveal his secret? He was a terrible guard.

All the better for her. Suffering through his revolting snorts had convinced her to steal two pennies and finally end her struggle for money. In the past week, the townsfolk had kicked dust in her face and called her demon-possessed or stricken for her past sins. Aelfric's accusation that she had kidnapped Godwin was the last she could take.

He needed to learn a lesson.

She studied the triangular shelter he had built opposite the smokehouse. On her hands and knees, she crept in between the fire pit and where he lay snoring. The embers warmed her side, but dragging her knees over the rocky earth made goosebumps skitter up her arms.

Aelfric's blanket covered him from the chin down. One of his belt pouches peeked from under the side of his blanket, close to his exposed hand.

This pouch had jiggled with what sounded like coins when she'd first met him. Aliwyn waited until he snored again before snipping the stitches on his bag. She began to shred the cloth with extra cuts to make it seem torn.

Aelfric's fingers twitched. She froze, but he didn't move again. His body carried the scent of freshly cut grass, probably thanks to Godwin's antics in the sunbathed meadow. A lump lodged in her throat as her scissors made soft clipping sounds. She had already snatched a load of laundry from Thrunscoe, fled to Mablethorpe, and cut up the garments to sew accessories. It was a foul thing to have done, and few people bought her wares anyway.

Why was she stealing again?

But the hole she was snipping grew in size, and Aliwyn steeled herself. Aelfric had been so fortunate with everything, including his narrow escape thanks to her. His musical talent was a blessing she couldn't imagine having. There were days when only his music had given her hope that she'd find another family to love her.

But the musician whose music had spoken to her heart was just another whelp who doubted her goodwill and scorned her for her rash.

Aliwyn blinked back her tears. She had fasted and repented even before stealing clothes, but she hadn't gotten better. Recently, her gums bled when she ate. No one cared enough to sympathize with how frightened she felt except for the constable, Wulfstan, but he was too busy to talk.

Slipping her fingers into the new hole, Aliwyn probed Aelfric's belt pouch, searching for pennies. Her fingers skimmed over a saucer-like object, and she rubbed its contours with a deepening scowl. A clamshell? The belt pouch was full of clamshells? She pulled out the object halfway before pushing it back in.

Indeed, it was a shell!

After all this trouble, she couldn't settle for seashells. Her fingers probed deeper, and she pulled out the first thing that felt different.

Out slid Aelfric's recorder, and she gasped. This marvelous object wove magic with sound and had carried her into other worlds. She stroked the smooth wood with her thumb, admiring the shape of the worn fingerholes, but the instrument was lifeless and ordinary without a musician to play it.

Aliwyn couldn't take his recorder. With trembling fingers, she tried to slip the instrument back through the small hole, but the seashells gave resistance. Finally, she gave a desperate shove, and the shells rattled within the bag.

Aelfric stopped snoring, and her throat seized. When he began to turn, she clambered to her feet. She stuffed the recorder and scissors into the same pocket and hurried for the smokehouse. If he woke up, she'd say she had exited to replenish her costrel at the well.

Before slipping back indoors, Aliwyn glanced at Aelfric and his forehead of messy black hair. His eyes were closed, but he tossed and turned as though no position was comfortable. She entered the smokehouse with its enveloping warmth and shut the door. Shivers rained down her back as she rolled the instrument between her fingers.

Dear Heavens. What had she done?

Outside, Aelfric sneezed, sniffled, and then sneezed again. Aliwyn pressed her ear against the door and heard the rustling of his mattress, followed by a heavy sigh. She couldn't give back the instrument without revealing she had robbed him. What if he became angry and attacked her?

She peered out the crack of the doorframe to find Aelfric squatting before the fire pit, rubbing his hands over the embers. His eyes were downcast and puffy in the morning light.

The uplifting melodies he had once played echoed in her mind, and tears welled in her eyes. She'd wanted to teach him a lesson for being so conceited, but who was she to teach him anything? She was a thief and a repeat offender.

Rustling and footfalls sounded outside, and Aliwyn struggled to see through the slit of the doorframe. A yawning Aelfric walked into view while swinging his knapsack over one shoulder. His headscarf fell in a shapeless cascade over his shoulders.

Aliwyn couldn't breathe. Her arm jerked for the door handle, but fear paralyzed her. If he attacked her for picking his pockets, she was no match for him. She pressed her forehead to the doorframe and watched how he stood facing the smokehouse with his lips pressed together. He studied its towering frame as though wondering if it were real.

Aelfric pulled out a flattened bag from behind his gown and untied its many laces. Retrieving something shiny, he knelt before the smokehouse door. His head swung within a hand's width from her face on the other side. Aliwyn toppled backward and caught herself before she fell. To her amazement, a pair of fingertips slid two halfpennies through the space beneath her door.

Aliwyn covered her mouth. Tears splashed onto her hands, and her head spun. She only came to her senses when Aelfric sneezed again, this time more distant.

He was leaving! What if it was for another country?

She reached for the door, but her shaky and wet hands struggled to grasp the handle. Finally, she swung the door open with the hinges squeaking in protest. A swirl of spring air rushed inside, carrying scents of the ocean air laced with fish and salt.

To her far left stood a row of taverns and shops. A few sailors strode along the wharf while others haggled with merchants at their storefronts. In the distance, the morning sun spread its rays upon the North Sea like yellow petals floating on the water. Sailing ships dotted the horizon.

But Aelfric was nowhere to be seen, and her heart dropped like a stone.

Even if it became clear she had robbed him, she had to return his recorder.

Aliwyn swerved back inside the smokehouse and found Godwin lying on his mattress as before, asleep in a darling bundle of blankets. Yesterday, she had been able to scoop him into her arms, stand up with his weight, and run. Her body was too sore today.

Aliwyn shook the boy's shoulders. "Godwin. Godwin, my dear…"

The church bells on the opposite end of the docks struck Prime, the first hour of daylight. She tugged the blanket off the boy, but he swatted away her hand with a whimper. Ignoring his objection, she pulled him

CHAPTER 4

into a sitting position. Godwin thrashed and filled the smokehouse with a piercing wail. Aliwyn grimaced and held his arms down.

"Godwin, please! We can't let Aelfric leave without his recorder!"

She adjusted the child's cloak around his shoulders and pulled him to his feet. Her mind clouded with exertion as she stood and pulled him toward the door. Godwin shrieked and fell in a heap, bouncing on his bottom. Heat rose to her face. She mustered the strength to pick up the child and turned for the door, but two shadowy bodies stood at the entrance and blocked her way.

Aliwyn gasped. Constable Wulfstan glared at her with his brows furrowed and his bearded jaw set. Next to him stood a plump woman with her lips twisted in a snarl. Aliwyn clutched Godwin to her chest. It was Cwenhild, the woman whose laundry she had stolen from the neighboring town.

"We need to inspect the clothes you have stashed here," Wulfstan muttered.

"No need. I remember seeing this girl the day I was robbed." The woman jabbed a finger at Aliwyn's face. "This time, you won't get away!"

With Godwin wailing in her arms, Aliwyn staggered back, and the constable and woman marched into the smokehouse.

Chapter 5

Aelfric

A FEW MILITIAMEN MILLED around the docks, but there were too many ships boarding and too many passengers for them to question everyone. Smirking, Aelfric tugged on his headscarf and shuffled into the line waiting to board a magnificent cog ship with a red cross on its sail.

Mablethorpe's militia was not responsible for patrolling the quays anyway. Instead, each ship's crew was responsible for the safety of the passengers and cargo. How much had Cuthbert paid the militia to search for him? Well, they'd never get him, those cod-witted dolts.

Aelfric took a bite of yesterday's hot cross buns and eyed the ragtag assembly of families, merchants, and armored men—probably mercenaries. He had better guard his money once he boarded. Seagulls circled the painted skies overhead, and Aelfric tried not to inhale the body odor wafting around him.

A few women in line carried children the size of Godwin. Aliwyn's hollow cheeks and sharp chin resurfaced in his mind, and he scratched between his eyebrows until it stung. How they had ended their brief encounter still left a dark cloud in his memory.

Aelfric frowned at the horizon and adjusted the knapsack over his shoulder.

"Da, I found a pretty seashell!" a boy cried behind him.

Aelfric grinned to himself. He also admired the iridescent color of seashells and the way they glimmered on a beach.

CHAPTER 5

He strolled up to the fare collector and placed a fistful of coins on the man's desk. The collector, a bearded man with a mole on his nose, sorted the money with one finger.

"You're a half penny short," he said.

Aelfric tried to stop staring at the man's hairy mole and reached into the satchel he had kept against his sternum. Out came only one quarter penny, and heat flushed down his neck. Unless he had miscalculated, giving Aliwyn two half pennies still left him enough to pay the fare. He rummaged through his belt satchels and plunged into the emptiness of his seashell pouch.

His recorder was gone.

Aelfric's vision blacked at the edges. He dug frantically through the clinking shells until one tumbled onto the wooden planks of the quay.

"Hmph." The fare collector jutted his chin. "You have a leak there."

Aelfric grabbed his bag of seashells and squeezed along its bottom until his finger poked into the ragged defect. A tear!

Had he torn his belt pouch while crawling into the smokehouse? While chasing Aliwyn down the hill with branches snagging onto his clothes? If his recorder had fallen into the undergrowth, he might never find it. Or maybe Cuthbert would find it first. Aelfric grimaced. Without thinking, he pulled out a handful of shells from his defective pouch and squinted at them in the morning rays. Shells clattered onto the quay, but the instrument didn't miraculously appear.

"You have a quarter penny there." The fare collector slid his foot toward the mess Aelfric had made. "Give it to me, and stop holding the line."

Aelfric stooped to gather the fallen objects. He couldn't leave England without his recorder, his best friend and his father's spirit in one. Standing again, he dropped his seashells into another belt pouch. He shook his head apologetically at the stone-faced collector and gathered all the fare money back into his purse.

Aelfric exited the line with pins sinking into his scalp. What had he done to deserve this rotten twist of fate? He marched down a row of questioning faces and couldn't shout to ask if they had found a recorder anywhere.

Neither could he risk being identified as the piper who had earned over ten pennies per week.

The pain in his throat grew. Never before had he been so silenced, without a voice and without music.

"Excuse me, young lady," said a man's voice. "This must've fallen out of your collection."

Aelfric looked up at the bearded man offering to return one of his seashells. Next to the man stood a boy whose brows were drawn with disappointment. He was probably the one who had found a shell earlier.

Aelfric remembered the boy's excitement, and he forced a smile.

"Keep it." At least Aelfric could pass as a girl when he whispered.

The boy's face brightened. "Oh, really? Thank you!"

Judging by their facial resemblance, the man and boy were father and son. Aelfric also looked like a miniature of his father, although he lacked his father's lucid green eyes. Now, more than ever, it pained him to see a father and son happily together. Aelfric tore away before they could see his face flushing.

He pushed his knapsack higher over his shoulder and scrutinized the ground as he trudged toward the smokehouse. Maybe he'd lost the instrument while walking to the quays. Yet he shouldn't keep staring at his feet. Aelfric looked up and searched for Cuthbert or Edgar, the constable, or the militiamen. Merchants and donkeys filled the roads again, ignoring him and obscuring his presence. Chills nonetheless rained down Aelfric's back. He was endangering himself by staying in Mablethorpe, but he needed his recorder.

Or maybe he should give it up and leave the town. Aelfric dragged his feet. He couldn't spend anything on food when he needed every penny for the ship's fare.

Possibly begging for money crossed his mind, but he tensed and kept walking. He was not about to stoop that low.

Aelfric had to backtrack to the smokehouse while searching, but that came with a grave risk. Aliwyn could have betrayed him already. If so, it was only a matter of time before the militia pounced on the fake girl in a blue dress. He wiped his eyes, his chest so tight he couldn't breathe.

CHAPTER 5

A toddler's familiar squeals reached his ears. Was he losing his mind, or was that Godwin? Aelfric paused and steadied himself, but the noise persisted. Now, the boy was shrieking. Aelfric sucked in his breath. He shuffled toward the alleyway where the crying came from.

Something was wrong with Godwin, unless he couldn't tell one screaming toddler from another.

Jittery all over, Aelfric waited between two buildings. Wulfstan the constable walked into view from his left, carrying a thrashing Godwin in his arms. The tot grasped at Wulfstan's beard and eyes despite the man's attempt to hold him backward and at arm's length. Aelfric's mouth fell open. Shouldn't Aliwyn be carrying the child instead?

He couldn't afford to care; he needed to find his recorder and leave the country. Even so, when Godwin spotted him and shrieked with renewed fervor, Aelfric's feet trailed behind Wulfstan on their own. His heart raced as he slid alongside the shadows of the wheelwright's workshop and multiple taverns. Chickens trotted out of his way, but no passerby paid him more than a glance.

Aelfric wanted to take Godwin and return him to Aliwyn, but she was nowhere in sight. Could she have cast Godwin aside this morning for whatever reason? The thought left a sour taste in Aelfric's mouth. He now doubted she had stolen Godwin to help her beg.

So what had happened to her?

Up ahead, at the end of the waterfront, the church's back door creaked open. It was the same door Aelfric had darted out of yesterday. A stern Father Norbert, with his trailing black robe, walked out and turned toward the constable.

"What is all this ruckus about?" the priest called out, his rosary in his hand.

Aelfric straightened like a pole. According to Aliwyn, this priest had sold children as thralls, and Godwin's sobbing took on a new meaning.

Aelfric picked up his gown and bolted after Wulfstan. Too late, he spotted several militiamen wearing bright blue scarves stationed between the market booths. The sunlight glinting off their spears made his stomach plummet. Aelfric's mind screamed for him to turn back, but Wulfstan spun around to face him first. The man was flushed down to the neck.

"Ardith!" He thrust Godwin toward Aelfric's chest. "Take this boy. Aliwyn's in the market—"

Aelfric didn't hear the rest. Godwin squealed with his arms extended, and Aelfric grabbed the tot. He pulled up his gown and ran back toward the buildings.

The militiamen nearby laughed. None of them marched out to trap Aelfric in a circle of spear tips, and he released a sigh of relief. Aliwyn had not betrayed his identity to anyone after all.

Was she really in the market? Aelfric had better check the smokehouse first. He hurried toward the building with Godwin's wet cheeks rubbing against his neck.

Chapter 6

Aelfric

Aelfric arrived within earshot of the smokehouse with his throat searing from panting and Godwin clinging to his neck. To his surprise, the smokehouse door was wide open. Outside stood a stout woman with a drawstring sack by her feet, stuffed with something Aelfric couldn't see. He recognized her as one of the merchants' wives who, after watching all her friends toss Aelfric some money, had cautiously placed a quarter penny on his knapsack.

Today, she looked rather irritated. With her arms at her hips, she spoke with two militiamen who looked equally irritated at having to listen.

Aelfric circled the scene's periphery and struggled to see within the dim smokehouse. Aliwyn wasn't inside, and his shoulders slumped. The woman continued to mutter about the laundry racks being unsafe. What a strange thing to complain about. Aelfric wanted more details, but he couldn't hear her well.

Regardless, Aliwyn was gone, and so was his recorder. He glanced down and wrinkled his nose at Godwin, who had covered Aelfric's neck in tears and drool and was still sniveling.

"Did you sneak off when Aliwyn went to the market?" he whispered.

If so, it was futile to search for her. The marketplace was even more crowded than the harbor on Mondays, especially the Monday before Easter. The townsfolk would probably be playing egg-rolling and egg-dancing games along every street.

Godwin's lips curled downward.

"Ada," he sobbed.

Aelfric drew in a slow breath. He had never taken care of a child. He had once tried to keep garden snails as pets, but even they had slid away overnight. Childcare shouldn't be difficult, though. After all, all the women did it.

Aelfric gazed into the boy's hazel eyes. "Behave yourself, and I'll keep you until Aliwyn comes back."

With this, he shifted the boy's weight in his arms and began walking. A heaviness settled over him again as he studied the looming hillside he had trudged up the day before. Women and children walked on the dirt path, kicking up dust in between the undergrowth. His recorder could be anywhere. What if one of the children had found it and had taken it home?

Aelfric tried not to fear the worst. He walked up the path and searched the ground and woodland flanking the trail. Not even a third of the way up the slope, Godwin burst into shrieks. Aelfric almost dropped the boy. He pulled back, his ears ringing from the noise, and Godwin sucked his fist with tears streaming down his face. Aelfric had the sense to pull out his half-eaten hot cross bun and push it into the boy's mouth. Godwin chewed it, whimpering.

A gust of wind chilled the sweat along Aelfric's hairline. He had forgotten to buy food. With all that had been happening, he wasn't hungry, but Godwin was.

"We've gone too far uphill," Aelfric whispered as if the boy would understand. "I didn't eat much either, so just hang on until I find my recorder."

Godwin didn't listen. He fussed and kicked, and Aelfric couldn't carry the thrashing tot the way Wulfstan could with his longer arms. His chest heaving, Aelfric lowered the boy to the ground and pulled him by the hand. By the time they plodded to the fork in the road, Godwin's crying was so intolerable that Aelfric wanted to scream himself. The passing women stared at him, some with sympathy and others with disdain.

The recorder was still nowhere to be found.

Godwin would blow Aelfric's cover if he continued crying like he was being slaughtered. Aelfric dragged him toward the meadow where the boy had happily pulled up grass the day before. One more wail pierced his ears, and Aelfric's emotions boiled over.

He pressed the boy down on his bottom and gripped his small shoulders. "Stop your blasted crying!"

Godwin inhaled a staccato breath. Out came a fresh surge of tears, and Aelfric narrowed his eyes. An ache deepened in his throat. He had been terrified of the way Cuthbert used to threaten him, so why had he acted the same way toward Godwin? When the boy wailed again, Aelfric loosened his hold.

"Godwin, I'm sorry." He hung his head. "I'll find food for you."

And how would he, short of spending money he needed for the ship's fare tomorrow? It was time to swallow his pride and beg. Aelfric picked up the boy and approached the first woman he saw washing her clothes. She had a small parcel beside her which emanated the fragrance of fresh bread and rosemary.

"Can you spare any food?" Aelfric whispered. He extended an upturned hand.

The woman glanced up. Curls of dark hair escaped from her headscarf, and she lifted her wickerwork basket away from where he and Godwin stood. Without a word, she reached into her belt pouch, sprinkled some ash on the wet tunic she had been washing, and resumed scrubbing.

Aelfric swallowed. His stomach burned from the tantalizing aroma of bread, but he'd get none of it. He led Godwin to two dozen other women along the hillside while he searched for this recorder. Godwin kept quiet by eating dandelion flowers and sipping water from his costrel. Finally, one mother with three youngsters of her own handed Godwin a carrot. One tiny carrot, and no more.

The sun beat down on Aelfric's stuffy headscarf, and the sole of his right shoe was so detached he could scoop in pebbles and kick them out at will. By the time Godwin finished gnawing on the carrot, he was listless and sagging in Aelfric's arms. The recorder was still missing.

Aelfric halted and glared at the people passing by him as though he were invisible.

Stroking Godwin's hair, he cradled the boy against his chest. This would not do. He carried the child downhill.

One thought weighed on his shoulders like a stone mantle. He appeared to be exactly what he'd suspected Aliwyn to be—a panhandler who used Godwin's presence to gain sympathy. But Aelfric wasn't keeping Godwin for his own gain, and Aliwyn probably hadn't been, either.

Hauling around a toddler to beg wasn't worth the trouble. Maybe that's why Aliwyn had been so upset when he'd doubted her story.

The smokehouse door was still open when he approached it in the early afternoon. Aliwyn hadn't returned, and Aelfric's head buzzed with fatigue. Fearing capture had drained him, and all the anxiety had been for naught. With aromas from the seaside booths stoking his hunger, he finally spent a halfpenny on walnuts, bread, and honey apple tarts. The man who sold hot cross buns yesterday recognized Aelfric as his enthusiastic customer, and he gave Godwin a leftover bun for free.

AELFRIC SETTLED THE BOY down on a dirt slope facing the sea and laid their provisions on a boulder. The tide lapped at the shoreline, providing a soft rhythm to the gulls' persistent cries. Godwin devoured his food. Aelfric only squinted at the bright waters and the square-sailed ships in the distance. His boat to Scotland had sailed long ago, and he had just spent a halfpenny he needed for the fare. He pushed walnuts into his mouth but struggled to enjoy the fatty taste.

"Da," Godwin said. His face showed remnants of everything he had eaten.

"You're welcome," Aelfric mumbled.

"Hot bun." The boy took the gifted bread and mashed it in his hands.

"Mmm...cold smashed bun."

Godwin shifted onto all fours and crawled onto his lap, and Aelfric stiffened.

CHAPTER 6

The boy snuggled against him and kicked his legs as they hung off the other side. "Da."

"I'm not your father, wee'un."

Nonetheless, the child's ball of warmth, so trusting and fragile, made his eyes blur. Aelfric used to climb into his grandmother's lap and smile at her freckled face when he was eight years old and too big to fit there. His older sister would laugh at him. He hated that.

But her life had been cut short. She was forever gone from this side of eternity, no matter how much Aelfric missed her sometimes. The Normans had razed Durham last winter to stop an English uprising. Aelfric had clung to hope that his loved ones had escaped until he'd seen their belongings on sale a month ago, during an auction in Hull.

The sight of his family's clothing still left him sleepless some nights. His sister's and mother's gowns had been bloody and charred, his father's recorder a blackened and crumbling tube. No one had wanted to buy their belongings. Aelfric had taken everything and buried them.

His eyes clouded. He chased from his mind the memories of shoveling a hole in the church cemetery.

After a moment, Aelfric wrapped his arms around the boy babbling on his lap. "Say Godwin, how can I get out of Mablethorpe? The militia is after me, and I don't have enough money to sail anymore."

And no recorder to play and earn anything. He couldn't work odd jobs either as a girl and risk being identified.

Aelfric rested his chin on the boy's curls and gazed at the ocean to freedom he couldn't traverse. A quay in the distance featured a red ribbon fluttering from a wooden post, signaling to passersby that the captain sought a cabin boy. Aelfric had seen the ribbon on different quays during his three weeks in Mablethorpe, but he had turned away with his nose held high. Why should he work when he could be a paying passenger and have others serve *him*?

Maybe, just maybe, he had been too full of himself.

A shiver ran through him. He'd had one plan—leave England—and that was now torn to pieces.

Godwin looked up with his round eyes and smiled, his cheeks bulging with bread. Aelfric grinned back despite the choking sensation in his throat. Perhaps Godwin enjoyed his company, but Aelfric didn't know how to care for a child. Somewhere out there had to be his mother and father, much wiser and more experienced than he was, praying for the return of their precious son. Aelfric didn't have proof of this any more than Aliwyn did. But he wanted to believe Godwin wouldn't grow up facing the same uncertainty that he faced now.

Was this why Aliwyn was so convinced Godwin's parents were alive?

Worry for her whereabouts trickled through Aelfric's exhaustion. He stretched and suppressed a yawn. Aliwyn should've returned by now unless something had happened to her. He hoped she was all right.

Aliwyn had lived in Mablethorpe for a longer time. Maybe she'd know of a hidden tunnel or a breach in the town walls he could sneak out of.

"Ada." Godwin touched Aelfric's chin with tiny fingers.

"You miss Aliwyn?"

The boy kept babbling.

Aelfric adjusted his headscarf and prayed his disguise would hold even if he entered the market. Many other peasants would be milling around; he just had to keep his head down.

"All right, let's go." He stood up and shook out his legs. "We're going to find Aliwyn."

Aliwyn

ALIWYN STOOD AT THE edge of the line while bracing an empty bucket against her chest. After spending hours with her ankles locked in the stocks, the last thing she wanted to see was another crowd. The peasants

CHAPTER 6

at the market had hurled everything from rotten apples to dead rats at her face while spitting and shouting obscenities.

Thief! Thief! Aliwyn winced at the memory. Constable Wulfstan had given her a bucket of warm water so she could wash herself on her way out. Her clothes and hair were damp, and her forehead stung with scratches and bruises.

The throng extended from the church's back door and congested the main road. Aliwyn searched the line, hoping to find an opening to slip through. Why was there such a large gathering? Bits of conversation informed her that the constable and a few merchants had donated food so the church could serve free pottage. With meat, eggs, and dairy prohibited for Lent, the populace appeared hungry for what was still allowed.

A young man with black hair entered the line from the side, but it wasn't Aelfric. He must've sailed away by now, and it was a good thing. The militiamen outside the market and guarding the town gates had stopped every passerby to question their plans. Cuthbert and his son had prowled the marketplace all day for Aelfric and the other escapees, but they'd left frustrated and empty-handed. On her way here, Aliwyn had seen them taking a swig of ale outside the Red Hen tavern.

A child's laughter pierced through the background voices. Was it Godwin? Aliwyn steeled herself and approached the gathering, ready to push her way through. Wulfstan had told her he'd have his mother watch Godwin at home until Aliwyn's punishment was over. She had to fetch the boy now, even if Cwenhild had told her to leave town, or else.

Someone with a headscarf wove through the crowd and waved an arm. Was it one of Cwenhild's sisters? Aliwyn ducked with the bucket shielding her face, but no rotten fruit flew in her direction. Lowering the bucket, her eyes refocused on the sight of Aelfric carrying Godwin in the golden afternoon sun. He waved again as he approached, and grins brightened both their faces.

Godwin squirmed in Aelfric's arms. Aelfric lowered the boy to the ground, and the child tottered toward her. Aliwyn knelt and opened her arms with a quivering smile. Was she dreaming? Why had Aelfric stayed knowing the Staddons were still here?

Godwin snuggled against her, and she embraced the child with tears rising in her eyes. This wasn't a dream. The boy's hair tickled her chin, his small body familiar and robust. The scent of spiced apples wafted from his tunic. Aelfric must've bought him a treat earlier that day.

Her surge of gratitude was soon stamped out by dread. She still had Aelfric's recorder in her pocket, cleaned and wrapped in a handkerchief, along with his two half pennies she didn't deserve to keep. Now, she had to give it all back.

"What happened to you?" Aelfric squatted beside her and seemed to study her new bruises. The concern in his eyes made her shiver.

She loosened Godwin's arms from around her neck and fumbled with the flap of her belt pouch. "I was put in the stocks."

"What? Why would the constable put—"

"Shhh. I have your recorder."

Her arm shaking, Aliwyn took out the parcel and pushed it into his hand.

Aelfric's eyebrows shot up. He grabbed the bundle, felt its contours, and barked a laugh. Had it not been for the noisy gathering, his voice would've ruined his disguise. He threw up his arms as though to embrace her, and Aliwyn shrunk back.

"Where did you find it?" he asked.

"I didn't find it."

Aliwyn could barely speak through the knot in her throat. She reached into her belt pouch again and pulled out her scissors. Her face hot, she pointed the tips at his waist, where the holey satchel still hung from his belt pouch. She made a few snipping movements. The sinister metal clinked in her hands.

All joy drained from Aelfric's face. Shadows crept into the grooves of his frown, and he stuffed his recorder and the two halfpennies into another belt pouch. When he rose to his feet, she squeezed her kneecaps.

"I'm sorry." She looked up at him. "I really am."

His face flushed, and he opened his mouth but said nothing. She knew he could kick her from where he stood, and goosebumps skittered across her arms. Gathering Godwin close to her, she was desperate to flee but wasn't strong enough to stand while carrying him.

"I just wanted to help Godwin," she stammered. "Please don't hurt me."

"Da." Godwin looked up at Aelfric with a big grin.

To her amazement, Aelfric took a step back. No kicks came, and Aliwyn dared to breathe again. She released Godwin and struggled to push herself up by her knees, but an angry shout from the crowd made her freeze. An instant later, what felt like a rock struck her left temple.

Aliwyn shrieked and fell on her side. She had barely pushed to her elbows when hands tore at her cloak from behind. Aliwyn gagged until her cloak was finally pulled off.

"Wench!" cried the same voice. "I told you to scram!"

It was Cwenhild, the woman whose family Aliwyn had robbed. The stout woman grabbed Aliwyn by the back of her gown and tossed her onto the ground. Too terrified to scream, Aliwyn skidded and rolled with her arms covering her head. Other voices joined in and grabbed at her hair, kicking her back, and Aliwyn could only curl into a ball.

Aelfric, run! He was wearing the one gown she had stolen but had found too beautiful to destroy. These women would recognize it soon enough and beat him, too.

But the kicking stopped, and Aliwyn lay shuddering on the ground. Through her sobs, she heard the other women screaming.

Aliwyn lowered her arms from her wet eyes. Aelfric had taken her empty bucket and was whacking all three of her assailants with wild sweeps of his arm. Godwin stood on his own, as still as a statue, as he sucked on his hand. No one from the crowd stepped forth to intervene. Her teeth chattered. The back of her ribs spasmed in pain, but she dragged herself until she was next to the boy.

"Godwin, run!"

To her horror, the boy only plopped next to her and continued sucking on his hand.

"Enough!" The constable's voice bellowed over the cacophony. "Stop fighting!"

Aelfric stopped swinging. He hung the bucket handle over his arm and backed toward where Aliwyn lay beside Godwin. He glanced at her, his teeth bared and his fists still raised to punch.

"Run!" she wheezed.

He had flung his cloak aside for everyone to see the stolen blue gown he wore, and Aliwyn's limbs turned to lead.

"Why are you fighting?" Wulfstan's boots marched into view.

Unable to talk, Aelfric turned to her again with desperation wrinkling his forehead. Aliwyn struggled to sit up.

She faced a teetering wall of faces, and her temples pulsed from the beating. "Cwenhild attacked me, and my cousin tried to defend me."

"That's my sister's dress!" Cwenhild jabbed a finger at Aelfric. "So she's the one who stole it!"

"No, I did!" Aliwyn cried. "I stole everything!"

Cwenhild stomped toward Aelfric, her snarling face rising a head in height above his. "Take off my sister's gown and give it back."

What would Aelfric do now? Aliwyn crawled to his side, her mind scrambling for what to say. Before she could open her mouth again, he reached into his pouch and pulled out a fistful of coins. He extended it toward Cwenhild and unfurled his fingers.

Cwenhild's sister, who was older and shorter, stepped in front of Cwenhild. She swept the small mound of pennies onto her hand.

"I suppose this would pay for new Easter dresses." She glared at Aelfric, then at Aliwyn, before wrinkling her nose and backing away.

Aliwyn squeezed her eyes shut. She wanted to sink into the ground and disappear.

The crowd began to shuffle back into a line for pottage. Wulfstan approached her, his imposing stature amplified by his scowl, and Aliwyn tightened her hold around Godwin's arm. What if Wulfstan deemed her unfit to care for a child and took him away?

But the man turned to Aelfric instead, who stared at his feet with his face flushed. Wulfstan gestured for the bucket, and Aelfric shook the handle off onto the man's hand.

CHAPTER 6

"Ardith and Aliwyn," Wulfstan said. "Both of you must come with me to the smokehouse."

Too choked to speak, Aliwyn struggled to stand. The sight of the pinprick rash and bruises on her forearms made her legs wobble. She couldn't get up until Aelfric and Wulfstan gripped her elbows and lifted.

Aliwyn staggered to her feet. Aelfric was still panting, and she couldn't bring herself to look at him. Neither did she dare to ask Cwenhild for her cloak back, and she shivered in her damp and dirty dress.

Straightening out her clothes, Aliwyn caught sight of the woman muttering to her sisters. The way her eyes skimmed over Aelfric made Aliwyn stiffen.

Did the woman recognize Aelfric after seeing him up close? Aliwyn was about to grab Aelfric and turn him away when a boy who resembled Cwenhild emerged from the crowd. He took her hand and led her back into the line for pottage. Cwenhild's sisters followed, and Aliwyn released a sigh of relief. It had been another close call for Aelfric.

Godwin walked in between Aliwyn and Aelfric. The child reached up and wriggled his small fingers into Aliwyn's hand, then extended another hand for Aelfric's.

After all that had happened, she was even more grateful to have him. Aliwyn, Aelfric, and Godwin left the crowd and followed Wulfstan toward the smokehouse.

Chapter 7

Aliwyn

ALIWYN TRIED TO IGNORE the throbbing of her bloody lips as they walked. Why had Aelfric defended her? She glanced at him walking beside her. He had picked up Godwin so they could walk faster, and the bitterness in his glare made her quiver.

"I missed my ship to look for the recorder you stole," he hissed.

Aliwyn chewed on her lip. Now wasn't the time to talk. The constable had his back turned and was too far ahead to hear, but they were about to pass the busy Red Hen tavern on the opposite side of the street. The upstairs shutters were open. A familiar bald man leaned outside with a frown wrinkling his forehead. A younger man and woman stood behind him.

Aliwyn's eyes widened. Cuthbert, Edgar, and perhaps Edgar's wife were watching them.

Aelfric spoke again. "Why did you steal—"

"Shh!"

She gripped his arm and shook her head, but Aelfric only jerked away in a huff. At least he was quiet now. Didn't he know the penalty for runaway thralls in Mablethorpe was fifteen lashes at the pillory? Perhaps he didn't.

She and Aelfric slipped past the Staddons' watch. When the inn was far behind them, chills prickled her scalp. They may have avoided another disaster, but Aelfric's brashness would get him caught soon enough. She should try to keep him safe overnight until he could board another ship. It was the least she could do. Had she not stolen his recorder, he would've sailed away that morning. Aelfric might be seething mad, but he'd defended her even when she hadn't deserved it.

Aliwyn stole another glance at him. He carried Godwin as though the boy was part of himself. How had the two of them become this close? But that was nothing either of them could celebrate. Aelfric's eyebrows twitched in between fury and sorrow as he gazed ahead, and she blinked back her tears. He had just given up money to make peace for a problem she had caused.

It felt horrible to see someone this angry with her. She still wanted to help him leave Mablethorpe, but maybe he'd run away from her the first chance he got.

Wulfstan paused by a well to fill the bucket before resuming his pace. Aelfric walked in a wide circle to avoid the same well, and Aliwyn frowned at his strange behavior. He offered no explanation.

Ahead of them, Wulfstan stood waiting beside the smokehouse he had unlocked.

"Stay inside until tomorrow," he said. "Do you have food for tonight?"

"Yes, I do, sir. Thank you," Aliwyn said. Despite his stern exterior, he had been one of the only people who had shown her sympathy in Mablethorpe.

Wulfstan's tired eyes shifted from her to Aelfric, who stood with his headscarf pulled in awkward directions and his surly gaze unwavering. Godwin was asleep against his shoulder.

Finally, Wulfstan drew a slow breath. "Lock the door for security. I believe Cwenhild is leaving town tomorrow night. Don't leave the smokehouse until then."

Aliwyn nodded with an iciness tingling down her back. The residents of Mablethorpe resented her, and now Aelfric as well. How could they stay together in this small space?

They entered the smokehouse with the same two barrels, the mattress, and a hole in the thatched roof. Wulfstan left the bucket of water beside the door as Aelfric lowered Godwin onto a bed.

Aliwyn's heart raced as the man turned to leave. He was a busy man who sold wool in addition to serving as the town's constable, and yet he had taken time to deliver a mattress and cookware to this smokehouse until her health improved. In return, she had only caused him trouble. She hadn't even returned everything she had stolen.

"Sir," she called out.

Wulfstan turned around, and Aliwyn dug into her largest belt pouch to pull out the mittens she had sewn. They were a damp and matted mess by now. Her lips trembled as she offered them with both hands.

"I sewed these with the cloth I cut from the dresses. I shouldn't keep them. Maybe you'll find someone in the sanctuary who needs mittens…"

Wulfstan smiled, but the warmth in his gaze only made sobs rack her body. He looked like her father, much like any other man in his thirties with dark hair and a beard. And her father, had he been alive, would be so ashamed of how she had deteriorated into a petty thief.

"Thank you." Wulfstan collected the mittens from her hand. "I do know of people who can use these. A refugee family who just arrived from up north."

Aliwyn mustered a grin as he continued. "I forgot to ask Father Norbert to see you for your injuries. Should I send him to you?"

"Oh, no. I'm better off without him."

"I can see that nothing has helped your condition." Wulfstan's lips thinned. "I have some deliveries to make, but I'll return at sunset to check on you."

He departed in the bright afternoon sun, and she bolted the door with an echoing click of the metal latch. It felt good to have nothing left of what she had stolen, but her relief didn't last. Behind her, Aelfric growled and stomped the floor.

Her back stiff, she turned around.

Aelfric tore off his headscarf, crumpled it, and threw it down. The way he had so violently beaten off the three women now haunted her. What if he took out his anger on her next?

But he only slowed his pacing, his face contorted with misery.

"Aelfric," she whispered. "Again, I'm really sorry."

"Why did you do it?" His voice rose and fell with the jerking of his chest. "My recorder won't sell for much, but my father made it for me, and I can't live without it."

CHAPTER 7

"I didn't mean to steal it. I thought your bag of seashells was full of pennies, so I cut it open. I grabbed your recorder by accident." She held her breath when Aelfric's brown eyes pierced her once more. "Then you woke up and left. I tried to follow you, but I was arrested."

Aliwyn suppressed a sneeze and tasted blood. She licked her lips only to taste more. Her gums were bleeding again, and she covered her mouth with her face burning. She must look disgusting. On the opposite side of the smokehouse, Aelfric looked down and tugged on the hole in his belt pouch, his expression unreadable behind a curtain of black bangs.

"I can sew the hole for you," she said.

"I'll sew it myself!"

"I-I saw you pay for the gown I stole. I'd pay you back, but Cwenhild took all my pennies. If I can still make it up to you—"

"You can't. Not unless you make money fall from the sky." He pointed at the ceiling. "I don't have enough money to sail for Scotland anymore."

He walked to the opening under the roof and sat there with his back turned. He yanked out what looked like a wooden sewing kit from his knapsack, and Aliwyn swallowed more blood leaking into her mouth. It happened so often that she no longer felt afraid, but the metallic taste made her nauseous. Being stuck with Aelfric made everything worse. Why had he defended her if he loathed her this much?

There was nothing else she could do. She kneeled by the hearth and retrieved her flint, fire striker, and charred rag from the tinderbox in her belt pouch. Her heart thrumming, she kept Aelfric in her peripheral view. He sat cross-legged. Under his folded knee, the sole of his shoe was so detached it looked like parted duckbills. An old whip scar peeked from his hood and snaked around his nape. The full brunt of the dangers he still faced crashed onto her, and she squeezed the frigid metal striker.

She wanted to help Aelfric evade the Staddons for as long as she could. A plan formed in her mind that would help them both, but how could she earn his trust?

Aliwyn whispered the first thing that came to her mind. "Aelfric, I just want to say...thank you for defending me today."

Aliwyn meant every word she said, but Aelfric showed no reaction.

Her eyes blurred. She struck the flint to ignite the charred cloth, but the metal hit her thumb instead. Aliwyn hardly acknowledged the pain, and she let the objects slip from her grasp.

Aelfric

AELFRIC HELD HIS BREATH as Aliwyn's words of gratitude swirled in his head. Finally, he turned around at the sound of objects thudding onto the ground. Aliwyn was kneeling before the cold hearth with a bleeding hand pressed against her sleeve, and the ache he had been nursing in his throat expanded. He had never seen anyone bleed so easily. Thank Heavens no one else in Mablethorpe seemed to have what she had.

"How did you just hurt yourself?" he asked.

She gestured at a metal striker on the ground, her lips parted. Without her cloak, she shivered in her filthy dress.

"I'll start the fire." Aelfric broke the sewing thread with his teeth and slipped the needle back into his sewing box.

He checked on Godwin as he stood up. The boy slept on his belly with his chubby cheek squished against the mattress, and Aelfric grinned. Nonetheless, a heaviness settled back over his shoulders as he eyed Aliwyn's bloody hand.

Aliwyn's light blue eyes widened as he approached, and he tried to relax his frown. The sight of Cwenhild and her sisters throwing her aside and kicking her flashed in his mind. It was the way Cuthbert had once broken Aelfric's ribs, and he still reeled at the memory.

Stooping, he picked up the flint and a piece of blackened rag. He struck the flint until the charred cloth began to smoke. His breaths brought life to a tiny flame, and he lowered the cloth onto a bed of wood shavings. Aliwyn rose to fetch firewood from behind the door. They fed the hearth until golden flames licked their way up between the logs, chasing away the shadows and bathing them in an orange glow.

Aelfric opened his hands toward the warmth. "It bothers me that no one else tried to help you. The whole crowd watched but did nothing. It was awful."

"It's not surprising. People think I'm cursed by God."

"What? Why would God do that?"

She was silent for a moment. "For…for sinning in the past."

Aelfric shook his head. His father had explained why this way of thinking was wrong, but he didn't remember exactly what he'd said.

"I don't believe it," Aelfric muttered. "There are thousands of Normans in England, and they're living mighty fine lives despite all their killing and stealing. If we all got cursed for doing bad things, we'd all be dead."

He didn't expect her to smile.

"I appreciate that," she said. "I wish I could read the scriptures myself to see what they say. I don't believe I'm cursed, either, but the priest convinced his congregation to avoid me."

"Why does Father Norbert hate you so much?"

"I yelled at him for betraying his faith and selling helpless children."

"Well, then." Aelfric shifted his weight. "You have your answer. This is not about God. That man is mad at you, so don't believe what he says."

She kept her gaze lowered. "But the rest of the town believes him. They avoid me because Easter is such a holy holiday."

Aelfric scoffed. Cwenhild and her sisters could wear gorgeous Easter dresses, appearing as holy as ever, but inside they'd still be full of cobwebs. The thought sent chills prickling down his scalp. He could criticize them if he wanted to, but he felt just as bitter toward Aliwyn.

Until he got his money back and escaped England, he couldn't just forget all the ways she had wronged him. How did he expect her to pay him back, though? Aelfric wrestled with himself until his face grew hot. Finally, pushing those thoughts to the back of his mind, he changed the subject.

"So, about your ailment," he said. "Let's agree it's not a curse. Have you sought treatment?"

"Yes. From many different priests and healers. They've given me boiled pork liver, fish heads, some bitter teas, hot baths, and ointments of all kinds. They also tried bloodletting."

"Bloodletting?" Aelfric raised an eyebrow. "I'll wager that just made you worse!"

Aelfric's grandmother had told him bloodletting never worked, but he regretted speaking so glibly. Aliwyn kept her eyes downcast. The fire cast a warm glow over her features, and he could almost imagine what she'd looked like in her healthier days. With her gently curved eyebrows and large eyes, she would've looked very different.

Aliwyn pulled the cork out of her water costrel and took a sip. "A-anyway, I wanted to ask you something. How many pennies do you have left?"

He hardened his lips. "Why do you ask?"

"It's cheaper to sail from Barton-Upon-Humber. They have a bigger port with more ships, and the captains keep prices low to compete for passengers. The fare to Scotland cost only fifteen pennies about a month ago."

"Really? How do you know?"

"Because I stayed in Barton-Upon-Humber for a while. I can help you get there." She smiled at him. "There are carriages departing for Barton every day. We can board one together, and I'll do the talking."

Aelfric couldn't shake the feeling she had ulterior motives. "How much does the fare to Barton cost?"

"Two pennies per passenger."

"And if you come with me, I'll have to pay for your fare?"

Sorrow wrinkled her forehead. "Well...yes."

"Look, Aliwyn." He rubbed his nose. "I don't have proof the fares to Scotland are cheaper in Barton."

"Just ask any merchant in Mablethorpe. They'll confirm what I said."

"Even if they do, I'm not paying for your ride."

Barton-Upon-Humber was situated north and closer to Beverley. Aliwyn was simply negotiating herself a free ride to Barton.

She sat back and hugged her knees to her chest. Shafts of afternoon sunshine beamed through the broken roof overhead. Her eyes were tearing again, and Aelfric struggled for words. Had she not been a thief who'd wrecked his plans, maybe he'd trust her more by now.

The crackling fire filled the silence between them.

"You don't know of some hidden tunnel leading out of town?" he mumbled. "Or some other way I can sneak out?"

"No..."

Aelfric sighed with the sinking feeling of doom. He toyed with the idea of setting rooftops on fire to create a distraction, but how could he live with himself afterward?

"If putting me on a carriage is your best plan," he muttered, "I might as well sneak out of Mablethorpe by myself and keep you out of this."

Aliwyn didn't move. The background churning of his stomach intensified into loud gurgles, but he was in no mood to eat. All the odds kept stacking against him. What had he done to deserve such bad luck? And if Aliwyn was right about the fare being cheaper in Barton, did he even have fifteen pennies left?

Aelfric turned aside and fished out his remaining money. He counted the shimmering objects in the firelight. Though it was pleasing to count more and more, his heart began to race. Aliwyn must be staring at him.

Aelfric counted his money several times until he was sure he had more than fifteen pennies. Aliwyn had better be telling the truth about a cheaper fare in Barton. But he still needed to sneak out of Mablethorpe first...

Aliwyn rose and adjusted Godwin's blankets before approaching the twin barrels by the wall. Bracing onto one of them, she began to scoot it away from the other.

"Do you like turnip stew?" She looked back at Aelfric.

"I eat most things. Why do you ask?"

"I'll make stew for us."

Aelfric tried to ignore the aching of his stomach. Now, she'd charge him ten pennies per bowl to wring money out of him. He squeezed the pennies he had been counting and crossed his arms.

Aliwyn stepped in between the two separated barrels. Both objects had splintered on the side and were fit for smashing into firewood. Yet, placed together with their holes facing each other, the two complemented each other's shortcomings and served well as storage space.

She kneeled and retrieved a clay pot and metal stand from inside one of the barrels. A drawstring bag of what could be grain protruded from within the pot, and a few turnips tumbled by her feet. Aliwyn gathered the turnips into the pot.

Smiling, she carried everything toward him.

Aelfric glowered at her. "How did you afford cookware and all this food?"

"Wulfstan let me borrow his pot and gave me some smoked meat. I paid for the rest of the food myself by selling mittens." Her expression sank. "Nothing I'm holding is stolen, if that's what you're asking."

That was precisely what he was implying, and Aelfric shuffled in his seat. "H-how much do you charge per bowl?"

"Nothing. It's free."

"What? Why?"

Aliwyn didn't answer. A scowl now shadowing her face, she placed the stand over the fire and lowered the pot beside him. She left to fetch the bucket of water by the door, and the coins on Aelfric's palms grew damp and heavy. He slipped them back into his pouch.

His hand glided over the recorder she had returned wrapped in a handkerchief. He pulled it out and unwrapped the cloth. Inside, his instrument was clean and without cracks, and Aliwyn had returned the two half pennies he had given her.

He scratched his eyebrows. That morning, he had been generous because he wanted Aliwyn to bring Godwin to his parents. Now Aliwyn had returned his donation and was sharing her food without charging him. How would she go to Beverley now, or even buy her next meal?

"Aliwyn," he said. "Did you say Cwenhild grabbed all your money?"

"Yes, and my cloak." She poured water into the clay pot.

"That isn't right. You should ask for everything back."

"Well, I ruined her nicest dresses. That wasn't right, either."

Her face reddening, Aliwyn sat and peeled a dirty turnip with her eating knife. Reddish bruises covered her wrists and forearms where the women had struck her. Aelfric could imagine her hurting herself again, and he extended his hand.

"Let me do it."

She passed him the turnip and knife with tears welling in her eyes. The heaviness behind his ribs worsened. She needed more than someone who could peel her vegetables. He took pride in earning all his pennies through lawful, hard work, but he saved them for himself. Aliwyn might be a thief, but she didn't keep things for herself even when she had little left. Shouldn't she be pacing the room in a panic instead of cooking?

Aliwyn carried the peeled turnips to a barrel to slice them on top. She boiled the slices with pieces of smoked meat, barley, and dried thyme, and the irresistible fragrance of hot stew filled the room. Soon, Aelfric was too busy swallowing saliva to think of anything but eating.

When the stew was ready, she served them both and said grace. Aelfric cupped his bowl and sipped, relishing the medley of flavors that poured over his tongue. Salt, fat, and chunks of meat! What could be better? His spirits lifted as the meal soothed his gurgling stomach. He ate so fast he burned his mouth, but Aliwyn only sat and watched him.

"Do you like it?" She grinned.

He wiped his mouth. "Obviously, I do."

Her smile broadened, and her lips parted with a flash of bright scarlet. Was that blood smeared all over her teeth? Aelfric almost coughed out his food, and Aliwyn ducked her head.

She left for Godwin's side and patted the boy's shoulder. "It's time to eat, sweetheart."

As the tot stirred and sat up, Aelfric stared at her with his back stiff. Maybe he had just imagined that terrifying smile.

"Take as much as you want," Aliwyn said. "Just leave my bowl to cool for Godwin."

He began licking his bowl. "I'll eat it, all right. Why aren't you charging me?"

"Does everything have to cost money?"

"I guess not."

Ravenous for more, Aelfric helped himself to another bowl. Aliwyn turned around to take the serving for Godwin but didn't look at him again.

Aelfric finished two more bowls while she fed Godwin on her lap. She sang and spoke to him, and her gentle melodies filled the room. Her sweetness with the boy made Aelfric's throat swell. His grandmother and mother also used to sing to him, but missing them was a feeling he had numbed for years.

Aliwyn wiped Godwin's face and hands with a handkerchief and tucked him in again. When she turned around to serve herself, Aelfric's face flushed. He'd eaten almost everything. The storage space formed by her two barrels was now empty.

"What are you eating tomorrow?" he asked.

She sipped her meal. "I'll beg outside the church."

Aelfric squinted at the glowing embers beneath the cauldron. Begging had been a terrible experience he never wanted to repeat. Had Aliwyn turned him in for a reward, she might be on a carriage to Beverley by now. He shuddered at the memory of Cuthbert's face and how Aliwyn had also protected Godwin from capture. She may be a thief, but she kept her word.

Perhaps he should accept her help to escape. It wasn't as though he had any grand ideas.

"As for you," Aliwyn said. "What are you doing tomorrow? How do you plan on leaving Mablethorpe?"

"I..." He grimaced. "I guess I could..."

He froze when her gaze lifted toward him. The statement that he'd pay for her and Godwin's fare to Barton-Upon-Humber stuck in his throat. He wanted to count his pennies one last time to ensure he had enough for everyone and a ship's fare for himself, but his hesitation made him want to punch a wall.

"You're sure you want to sneak me out of here?" His voice was squeaky. "Because if you get caught, you'll also be in trouble."

She set down her bowl and smiled. "I'm willing to do it."

"Then I'll...pay for all of us to go to Barton."

"Really?" Light returned to her eyes. "Thank you so much. What made you change your mind?" She chuckled. "Don't tell me it's because I fed you."

"Well, I like your stew, but…" He scowled, trying to put his thoughts into words. "I want Godwin to go home. And also, I'm glad you helped me hide—"

Before he could finish, a scuffling noise emerged from the hole beneath the smokehouse wall. Aelfric dropped his empty bowl and shot to his feet.

Chapter 8

Aliwyn

ALIWYN PUSHED HERSELF UPRIGHT. Her knees throbbed from the sudden movement, but she ignored it and hurried to where Aelfric had thrown down his headscarf. She grabbed the cloth, swerved back to his side, and wrapped it over his head and shoulders.

The two of them stared at the escape hole. Neither Cuthbert nor a militia man dragged himself through. Instead, a timid voice spoke from the shadows.

"Hello, Mister Piper?" It sounded like a young boy. "Thank you for the seashell. It shines like a star. Da says my mum is also a star now, up in the sky."

Aliwyn froze with her eyes widened. She didn't know when Aelfric had given the boy a seashell, but the child had unraveled Aelfric's identity as the town's former piper. How did the boy know?

The child continued from outside. "My Da said I should tell you to run. An angry lady and her friends are coming. Goodbye."

The boy's footsteps scampered away, and Aliwyn's vision washed with stars. The angry ladies could only be Cwenhild and her sisters. Aelfric dashed for the smokehouse door, unbolted it, and pulled it open a slit. He peered outside, and Aliwyn skidded to a stop behind him. Her throat throbbing, she lowered herself and looked through the space below his head.

A crowd of militiamen with vivid blue scarves in the distance marched along the waterfront and toward the smokehouse. Three women walked amongst them, just close enough to be recognized as Cwenhild and her sisters.

She must've seen Aelfric too closely during their scuffle and had recognized him. Or someone else in the crowd had pointed him out after the fight. Regardless, Aelfric was moments from being caught. A bald man marched at the side of the procession—Cuthbert Staddon.

"By the Devil's tail," Aelfric wheezed.

He began to swing the door open, but Aliwyn grabbed his arm and flung his hand off the door handle. She threw herself back against the door and forced it shut again.

"Stop," she whispered. "If you run outside now, everyone will see where you're going. They'll grab you!"

All color had drained from his face, and his jaw quivered. "You can't help me anymore. I have to go."

"Then don't run out the door. Go out the back tunnel, and I'll come with you. I have an idea."

"You can't help me!"

His forehead wrinkled in misery, and he tried to wiggle his hand behind her back to grab the door handle again.

Aliwyn pushed him back by the shoulders. "Stop! I said I have an idea. There's an underground cellar with a trapdoor close by. You can hide in there."

"W-who's cellar is it?"

"I'll tell you later!"

The cellar belonged to Wulfstan, who had sheltered her there for a week before moving her to the smokehouse. The cellar wasn't a brilliant place to hide, but nothing was worse than Aelfric charging out the door and exposing himself. She pulled him toward the wall's defect with all her might. He was strong despite his slim build. Blood rushed to her face before he relented and followed her lead.

When he fell on his belly to crawl, Aliwyn doubled back to collect Godwin from his mattress. Her head gave a nauseating spin. Before she knew it, she had landed on all fours by the tot. Pain shot up her kneecaps and jolted her to her senses. She froze for a moment, panting.

Was helping Aelfric the right decision? The punishment for hiding a runaway thrall was also fifteen lashes. It was evident she had lied about who he was, but if they parted ways now, maybe she could still save herself.

She shuddered, her head hovering over Godwin's chubby and tranquil face. Aelfric's footsteps pounded to a stop beside hers. He had tied up his dress in a knot above his knees. Throwing back Godwin's blankets, he collected the limp child into his arms. The boy was content to slump against Aelfric's shoulder, and Aliwyn released a breath of relief. Aelfric hurried away with the boy cradled like a priceless parcel, and Aliwyn's heart felt too big for her chest.

She couldn't abandon him now.

"I'll crawl out first," she said. "Then you pass Godwin through the hole and follow me."

If Wulfstan caught them, he'd be administering the fifteen lashes to them both, but she refused to believe he'd do it.

Aelfric

AELFRIC AND ALIWYN RAN into the burned ruins and ducked between broken buildings, charred wood, and crumbling ash. The blackened scaffolding of a church towered over them in the distance, its roofless beams reaching into the sky like bony fingers. Aelfric swallowed his dread as he followed at Aliwyn's heels. His limbs hurried on with a strange detachment from his body.

Aliwyn had been leading the way but was already gasping for air and slowing down. Meanwhile, the jostling run had shaken Godwin wide awake. He squealed with a big smile and kicked his legs along Aelfric's side as if ordering his pony to gallop.

"Da, da, da!"

CHAPTER 8

Aelfric gritted his teeth. Godwin's noises could ruin all their efforts, but trying to silence the boy would probably make him cry.

Aliwyn stopped by the counter of the ruined blacksmith's workshop and doubled over, bracing her left side and panting. A gust of wind carried the stench of animal carcasses and mold to Aelfric's nose. His stomach lurched. He shuddered in a cold sweat and fought the urge to dash off without Aliwyn.

"So whose cellar is it?" he asked.

She grimaced but didn't look at him. Aelfric stared at her thin frame with his throat clogging. She should be back in the smokehouse and lying in bed after a hot meal, not out here.

He had been a fool for thinking a disguise would save him. The moment he'd exited the boarding line for Scotland was when he'd forfeited his freedom. Getting caught had only been a matter of time. Even worse, he'd dragged Aliwyn and Godwin into the same mess.

Godwin still kicked and babbled in his arms, and Aelfric wanted to burst. He struggled to loosen Godwin's grip from around his neck. What kind of danger had he thrown this boy into?

"Aliwyn, take him," he stuttered. "I'm sorry you had to deal with me."

"It's Wulfstan's cellar," she whispered at the same time.

"What?" Aelfric chuckled bitterly. "Forget it! Tell everyone I threatened to kill you unless you lied about who I am. I have to go."

Panic flared in her eyes. "Where are you going?"

She shouldn't care. Aelfric jerked Godwin's arms off from around his neck. Lowering the boy to the floor, he tensed at how Godwin stared back at him, startled.

"Aelfric." Aliwyn tried to take his arm. "We're almost there."

He dodged her grasp and ran.

Aelfric turned left and skirted along the shadows of the burned church, but soon his legs faltered. There was nowhere to run. The smokehouse must be surrounded by now, and the militia at both town gates must be on high alert. Aelfric pressed himself against the crumbling foundations of the chapel with his heart hammering. His eyes darting left and right, he imagined men with blue scarves pouncing from around the corner, but none appeared. The smokehouse was lost behind a maze of buildings and overturned carts.

Maybe Aliwyn had led them this way to buy time. Her broken composure flashed in his mind. After all the trouble she had gone through, he'd abandoned her with a fantastical notion that he could still escape. A voice in his head screamed for him to turn back. If he had nowhere to go, neither did she.

Hiding in a cellar, even the bailiff's cellar, was better than not hiding at all. He should've listened to her.

Aelfric staggered back the way he'd come, toward Aliwyn and Godwin, or so he thought. Where were they? With his chin in the air, he strained to hear the tot's squeals above his ragged breathing. The sound of a whinnying horse reached his ears instead.

A cold finger traced down his spine. The militiamen didn't ride horses. They were the town's peasants who volunteered their time, and either couldn't afford horses or had no need for them. Had Cuthbert gone so far as to call upon the Norman knights for help?

Horse hooves striking the ground thundered from behind the buildings ahead. A girl shrieked.

By the Devil's tail!

Aelfric bolted toward the noise. More voices reached his ears—those of a man speaking and a girl whimpering. Most knights were foreign invaders, and their warhorses could kick and maim. Aliwyn didn't stand a chance. If he turned himself in, would the man on horseback spare her?

He sped on with the fear of finding Aliwyn battered and bleeding storming his mind. Before long, the musky smell of wool blew to his nose. There had been no sheep or remnants of any in the area. The scent made no sense, but now was not the time to wonder.

His vision blackening from exertion, Aelfric dashed past a street corner. To his right, he caught sight of Aliwyn with a tall man. Aelfric swerved toward them. His teeth clattered to the pounding of his feet, but no knight terrorized the ramshackle streets. Instead, Wulfstan stood by a horse-drawn wagon with his hands around Aliwyn's shoulders. She looked like a ragged doll with her head hanging. He must be arresting her.

CHAPTER 8

"Don't hurt her," he blurted out. "I'm the one you want."

The cry had no force, as he had no air left. Aelfric's feet stumbled to a stop, and the muscles of his legs ached. He held up his hands in surrender and pressed forward, shaking. Wulfstan should lunge to arrest him now. The charred buildings seemed to tilt and swerve around him. No one grabbed his neck. Aelfric's eyes rounded when Godwin peered from behind Wulfstan's legs with a calm, curious smile.

"Aelfric." Aliwyn smiled. "I'm so glad you're back."

Her shoulders slumped within Wulfstan's hands. He stooped, hooked his arm behind her knees, and lifted. Aelfric gawked with his hands still raised as Wulfstan carried Aliwyn to the rear of the covered wagon.

"We didn't know how we'd find you." Wulfstan frowned at him. "Now get on, quick."

He jerked his head toward the wagon, his gaze locked on the ruins behind Aelfric.

No bloodshed, no arrest. Aliwyn wasn't hurt. Shivers racked Aelfric's frame as the nightmare he had conjured up crumbled like cinders around a fire.

Godwin scampered after Wulfstan in his usual wobbly gait, punctuated with little hops and swings of his arm. Wulfstan turned around, picked up the tot, and set him on the wagon. Aliwyn put her arm around Godwin and leaned out the back of the wagon, beckoning for Aelfric to follow.

Aelfric wiped his eyes. His heart skipped, and he ran to join her.

Burlap sacks cluttered the interior of the wagon. They were probably all filled with wool. A pungent sheep smell filled Aelfric's lungs as he panted and scrambled to squeeze between two bags. His back rolled against the wooden walls with a thump. The rough bags scratched the sides of his sweaty neck, and he suppressed a sneeze.

It was cool and dark. Aliwyn sat opposite him, her hood pulled over her head, and Godwin nestled between her knees. The whites of her eyes glimmered in the dimness, and she looked back at him with a blank face. Aelfric wanted to ask if she was all right, but it wasn't the time to talk. Wulfstan made the wagon rock when he sat at the front. As the evening sun silhouetted his shoulders, he set the wagon into motion. The momentum made Aelfric sway to his right.

He clutched his kneecaps as the scenery outside changed from blackened buildings to spritely green shrubs and forestry. The refreshing scent of evergreens tickled his nose. Aelfric recognized this route. Wulfstan drove the wagon toward the royal forest, a stretch of woodland protected for the king's hunting excursions and forbidden to others except by special permission. Aelfric had once wandered to the forest's edge, spotted a fat pheasant, and drooled over the thought of roasting it.

What lay on the other side of the forest, he didn't know.

Wulfstan glanced behind him and spoke above the churning wagon wheels. "You must have questions for me."

"I do." Aelfric leaned forward. "Where are we going?"

"Saltfleet," Wulfstan began. Without warning, his jaw clamped shut, and his head snapped back to the road.

The wagon jostled onward. Aelfric sucked in his breath when Edgar Staddon's cry rang from outside. "Wulfstan, sir! I need your help!"

The constable pulled the wagon to a stop, and Aelfric locked his arms around his knees. Across from him, Aliwyn gathered Godwin to her chest and buried the boy's face against her shoulder. Her parted lips quivered.

"What is it?" Wulfstan called out.

"Cwenhild identified the runaway." Edgar's footsteps halted beside the wagon. He was panting. "He was, in fact, the mute girl in the smokehouse we saw yesterday, but...my father just told me the smokehouse is empty!"

"How unfortunate," Wulfstan said. "Why don't you all search in the marketplace?"

"We will, but we cannot enter the royal forest. Please tell me if you see the boy—"

"Yes, no problem. I have a delivery to make, so I must hurry on now."

With that, Wulfstan clicked his tongue, and the wagon jerked back into motion. Aelfric slumped back against the wooden boards. He closed his eyes to the rollicking movements of the wagon and released the tension in his limbs. Nonetheless, bouts of dread still made his ribs spasm. A long time passed to the rhythmic clopping of horse hooves.

When he looked at Aliwyn again, she had lowered her head. Godwin was curled on his side in her lap and was nodding off. Aelfric wanted to see her face, to apologize for abandoning her, but his words were lost in a swirl of emotions.

Conifer branches scraped over the top of the wagon. Wulfstan turned around again, his concerned gaze wandering between his passengers.

"Thank you, sir." Aelfric stammered. "I don't know why you helped me."

"It's a matter of principle." A breeze blew Wulfstan's wavy brown hair about his face. "We lament the Normans for mistreating our people, and yet we sell our own overseas the way we would sell sheep or barrels of salt. I am opposed to it, although I'm in the minority."

Aelfric scratched the back of his neck. He had never felt like he belonged to the English people. Cuthbert's beatings had made it clear Aelfric had been set apart since birth, but Wulfstan didn't see him that way. Of all people, he was the constable responsible for catching runaways.

"I wish I could pay you back," Aelfric said.

"Don't. The most valuable things in life are given, not bought."

Aelfric pressed his flushing cheeks into the sack beside him. No one—especially not Aliwyn—should see him tearing up.

"I couldn't have fetched you in time had you not run for my residence," Wulfstan said. "What prompted you to come for me?"

Aliwyn spoke for the first time, her voice timid. "I thought I could hide Aelfric in your cellar. And also, a little boy warned us people were coming to arrest Aelfric."

Wulfstan steered the wagon to the left, and a few rays of light penetrated the pine branches. "I believe I know that boy. His father volunteers in the militia and identified Aelfric on the waterfront this morning."

Aelfric pulled his face back from the sack with a shiver tingling his spine. He remembered the boy with the seashell and the spark of excitement in his eyes. All along, his father had recognized Aelfric as an escapee.

"But he didn't turn me in," Aelfric stuttered.

"No, and he wasn't the only one who recognized you but walked on," Wulfstan said with a sigh. "The others eventually reported your identity to me, and I…I waited for you to leave town. But you didn't. Cwenhild finally recognized you, and she had other plans."

Aelfric frowned at the floorboards. So much for thinking his disguise was brilliant and that the townsfolk were as dull as wood.

"I think many people loved your music," Aliwyn said softly.

Aelfric rubbed his nose. He had regarded the people of Mablethorpe as little more than walking purses. Every penny they tossed him made him smirk at how easy it was to dupe someone into giving up their hard-earned profits. After all, Aelfric wasn't a minstrel with proper training, and he simply made up music as he went. He'd felt like a clever imposter. Tears welled in his eyes again.

He was glad he'd given the boy a seashell. Hopefully, the child wouldn't face any consequences for warning Aelfric about the impending disaster.

"Will you get into trouble for helping us, Wulfstan?" Aliwyn asked.

"God willing, I won't get caught," he answered. "I often take this route for deliveries, so it seems nothing out of the ordinary. And if my deeds are exposed…" He dipped his chin. "Then I'll resign. I've wanted to for a while."

"What?" Aliwyn scowled. "But why?"

"Mablethorpe has not been the same since it was granted a town charter." Wulfstan picked up his costrel and took a sip. "Now, instead of governance by a lord, the town is ruled by greed. The burned homes you saw were left to rot because only the poor were affected. The inhabitants have been forced to leave, and workshops and taverns will replace their homes."

Aelfric drew a slow breath. He had never imagined such an ugly side could exist in a thriving town.

CHAPTER 8

"And there was the sale of children I couldn't stop a few weeks ago." Wulfstan passed his hand over his face.

"I know you tried to intervene," Aliwyn said. "Wulfstan, for what it's worth, I think you're a great constable."

He turned around and smiled. "Thank you."

The wagon continued in silence, winding its way through the forest path. Godwin's eyelids drooped shut, and Aliwyn yawned. Aelfric's stomach hurt from eating too much and then running, but there were more serious matters to sort through.

"Wulfstan," he said. "Are there ships to Scotland leaving from Saltfleet?"

"Yes, plenty because of the salt trade."

Aelfric's eyebrows shot up. "How much is the fare?"

"The ships don't take passengers, but you can present yourself for hire. Find a ship with a yellow sail. Those dock every weekday morning fresh from the North Sea. The crew wouldn't have heard of any runaways, and they'll sail to Scotland."

Aelfric's heart gave a great leap. He flexed his arms a few times. "Sure, I can find work."

He'd jump at the opportunity of being a cabin boy this time. Sailing from Saltfleet would be much faster than traveling to Barton-Upon-Humber and trying his luck there. Grinning, he drummed his fingers on the side of his thigh and looked at Aliwyn, but she only squinted miserably back at him.

The excitement drained out of him. Didn't she know all along they would go their separate ways?

"Wulfstan," Aliwyn said. "Where can we stay in Saltfleet overnight?"

"Saltfleet has a Norman convent sheltering English refugees. The sisters there want nothing to do with thrall owners. I've seen them drive Edgar Staddon away in the past."

"That's great," Aelfric said. "But does the shelter take boys? 'Cause I'm done with this dress."

Aliwyn frowned. "You should keep it on until you can set sail."

"Why? The dress didn't even fool—"

"The convent must have a way to shelter both men and women," Wulfstan interrupted. "Aelfric can decide what he wants to wear. But the nuns have also accepted many…"

"What?" Aelfric asked.

"Vasfians."

"Vasfians!" Aliwyn straightened, catching Godwin's head before he peeled off her shoulder. "But they're not refugees!"

"No." Wulfstan shook his head. "And I don't know why they're staying with the sisters. I hardly speak Norman French, so I couldn't ask."

Aelfric's heart sank at Aliwyn's deepening scowl. None of the English he knew liked Vasfians, but he didn't expect her reaction to be so intense.

The Vasfians were forest dwellers who lived independently of the king's rule and rejected the church's teachings. They spoke their own language and didn't interact much with those outside their hill forts. Cuthbert's clients had talked about their terrifying rituals of human sacrifice and headhunting, but Aelfric didn't know how true that was.

Both his grandmothers had been tribal women who'd moved to Scotland along with hundreds of other Vasfians. His paternal grandmother had taught both Aelfric and his father how to play the recorder. Cuthbert had beaten her often because of her freckles, although her red hair had turned silver by the time Aelfric had been born. She'd passed away in her sleep when Aelfric was nine.

He'd never met his maternal grandmother, who'd died back in Scotland.

Because of his heritage, Aelfric had always wanted to meet a Vasfian living in a tribe—without getting killed.

Aliwyn pulled on a tear on her sleeve. "Is there somewhere else in Saltfleet we can stay? The Vasfians are covered in freckles. They look more ill than I do."

"They're born that way," Aelfric said between his teeth.

Aliwyn scowled at him. "My little sister had a rash that made her look like a Vasfian, and it killed her."

Aelfric opened his mouth, but Wulfstan spoke first.

CHAPTER 8

"The convent is the only safe place to stay. The town is otherwise full of salt houses, not taverns. The Vasfian presence bothers me also, but staying in Mablethorpe poses a greater risk for all of you."

"I doubt Cuthbert would go to a place with Norman French-speaking nuns and Vasfians around," Aelfric said. "So staying at the convent sounds fine to me."

He glared at Aliwyn. Her frown deepened, and she averted her eyes.

Vasfian blood coursed through his veins. He didn't have their freckles or red hair, but everything Aliwyn had said about the tribes felt like a blow. Aelfric had to defend his own, even if his attitude made her suspect he had connections with the Vasfians. What would he do if she questioned him about his past? Lie about his family? His heart racing, Aelfric pressed his back against the wagon.

It was a good thing he wouldn't be with Aliwyn for long.

Chapter 9

Aelfric

As the sun dipped out of sight, the wagon emerged from the woodland and rolled onto muddy marshland. Clusters of trees still dotted the landscape, but many were rotting tree stumps. Perhaps too much salt had leached into the land and killed the trees.

Aliwyn and Godwin were asleep between the bags of wool. Aelfric changed into his spare tunic. For a long time, he rubbed his bleary eyes and fought to stay awake. Aliwyn's reaction to the news of Vasfians still bothered him, but as the wagon rolled onto the sandy roads of Saltfleet, the sharp scent of the sea intensified and stole his attention.

Aelfric had only heard of how the salt houses functioned, but he hadn't seen any until now.

He stretched his neck to look past Wulfstan's shoulders. Rectangular stone buildings rose from the otherwise flat and exposed landscape. Smoke billowed from the opposing corners of their sloping, straw-thatched roofs. The seawater must've been boiling inside. Workers shoveled shallow pools of brine between the buildings to collect the salt crystalizing along the bottom.

Wulfstan's wagon passed women selling their displays of spices and fresh herbs to cure meat. All along the streets, men pushed wheelbarrows laden with sacks of white minerals.

The wagon eventually rolled into a deserted area where only logs and giant tree stumps stood in the foreground of a flat beach. They stopped

CHAPTER 9

in the shadows of an enormous rotting tree whose hollowed center could have fit Aelfric lying down.

Wulfstan turned to face his passengers, but only Aelfric was still awake.

"The convent is a short walk from here," the man said. "It's protected by a thick wall. You can't miss it."

"Oh, I won't." Aelfric suppressed a yawn.

Wulfstan gestured for Aelfric to come closer. "There's something we need to discuss."

Had he done something wrong? With a tremor in his limbs, Aelfric crawled toward the driver's seat. He pushed up from his hands and knees and sat back. "Yes, sir?"

A beard covered most of Wulfstan's face, but the fine lines fanning from the corners of his eyes told of a man who smiled often.

"I'd like you to talk to Aliwyn about her ambitions," he said.

"About going to Beverley, you mean?"

"Yes. Godwin's the son of an English thegn who—"

Aelfric gasped. "What? His father's rich?"

"Let me finish. I know Godwin's father, Osbeorn. He has been evicted and must leave England by mid-April. A Norman baron has already taken his land, so chances are, the family has already departed."

Aelfric scratched his eyebrow. It was too bad the Norman king had evicted Godwin's family and not the Staddons, who regularly and shrewdly avoided their tax dues.

"Aliwyn never told me Godwin's father is a thegn," Aelfric said. "Does she know his family's been thrown out of England?"

"She knows, but Godwin's nurse convinced her to take him to Beverley anyway. From what Aliwyn told me, the household had agreed to meet at Beverley Minster on Easter if they ever separated. They reasoned there would be a Truce of God during Easter."

"Truce of God? What's that?"

Wulfstan gave a half-grin. "It's when both sides acknowledge they believe in the same God and put down their arms for a few days. Then they start fighting again."

The bitterness in his voice made Aelfric nervous. He'd never considered that the Norman knights, full of themselves and armed to their teeth, also believed in God.

Wulfstan sighed. "Osbeorn wagered the Minster was so sacred even the Normans wouldn't burn it. He was right. A new Norman knight governs Beverley and has stabilized the area. If Osbeorn were to return, the Minster still stands."

So, Godwin was a rich man's son. That was why he had been given such a distinguished name. Most peasants Aelfric knew were named after their livelihoods or something mundane—not the divine.

Aelfric glanced back at Aliwyn, who was hardly visible in the dimness. He was talking behind her back, in a way, and he wasn't proud of it.

"So after all you've told me," he said, "there is still a chance Godwin would find his family at Beverley."

"Correct," Wulfstan said. "But Aliwyn is gravely ill. I wouldn't oppose her plans if she was healthy, but she needs to stay in the convent until she recovers."

Aelfric hung his head. "If you want me to talk her out of it, I can't. She won't listen to me. I just met her yesterday."

"Really?" Wulfstan asked. "The way she tried to save you, I thought you two were close friends."

Aelfric looked up at Wulfstan's smile, catching the sparkle in his eyes. Why did the man look so merry all of a sudden?

"Why can't you take Godwin to Beverley?" Aelfric mumbled.

"I can't leave Mablethorpe for more than a day. The town is still full of refugees and other children needing protection."

"But I told you she won't listen to me. I also want to set sail tomorrow—"

"Aelfric?" Aliwyn's voice came from behind him. "Where are you?"

She sounded frightened, and Aelfric turned around. "I'm here. We're in Saltfleet."

"And I have to leave you all here," Wulfstan said, his expression somber again. "Aliwyn, I'll help you get off."

CHAPTER 9

Wulfstan walked to the rear of the wagon and offered Aliwyn his hand. She stepped out beside the hollowed tree stump.

The evening shadows accentuated her scowl. "Did you see any Vasfians?"

"No," Aelfric mumbled. He jumped off beside her and tightened his hold around Godwin.

"The convent is spacious," Wulfstan said. "You should be able to avoid them."

Aliwyn's frown didn't ease. "My mother and I once saw the redheads surrounding a dead beggar in the forest. They had killed the man to take his head."

"It's possible. They are pagans, after all."

Aelfric wiggled his toes within his holey shoe. "How do you know they weren't burying the man?"

Aliwyn glared at him. "Because they dump bodies into village rivers!"

"Enough." Wulfstan turned back to the wagon. "I'll give you both something before you go."

Aelfric crossed his arms. Why couldn't anyone start nice rumors about the tribes? He had better keep his Vasfian heritage a secret or watch Aliwyn run away screaming.

Wulfstan leaned into the wagon's back opening and retrieved two dark blue cloaks, both neatly folded.

"Take them," he said. "Cuthbert isn't looking for anyone wearing these colors. Keep your heads covered." He opened one of the cloaks and showed them a pocket sewn inside it. "Hide your eating knives there in case there's trouble tonight. And Aliwyn, keep your scissors with you."

Aelfric nodded, his shoulders rigid. He shifted Godwin against his shoulder and took the cloak with his other hand. It was made of much softer material than his clothes, and its innermost layer was waterproof goatskin. Such clothing was not cheap.

"Thank you for everything, sir," he said.

Aliwyn also took a cloak with her lips pressed together.

Wulfstan smiled. "Godspeed to all of you."

He turned to Aliwyn and continued. "I saw the beautiful clovers you embroidered on those mittens. You deserve something for your work."

"But I..." Aliwyn wrung her hands.

Wulfstan reached into his belt pouch and took out four silver pennies. She gasped. "I don't deserve—"

"Yes, you do." He took her hand and folded her fingers over the coins.

Aelfric smiled. For all the nastiness that Cwenhild represented, there were also people like Wulfstan.

"Thank you," Aliwyn said in a foggy voice. "If I return to Mablethorpe one day, will I see you again?"

"I don't know. I'm tired, but I'm afraid the town will degenerate further if I leave. Please pray for me."

Both Aelfric and Aliwyn nodded.

Aelfric didn't expect the constable to turn to him one last time.

"My mother was a thrall who was freed upon her master's death," he said. "May you find freedom, too."

At the thought of being free, warmth flooded through Aelfric. Wulfstan's mother had been fortunate, and her son had made good use of his freedom. Aelfric wanted to be just as wealthy and successful as the constable one day.

As the man turned to leave, Aliwyn rounded on him. She wrapped her arms around his torso with tears streaming down her cheeks, and Wulfstan bowed his head as he returned her embrace.

A lump settled in Aelfric's throat. He should have no trouble finding work tomorrow, but he'd probably hurt Aliwyn again when he left.

Aliwyn released Wulfstan. He stepped onto the wagon and made it rock again with his weight. The wheels creaked into motion, and the wagon turned around a stretch of fallen trees. Wulfstan was gone.

Aliwyn took a few steps after the wagon, the back of her shoulders shaking. A salty breeze prompted Godwin to wiggle against the warmth of Aelfric's chest, and he sighed. His palm grew sweaty as he held his new cloak. How was he supposed to talk Aliwyn into giving up her plans when he also wanted Godwin to go home?

CHAPTER 9

The cries of waterfowl echoed in the distance. Thunderclouds blanketed the sky where the sun had set, and Aelfric forced himself back into the present. He was the reason Aliwyn and Godwin couldn't return to the smokehouse. If there was trouble tonight, he needed to be ready to protect everyone.

He had used a knife most of his life to carve wood. Though the weapon felt like an extension of his arm, he'd never attacked anyone with a blade. He hoped he wouldn't have to, but he could use the knife for something else immediately.

"Aliwyn," he said. "Can you hold Godwin for a moment? I need to cut off my hair."

She wiped her face. "C-cut your hair?"

"Yea. I don't want anyone to recognize me by my black hair. If the Vasfians give us trouble, I fight better without a headscarf."

She bit her lip. "May the Heavens protect us tonight. But if you want to cut your hair, I can do it with my scissors."

"Oh, right."

Aliwyn retrieved her scissors and pointed the tip toward the ground.

"Lean toward me a little," she said.

The glint of sharp metal blades made him stiffen, and he didn't move.

Aliwyn dipped her chin. "I won't hurt you, I promise. And why would I want to?"

Aelfric sighed. He had always been on guard against the other thralls, who were all older and bigger, but Aliwyn was no surly brute. Finally, he tilted his head toward her.

Aliwyn reached for his forehead with a smile. Her gentle hand combed through his bangs, and she worked quickly. She gathered his strands in her free hand as she snipped. With time, Aelfric's dread fell away like the occasional black wisp floating onto the ground.

No one had touched him like this since he'd lost his family. Godwin stirred against him, and Aelfric rubbed the boy's back with his thumb. With time, the memory of his mum also cutting his hair made his throat tighten.

He needed to distract himself. "Did you ever fight anyone with those scissors?"

Aliwyn shifted to work on his temples. "I had to threaten many people who tried to rob me in the churches. They had daggers."

"I...I thought weapons weren't allowed in sanctuaries."

"No one could enforce the rules. People were starving and crammed together."

What a terrible experience. Aelfric glanced at her sunken eyes, and the tension in her gaze made him fall silent.

Aliwyn collected his hair into a pile on the ground with her feet. She found a stick and began digging a hole to bury it all. Aelfric watched the top of her head and tightened his hold around Godwin. What she had told him made his stomach turn.

As they scraped his hair into the pit, it sank in that he'd never be Mablethorpe's piper boy again. He barely knew the two people he'd had to flee with, and Cuthbert could still follow them here. If the Staddons attacked Aliwyn and Godwin, how far would he go to save them?

Chapter 10

Aelfric

They set out for the convent as soon as Aliwyn finished burying Aelfric's hair. Godwin began crying in Aelfric's arms as his shoes crunched on a layer of crystallized salt. Next to him, Aliwyn struggled to keep up.

The slate rooftops of various buildings in the convent loomed ahead, and the tower of its church reached toward the dimming sky. Everything was surrounded by high walls of more stone, and the gate to the courtyard was of heavy timber reinforced with iron fastenings. The Normans were known for building foreboding castles, and they built convents the same way.

Aelfric glanced at the scraggly girl walking beside him. At least Wulfstan's cloak hid most of her face and, therefore, her rash. Likewise, Aelfric's new cloak hid his dress.

"Make up a name for yourself," he murmured.

"I'll be Esla. It was my sister's name."

"Fine. I'll be Blane, my father's name. And from now on, Godwin is Grafton."

Ahead of them, the convent gate opened to give entry to a donkey cart and driver, and Aelfric quickened his pace.

As he'd hoped, they slipped inside the gate before anyone could close it again. Ahead of them lay a spacious meadow with a garden to their right and a fish pond to their left. The donkey cart rolled toward yet another gate to the inner courtyard and disappeared within. A sister standing outside this second gate approached Aelfric and the others.

Her full habit of black and white trailed on the ground as she walked, and the large crucifix hanging from her neck swayed with her movements.

"Good evening," Aliwyn said, crossing herself.

The sister said something in Norman French and placed her hand on her chest. "Lucette."

Both Aelfric and Aliwyn introduced themselves by their fake names.

The thin skin around Lucette's eyes wrinkled as she smiled, but her cheer disappeared as her gaze flicked over Aliwyn. Aelfric tensed when the sister shuffled back. She crossed herself and whispered something incomprehensible.

"She's not contagious," Aelfric set one foot forward. "Let us go in... please."

There was nothing like a sniveling toddler to drain his patience. Shifting Godwin from one aching arm to another, he pointed toward the inner courtyard and resisted shoving his way in. Wasn't it obvious the three of them sought shelter?

Lucette unfurled her fingers one by one, on both hands, while speaking gibberish.

Aelfric squinted at her. "Are you asking how old I am? I'm almost fifteen, and she's—"

"I'm thirteen," Aliwyn said.

"Way too old to be locked in an orphanage, if that's what you're thinking. And we'll keep this one." Aelfric dodged a smack from Godwin's drool-drenched hand.

Lucette finally stepped aside with her lips pursed. She left the second gate and beckoned a wide-eyed Aelfric to follow.

"But I want to go inside!" He jabbed a finger at the partly opened door.

Aliwyn shook her head. "Maybe the shelter for refugees is elsewhere." She hurried to follow the nun.

Aelfric swallowed several times before scampering after the other two. His foot within the holey shoe burned from all the grit jammed inside. The procession walked over a carpet of last year's leaves, and two cats darted across their path and into the bushes. They passed a sloping cemetery of

CHAPTER 10

simple wooden crosses before arriving at a building with firewood stacked along one wall.

"Oh, this must be a warming house," Aliwyn said.

"A warming house?" he asked.

"Yes. I stayed in several of these on my way down to Mablethorpe. There's a fire inside."

Aelfric barely heard her over Godwin's cries. He squinted at what seemed to be smoke drifting from the corners of the triangular rooftops. Lucette swung the door open with tension wrinkling her forehead. She crossed herself again before gesturing for the others to enter.

"Thank you," Aliwyn said as she stepped inside.

The smell of burning pine branches greeted Aelfric as he followed her, and his footsteps rustled the rushes strewn on the ground. A central hearth cast a flickering glow on the walls. Three stools surrounded a single mattress, all positioned at a safe distance from the flames. In the far corner stood a large, empty basin. Aelfric eyed the basin, but he was too tired to ask what it was for.

Aelfric lowered Godwin onto the mattress before tossing down his knapsack. Crouching, he rubbed the tot's back until Godwin sucked his hand again and stopped crying.

"You're hungry, Grafton?" Aelfric smiled at the boy's glittering eyes. "Me too."

Aliwyn approached Lucette and bowed.

"May we have some food, please?" She tapped her fingers against her lips.

The nun nodded. She turned to Aelfric and beckoned for him to follow. He frowned at her. "What? Why do you need me?"

"Maybe you can help her carry something," Aliwyn said.

"But what if I'm gone a long time? We need to talk about your plans for tomorrow."

Aliwyn kneeled beside Godwin and hugged the boy. "That can wait until we have food. I'll bar the door while you're gone."

Aelfric stood and scowled at his feet. Wulfstan must've given her money to buy food or new clothes, not to plow on to Beverley. Four pennies weren't enough to pay for wagon rides all the way there, and she was too weak to walk the remaining distance.

Who would return Godwin to his parents then?

Lucette called out to Aelfric. He snapped to his senses and dragged his feet after the sister. When he looked up again, shadowy figures had crowded around the exit. One of them held a torch, and they blocked Lucette from exiting. Aelfric widened his stance.

Cast in the torch's glow, three women in flowing fur cloaks stared back at him. Firelight illuminated the freckles covering their cheeks and the tendrils of red hair escaping from their hoods.

Vasfian women!

Lucette spoke to them in the Norman language. The redhead carrying the torch looked straight at Aelfric and smiled.

"Hello, Englishman."

Aelfric's eyebrows shot up. How come she spoke English? Before he could respond, someone scampered to his side and yanked his arm. He yelped and nearly toppled over. Aliwyn stepped in front of him and raised her arms on either side.

"Don't talk to redheads!" she shouted. "They might hurt you!"

Aelfric stared at her with his mouth hanging open.

"You're yelling for nothing," he stammered. "Stay here and bolt the door."

He stepped past her and hurried for the exit. Almost kicking Lucette's heels, he slipped past the three Vasfians and marched into the night. The night air tickled his nearly bald head, but heat rose over his cheeks. How could Aliwyn be so polite yet become so rude within a span of heartbeats?

The Vasfian women followed him and Lucette, who ambled over the rolling meadows as though nothing was amiss. Aelfric glanced behind him. The Vasfian who had greeted him was the youngest one, probably no more than sixteen or seventeen, but she was already a head taller than he was.

His pulse raced. That girl spoke English and Norman French. If he and Aliwyn were to get by comfortably tonight, he needed a translator. He should talk to the girl again and try to make a connection.

He turned around and walked backward. "S-sorry about my friend back there."

Her full lips parted into a smile. "Most outsiders are terrified of me. How come you're not?"

This was not how he imagined the conversation would go. Sweat broke at Aelfric's hairline, and he almost tripped over a rock on the road. The merchants who visited Cuthbert's shop once recalled how the tribes had beheaded a trespasser and burned his corpse beside their sacred hot springs. His body had been found a few days later, thrown outside the town gates along with a wooden mask painted red.

Why wasn't he being more cautious?

He walked faster and almost surpassed Lucette as she led them past a series of imposing wooden buildings.

"Who taught you English?" Aelfric called back at the Vasfian. "And what are you doing at a convent?"

Lucette stopped before a door of one building with a glowing parchment window. Her silent but stern frown pricked Aelfric with guilt. Was yelling prohibited in a convent?

Aelfric wiped his damp palms on his cloak and passed over the contours of his knife in his inner pocket. He caught his breath. Wulfstan believed he might need a weapon, but he would only wield it as a last resort. Aelfric shouldn't let all that gossip about the Vasfians get to him. The redheads at the convent hadn't threatened anyone.

With his body tense, Aelfric lowered his hand.

The door opened for Lucette. She greeted several sisters who sat embroidering a tapestry by the light of a rush lamp. Lucette stepped inside, and the door shut again.

Aelfric spun around when the Vasfian woman approached him from behind.

"Let's start over." She smiled and extended a hand. "My name is Reiya of the Mehi tribe. And you?"

Freckles covered her straight and slender fingers like stars in a night's sky, and Aelfric's scalp tingled. His grandmother had had just as many freckles. Aelfric, on the other hand, had none that he knew of.

"Am I doing it wrong?" Reiya rotated her hand a few times. "This is a handshake, is it not?"

"Y-yes." He grabbed her hand and squeezed. "I'm...Blane."

"A Scottish name! Are you from Scotland?"

Aelfric swallowed. He should've named himself something else. "How come you speak English?"

"Many English priests visited my mother's hill fort. I wanted them to teach me English. Or rather, I insisted." She raised a ginger eyebrow. "The priests didn't dare displease my mother."

What was she, a Vasfian princess? Given the gold torque around her neck, she must've been from a wealthy family. Aelfric studied Reiya's long eyelashes and slightly upturned nose as she turned to her two companions.

"Apisai." She made a circling gesture around her forehead and brought her hand down over her chest. The other two redheads smiled and did the same. Taking a step back, they bowed and left.

That was it—she was a Vasfian princess. Under the torchlight, Reiya's hair glowed under her hood like a fiery crown.

Her vivid green eyes turned back to him. They were the same color as his father's, but when matched with red hair on a young woman's face, the combination was ethereal. Aelfric's heart skipped a few beats.

"Was that a greeting between royalty?" he asked.

Reiya chuckled. "No. That's my people's way of saying hello and goodbye. It's also a sign of reverence to our god, Lenus." Her smile faded. "I'm visiting the convent to experience your Easter holiday. I didn't expect the sisters here to be so offended whenever I greeted my friends."

Aelfric's eyes trailed away. "I'm not surprised."

Before long, Lucette returned to them with a pile of blankets. Two other sisters brought bowls of pottage and a loaf of bread wrapped in cloth, and a third pushed a wheelbarrow full of stones to Aelfric's side.

"Rocks?" he asked.

Lucette smiled and spoke to Reiya, who translated.

"The sisters want your friend to take a hot bath. You should heat up the stones in the fire and throw them inside the washbasin."

That would explain the wooden basin in the warming room. Aelfric nodded and squirmed. There was nothing like a pretty girl who spoke three languages to make him feel inadequate. He pushed the wheelbarrow back to the warming house while Lucette and Reiya carried food and blankets. Their shadows crawled over the uneven ground to the orange light of Reiya's torch.

Reiya leaned toward his ear and murmured, "By the way, I've never seen this bath remedy work for anyone, and I've been here for two months."

Aelfric sighed. "Maybe it'll work for A—I mean, Esla."

"Esla is your friend's name? How long has she been unwell?"

Reiya asked more questions, and Aelfric answered them the best he could. As they walked within footsteps of the warming house, Reiya said, "There is a healer in Brocklesby named Miriam. She's English, but she trained with my grandmother and practices the medicine of my people. Is Esla willing to visit her?"

Aelfric drew his eyebrows in apology. "I doubt it."

"Well, if she ever is, my mother's hill fort is close to Brocklesby. Tell the healer to fetch me if you visit her."

Lucette knocked on the door of the warming room, and Aelfric adjusted his grip on the wheelbarrow's handles. There had been nothing frightening or dangerous about Reiya. Was it because he was lucky? How could he reconcile her pleasant nature with what he had heard her people could do?

Lucette knocked again on the warming house, and Aelfric released the wheelbarrow. He looked up at Reiya. "I hope you enjoy your Easter here. Eat as many hot cross buns as you can."

She grinned. "It's been hard to enjoy my stay when my French isn't great. I was relieved to hear English tonight. See you tomorrow, Blane?"

"Uh...I'm sailing at dawn."

"I see." Her smile disappeared. "Where are you going?"

"I'm..." Heat rose to Aelfric's face. He searched the darkness behind her for any signs the militia may have followed him here, but there was no one.

"Well, then." Reiya averted her eyes. "You don't have to tell me. It was still a pleasure to meet you."

"Y-you too."

Reiya and Lucette passed Aelfric their food items and the blankets hanging from their arms. Smiling, Reiya bid Aelfric goodnight. Both she and the sister departed into the darkness.

Aelfric dropped his gaze to the wheelbarrow of rocks. It would've been nice to ask Reiya about how the Vasfians lived. Tonight, for a moment, he had blissfully forgotten about whips, hot iron brands, and Cuthbert.

Behind him, the door of the warming house creaked open with an outward rush of heated air. He turned to face Aliwyn, who frowned at him from within the crevice.

"I told you not to speak to the redhead," she muttered.

Chapter 11

Aelfric

AELFRIC GLARED AT HER as he entered the room. "Well, I spoke to her anyway, and she didn't chop my head off."

Aliwyn chewed on her lower lip, then grabbed the bowls and bread from his hands. She carried them to a stool before the hearth and set them down. Aelfric licked his lips. Who was she to tell him what to do? Anger rose as bile in his throat, but he swallowed it again.

He pushed the wheelbarrow inside and barred the door. "You were overreacting."

"Don't let your guard down." Aliwyn crossed her arms. "Treachery runs in Vasfian blood. The tribes near my village would send their children to my church, pretending they wanted to learn about God. But those children only stole silverware and ran."

"You can find troublemakers in every village."

"The Vasfian adults are worse. They set snares everywhere to trap our woodcutters. My neighbor almost died when—"

"Stop it!" he shouted. "I don't want to hear it!"

"I..." Grief crumpled her face. "I just don't want you to get hurt."

Aelfric shuffled in a circle, rubbing his eyes until he saw stars. Those snare traps were probably meant to catch deer, and trapping men was just an accident. But what was the use of arguing with her?

Squinting at the hearth, Aelfric approached the low flames and sat. Aliwyn stood where he had left her and pinched her fingernails one by one. Her chin quivered.

Aelfric couldn't bring himself to apologize. Treachery did not run in his blood, and there had been nothing treacherous about Reiya. He needed to stand up for her.

"The Vasfian girl I spoke to seemed worried about you," he said. "She asked if you want to go to Brocklesby and see a healer trained in Vasfian medicine."

Aliwyn wrinkled her nose. "Why would I dabble in their demonic arts?"

Heat flared in Aelfric's chest again, but he kept his mouth shut. He picked up a bowl of pottage and slurped as loudly as he could. The skin of his hands appeared barren after he had seen Reiya's hands. Yet, had he been covered with freckles, Aliwyn would have attacked him with her scissors the moment they'd met. She would've thrown him back to Cuthbert, and Cuthbert would've dragged him back to Hull to be whipped and branded.

The thought pierced Aelfric with agony. He wanted to bolt out the door when Aliwyn sat beside him.

"Aelfric," she whispered. "Don't you know most towns have a militia to ward off the Vasfians? The redheads impaled my village priest when he tried to teach them about God. They threw his body in the river. We only found him when we drank the water and got sick. Your parents must've taught you to avoid the Vasfians."

"No, they didn't!"

He threw up his hands, almost hitting her, and Aliwyn recoiled. His vision tunneled, and his shout reverberated from the stone walls. Behind her, Godwin stirred under his blankets, and Aelfric shuddered. *By the Devil's tail.* He was awful today. Even as his stomach rumbled for more food, he set down his bowl.

"I'm sorry for yelling." He forced the words through his throat. "I haven't seen my parents in two years. Cuthbert sold them to another man up north, and the Normans burned that village. I saw their belongings at an auction, all bloody and burned."

His voice cracked. The family he had known was no more, and he was adrift like a leaf ripped off a tree. He may have felt a connection with Reiya tonight, but it was something he had neither the time nor the courage to explore. Tomorrow, he'd leave the country.

What kind of people awaited him in Scotland? He didn't even know what language they spoke. Cuthbert forbade his thralls from speaking anything but English. Tonight, stuck between Norman nuns and Vasfians, Aelfric had discovered how irritating it was not to understand a foreign language.

A delicate hand rubbed his back and shoulders.

"I'm so sorry," Aliwyn whispered. "I miss my family, too. I hope you find a new family in Scotland."

Only his relatives had comforted him with this kind of touch. The reminder of what he had lost made him want to shrink away. Aelfric gulped down his pottage, stood up, and explained the nun's prescribed bath to Aliwyn.

Her expression relaxed. She looked toward the corner of the room. "Two sisters came and filled the bin over there while you were gone. I'm willing to try their remedy."

"Then I'll help you warm up the water."

Maybe she appreciated the change in topic as much as he did.

Aliwyn picked up a piece of bread to eat, and Aelfric tossed stones into the hearth. Using metal tongs, he carried the rocks to the washbasin and dropped them in. Each stone splashed into the water with a burst of hissing and steam. He threw in more stones, testing the water after each one. The warm ripples cradling his fingers soothed his senses.

As Aelfric moved between the hearth and the basin, he passed over drawings of wagons, boats, and what looked like coins etched on the ground. Various tick marks lay in a row beside a rough map of the coastline, as though someone had been tallying up the costs of travel.

He glanced at Aliwyn. By her feet rested a wooden stick with one end coated in fresh mud. She was clever. When the nuns had come to fill the washbasin, she must've drawn images to ask them how to travel to Beverley. Thankfully for her, place names like "Beverley" sounded similar in both English and French.

Aelfric tossed another stone into the water, and a puff of steam rose to his face. "Are you still bent on taking Godwin to Beverley Minster?"

"Yes. The sisters told me how to get there with the four pennies I have."

He narrowed his eyes. Those sisters should've kept their mouths shut. "The Minster's big. Once you get inside, where exactly will you find his parents?"

"At the font where they baptize children. It's right inside the entrance. Godwin's nurse told me."

"Look." Aelfric released the tongs. "I also want Godwin to go home, but you're not fit enough to help him. Why don't you ask the sisters for help? I know of someone who can translate."

That translator would be Reiya, but he wasn't mentioning that now. Aelfric crossed his arms in the fire's light and faced Aliwyn's stare, tinged with sorrow.

"I'll be frank," he said. "You'll collapse on the way to Beverley. Then who will take care of Godwin?"

"First of all, I doubt the sisters would want to travel that far from their convent. And second, I'm also saving myself when I help Godwin."

"What? How?"

She pointed her toes toward each other. "I-If I tell you, please don't think I'm foolish."

"Fine." Aelfric drew a slow breath. "What is it?"

"I think my ailment is caused by loneliness."

"Loneliness?"

She gripped the edge of her stool, her knuckles white. "I had a father and three brothers just four months ago. The house was busy every day, and I was cooking and sewing every morning. In the afternoons, I speared eels and helped my brothers in the fields... I had friends and was happy." Her face contorted with a sob. "Then the Normans came and burned everything. I watched my family starve to death in the snow. I still don't understand why I survived."

Her words sketched scenes of suffering Aelfric didn't want to imagine. Goosebumps skittered over his arms. Judging by their clothes, his family members had met a much swifter end. He walked back to his stool and sat beside her.

"That...that's terrible."

"I finally escaped south," she said, "but I already had the beginnings of this rash. The lonelier I felt, the worse it became, and the more people avoided me. Godwin is too young to judge. He gave me a reason to get up every morning. I believe if Godwin's parents were to keep me as his new nurse, I'd recover. I just need a new family to love."

The crackling flames threw sparks into darkness, and her words echoed in Aelfric's mind. He ran his hand through his closely-trimmed hair.

"You don't believe me," she whispered.

He shook his head. "It's just different from everything I've ever heard."

Aelfric met her gaze, and the hollowness in her eyes swallowed him for a moment. It was an emptiness he was familiar with but had tried to fill with a relentless drive to earn pennies. While that had been amusing, money couldn't talk or listen or keep him warm at night. His purse sometimes stole his sleep because he was afraid of getting robbed.

"You could be right," he said. "No other treatment seems to have helped you, after all."

"You don't think I'm foolish?" She straightened. "Even Wulfstan said loneliness can't possibly do this."

"I don't know medicine, but I...I know how much it can hurt inside, even if no one can see it."

Tears rose in her eyes. Aelfric looked away and scratched the inner corner of his brow. He rummaged through his seashell pocket for the handkerchief she had given him when she had returned his recorder.

Passing it to her, he said, "Maybe in your case, the hurt inside came out, and now everyone can see."

"Thank you..."

She wiped her face with the handkerchief. The lingering coolness of the shells on his fingers gave him an idea.

"Here, let me show you something."

He fished out his seashells and spread them on the ground. Their edges were softened from the tide, and he flipped each one so only the pale outer covering would show.

"My father told me this many years ago," he said. "You see the shells from the outside? They don't look like much, but then you turn them over."

He flipped all the shells so that their colorful silver, pink, and green sides glimmered in a dazzling ring before the flames. "They're lovely on the inner side. Father said that's where someone's true beauty is found."

Aliwyn smiled. The way her face melted in the firelight, sweet and yet sorrowful, made a knot tie in his throat. Of all the people in the world, some of them downright evil, why did *she* have to fall ill?

"Can I have your blessing for my trip to Beverley?" she asked.

"My blessing?"

"Just to have your good wishes."

Aelfric sat back and crossed his legs. Wulfstan would probably be disappointed with how their conversation was going, but the constable also wanted Aliwyn to get better. If she was determined to try a special 'cure,' Aelfric was in no position to argue it would never help her.

His gaze lingered on Godwin, who had fallen asleep without eating. The boy's angelic face and the rise and fall of his little body made his shoulders sag. In an ideal world, this boy would never have been separated from his parents.

"I give you my blessing." It felt like a strange thing to say, and Aelfric smirked. "I'm not sure how much my blessing's worth. I'm not exactly lucky, or..." He lowered his eyes. "Or some good and holy person. But if I could go with you to Beverley, I would."

Aliwyn hugged her knees. "You need to save yourself, too. Thank you for your good wishes."

She lifted her hand as though to touch his display of seashells, but her fingers trembled, and she withdrew them.

Aelfric picked up the biggest shell he had and offered it to her.

"Here, I'll give you half my shells. You can dip them in your bath and look at them." He smiled and waited until she looked up. "And I promise to keep my back turned until you're done washing."

Aliwyn

THE HOT WATER so soothed Aliwyn's sore limbs that she wanted to fall asleep. She lifted her shells to bask in the hearth's glow and smiled at how the water drops sparkled over a rainbow of colors.

On the other side of the hearth, Aelfric sat with his back turned. He wiped his bare torso with a bucket of water he'd warmed with a rock, and she tried not to stare. The firelight lit up the rugged tone of his back, crisscrossed with whip scars that would likely mark him for life.

She rubbed the rough edge of the basin with a growing pain in her throat. Did the scars still hurt? She had robbed him to deflate his ego and teach him what it was like to live a hard life, but Aelfric didn't need a lesson.

She flinched when he sneezed.

"I'm almost done," she said. "I can help you draw a bath for yourself."

"No, it's too much trouble. I'm going to bed." He cleared his throat. "Are you staring at me? Please stop."

Aliwyn spun back around with a sheepish grin, and her bare shoulder bumped the side of the basin. Water sloshed under her chin and pulled at her wet hair. Her face flooded with warmth, and it wasn't from the heat of the bath.

A while later, she heard Aelfric rummaging through his knapsack for a change of clothes. The mattress rustled as he settled down and let out an exaggerated yawn. Most inns had only one bed per room, and the convent's warming house was no different. Back in her village, Aliwyn's family of five had slept on the same mattress to stay warm.

"I'm in bed now," Aelfric mumbled. "You can get out whenever you want."

By the time she was dressed again, he was asleep with his back turned and snoring. She snickered. Her brothers had snored, too, but Aelfric was louder than all of them combined.

Aliwyn stood in the echo of his snores as her cheer dissipated. After tomorrow, she'd never see him again, and the thought made her shiver. She found his clothes he had washed and jammed over the plank barring the door. With all her strength, she wrung them out again and hung them over the side of the washbasin, where they'd dry closer to the fire.

When Godwin awakened and whined, she fed the boy their remaining pottage and bread. She bathed him in Aelfric's bucket of water and sang to him on her lap until he was drowsy again. As soon as she lay him down, the tot rolled and snuggled against Aelfric's back.

Aliwyn adjusted the blankets over both of them, her heart full.

"I know, Godwin. He's a good person. I wish I could keep him."

The way Aelfric had run back to intercept the constable, his eyes bloodshot and his hands raised in surrender, would remain forever etched in her mind. He had turned himself in for the slim chance he could save her.

She sat on the side of the bed and stared at her hands and forearms. Pink scars from multiple rounds of bloodletting remained. Despite the bath, the red dots covering her body didn't fade. She rubbed her rash with her chin lowered. So many treatments had failed in the last two months that she had grown numb to each dismal outcome.

Her gaze fell on Aelfric's shoe with the gaping hole. With a gentle hand, she carried it close to the firelight and wiped it clean.

Threading a needle wasn't easy when her eyes were wet.

She was no cobbler, but she could drive her needle through shoe leather with a rock. Any stitches she made tonight would help his footwear hold together until he arrived in Scotland.

Long into the night, Aliwyn's fingers pushed and pulled at her needle. The shoe became whole again, one knot at a time, and her chest swelled with joy. Once in a while, she paused to smile at Aelfric's face in the firelight.

Chapter 12

Aelfric

"Blane? Time to get up!"

Someone knocked on the door, and Aelfric shot up in bed. The fear of Cuthbert bursting inside grabbed him by the throat, but the voice outside belonged to Reiya.

Aliwyn and Godwin were still asleep beside him in the dying light of the hearth. Aelfric rushed to the door, his shoeless feet rustling on the straw beneath. He peered into the crack at the edge of the doorframe and whispered, "Reiya, what are you doing here?"

She wore the same fur cloak as yesterday. "I thought you'd sleep through the morning bell, and you did, didn't you?"

Aelfric gasped. The bell in Hull was loud enough to wake the dead, but not so in the convent. He had the sense to throw on his cloak and pull up his hood to hide the scar along his neck. Lifting the plank barring the door, he pulled it open halfway. The morning light glowed through a blanket of clouds, and he rubbed his eyes.

"Rotten eels," he muttered. "I have to go."

"For the harbor front?" Reiya asked. "They've just started loading the ships, so you have some time before they leave."

Aelfric was about to spin away and put on his shoes, but Reiya carried a basket of what looked like fried dough folded within cloth napkins. One whiff was enough to make his stomach leap.

He glanced at Aliwyn, who hadn't moved underneath her blankets, thank goodness. Stepping outside, Aelfric closed the door quietly behind him. Reiya's cheeks were rosy, and her eyes bright.

His eyes trailed down to her basket. "Is that for me?"

"Yes." She grinned. "It's Lent for everyone except people who are unwell. Your friend is ill, so the sisters made her fritters." Reiya lowered her voice. "But if you eat most of it, I won't tell!"

Aelfric was already shoving fritters into his mouth. "So good. Thanks."

"You're welcome." Reiya chuckled. She checked the sky. "It might rain today. Why don't you wait until nicer weather to sail?"

"I can't." He forced a lump of dough down his throat. "I have my reasons."

Sheep bleated in the distant meadows. A few sisters strolled into view as lambs and ewes trotted on either side of them. Other sisters hurried in the opposite direction toward the church.

"I have to join the sisters for prayer soon," Reiya said. "Or rather, observe them. If you really have to go, I wish you a safe journey."

She extended a hand, and Aelfric shook it without hesitation.

A frown flickered over her eyebrows, and he withdrew quickly. He shouldn't have covered her hand in grease. With a sheepish grin, he wiped his palm on his shirt.

"You're not afraid of my freckles?" she asked.

"What? No."

Why did she look sad? Aelfric still wanted to rush to the harbor, but he didn't want to be rude.

"You're the first English person I've met who didn't react the way Esla did," Reiya said. "But you're also leaving the country."

Aelfric scratched his shin with the other foot. He wasn't the typical Englishman she assumed he was.

"Reiya, I'm..." A quick glance to either side confirmed no one was listening, and he dropped his voice to a whisper. "Both my grandmothers were Vasfians. They moved to Scotland when they were girls, and maybe they looked like you when they were young."

Reiya's mouth fell open, and a wave of excitement shivered through Aelfric. Finally, he had confessed his ancestry to someone who wouldn't be horrified upon hearing it. He couldn't stop grinning, but Reiya only knitted her brows.

"I understand now, but don't tell anyone else you're of Vasfian descent. They'll turn against you."

Aelfric rubbed his nose. "I know that. But you believe me when I say I'm part Vasfian?"

"Yes. There's no reason for you to make this up. It's not to your advantage, at least not now." She smiled wistfully. "I want to build better relationships between my people and the Outsiders. That's why I learned English, and I'm struggling with the French. One day, I want to be a different kind of chief."

Aelfric swallowed. With the reputation the Vasfians had, her goals seemed impossible, but what good would it do to show his doubt? He smiled at her. "Well then. I hope you can make a difference."

"Thank you. I hear Outsiders saying hurtful things about me all the time when they think I don't understand. Sometimes, I'm so tired of it that I make comments just to annoy them. Like when I mocked you last night for not being scared of me. Sorry about that, Blane."

He shrugged. "Forgiven."

Other sisters walked past in the grassy clearing, and Reiya greeted them. She passed her basket to Aelfric.

"I still hope to see you again." With a wary glance around her, she circled her hand around her head and smiled. "Apisai. That means 'peace be with you' in Vasfian."

"Apisai." Aelfric matched her gesture with his heart thumping. It felt as though he had entered into an exclusive society.

Reiya's smile grew before she turned away and joined the procession of sisters. Together, they approached a towering wooden church rising against the background of thick clouds. Aelfric hung his head. If he had more time, he'd talk to her for a week to learn about how the tribes lived and what they ate. Probably delicious food.

Aelfric went inside, set down his basket, and added kindling and firewood to the hearth. As a warm light filled the room, he shuffled to the shoes he'd left beside the washbasin and froze. Someone had repaired the gaping hole at the front.

He picked up the shoe and slapped it against his hand. The hole didn't reappear. He carried it to the firelight and studied the crisscrossed stitching. His eyes rounded. Aliwyn must've sewn his shoe, but she lacked a cobbler's awl, pliers, and other tools. How had she managed?

Back on the mattress, Aliwyn slept on her side with her hands curled by her cheek. Cwenhild's beating had left darkening bruises on her forehead, and the purple splotches on the back of her hands remained despite the bath.

Aelfric slipped on his shoes with a choking lump in his throat.

A scarf and cap he had not seen before hung over the edge of the washbasin, but their dark blue color was familiar. Aelfric felt the rough wool and frowned. It was the same fabric he had once worn. Aliwyn must've sacrificed the gown he had taken off to make him accessories.

Even if he had become nicer to her, he didn't deserve this. She should've saved that lovely gown for herself. And how long had it taken her to sew all this?

Aelfric collected the clothes she had draped neatly over the washbasin's edge. He folded them into his knapsack and sat on the ground. The cold earth sent shivers up his spine. Only his mother and grandmother had made clothes for him before. Aliwyn wasn't his blood relative, but she cared about him nonetheless, and at a cost.

Aelfric put on his cap and scarf to hide as much of his face as he could. Checking his reflection in a bucket of water, he smirked. He was unrecognizable.

Taking off his accessories again, Aelfric twirled his scarf around his arm. He still had to leave for the harbor, but the thought no longer spurred him on like before. Aliwyn wouldn't mind following him to the waterfront, would she? He approached the mattress to wake her up, and his feet passed over new sketches on the ground. He shuffled back for a better look.

Aliwyn had drawn an impressive scene with just a stick—a girl carrying a small child stood on the quays and waved at a distant, square-rigged ship. Smooth mountains rose behind the vessel, and seagulls flew on the horizon amongst the fluffy clouds.

Aelfric grinned. He drank in all the details, but when he studied the ship again, his smile fell flat.

Only a single person stood on the vessel as it sailed into apparent nothingness. Aliwyn's illustrations ended abruptly beneath a scattering of rushes covering the ground. He brushed aside the plants to uncover drab, blank earth, and a hollowness expanded behind his ribs. Maybe Aliwyn didn't draw his future because she didn't know what lay ahead. In truth, neither did he.

Aelfric sat back with his legs crossed and rubbed his eyes.

He had planned to work in Scotland as a traveling minstrel. How successful he'd be, he didn't know. Aelfric had met every prick of doubt with the raw reminder that he had to escape Cuthbert first. It was the only thing that mattered. Everything he'd endured before his grand getaway was passing the time, punctuated with bursts of pride whenever he'd filled his pockets. Surely, the freedom awaiting him in Scotland was the key to happiness.

Had he not met Aliwyn, Godwin, Wulfstan, and Reiya, maybe he'd still believe that was all true.

What brought him happiness, anyway?

Aelfric scratched the stubble of his hair. He no longer imagined himself as happy if he landed in Scotland with no one to talk to. His time with Aliwyn had convinced him of that. A ragged thief or not, she had become a sort of friend.

Aelfric stood up again and wiggled his cozy toes in his repaired shoe. In a different world, he'd have been born with all the freedom and money he could want. He couldn't change the circumstances of his birth, but he could help Aliwyn reach her dream of finding a loving home.

The map she had drawn on the ground, with circles marking the locations of different towns, gave him an idea.

Jittery with excitement, Aelfric hopped to Aliwyn's bedside and raised a hand to shake her shoulder. The sight of her swollen fingers folded beneath her chin made him halt. Sewing his shoe without the right tools had taken its toll. Aelfric lowered his eyes for a moment. He placed his hand on her wrist and patted it.

"Wake up. I need to tell you something."

Aliwyn

AELFRIC CALLED HER NAME several times, and the rising lilt in his voice made Aliwyn tense. She opened her eyes. Her limbs seemed to melt into the mattress. She tried to sit up, but pain shot up the side of her ribs and made her wince.

"Did something happen?" she asked.

"Nothing bad. I just had an idea." His eyes were wide and fastened on hers. "One of those salt ships could be stopping close to Beverley, right? So why don't you and Godwin sail with me?"

Aliwyn struggled to blink away her tiredness. "But Wulfstan said they don't take passengers."

"I'll negotiate. I'm sure one of those captains would take you and Godwin on board for the right price."

"Really? And how much would that be?"

"We'll see."

He sounded like a different person this morning. Aliwyn narrowed her eyes, but he was the same Aelfric, just wearing his spare beige tunic and not the dress.

"How many captains would you have to ask?" she said. "You'll draw attention to yourself. And what if none of the ships want to make a stop close to Beverley?"

CHAPTER 12

"Aliwyn, I want to try. Once you get off, I'll find you and Godwin a wagon to reach the Minster. Then I'll get back on the ship and continue to Scotland."

Something rough and warm lifted from her wrist, and Aliwyn held her breath. He had been holding onto her, and a flock of small birds fluttered in her stomach. She pushed herself to sit up and rubbed her eyes. Her hair must be sticking up, her eyes puffy, and her clothes all disheveled. She had only looked like this in front of her family. Heat spread from her face down to her neck, and Aliwyn squirmed.

Yet Aelfric's eyes never left hers. His grin accentuated the dimples on his cheeks. "Thanks for fixing my shoes and for making me a scarf and hat."

"You're welcome." She tried for a smile. "I wanted to give you something before you left."

"Well, I'll be with you for a while longer."

Aelfric left her side to fetch items from around the room, and Aliwyn pulled on her shoes with shaking hands. She'd love to travel with him, but he seemed to act without thinking. If someone identified him as he ran from ship to ship, begging the captains to accept a spindly girl and a toddler, she'd never forgive herself.

Aelfric returned with a basket emanating a sweet and heavenly aroma. His grin had faded into something more contemplative.

"What convinced you to help me?" she asked.

"You did." He placed the basket on her lap.

"Me?" she scoffed.

A steely glint shone in his eyes. "I want to leave England knowing you and Godwin are well on your way to Beverley. And watch this."

He pulled on his cap and wrapped his new scarf around his head. The scarf was just the correct width to conceal the whip scar winding up his neck, and the hat covered his striking black eyebrows. Everything fit as she had intended, and Aliwyn smiled.

"I'll also wear my hood," Aelfric said, beaming. "So unless you stare at my face mighty close, you won't be able to tell it's me."

He may have been right about blending in, but she had crafted the articles as a goodbye gift, not as something to make him bolder. The Staddons had been incredibly persistent for one thrall boy. How long could he go unnoticed in broad daylight?

She wasn't worth the trouble. Her whole body rigid, Aliwyn opened her mouth to protest.

Aelfric jutted his chin. "No arguing. I've made up my mind. If I can't find you a ship to board, you can still come back to this warming house."

He spun around and skidded to Godwin's side. "I'll carry him, and we'll talk on the way to the ships. You should eat something."

His voice was firm. Aliwyn picked up a fritter and chewed without tasting it. Aelfric's courage—or recklessness—made her heart race. Perhaps the distinction could only be made in hindsight. No one had been called courageous when nothing was at stake. Knowing he'd be with her a while longer sent a wave of strength through her limbs and dulled the pain from yesterday's bruises.

Aliwyn walked to the drawings she had made last night and erased everything with her foot. They mustn't leave a trace of their plans.

She approached Aelfric as he coaxed a whiny Godwin into the waking world. Picking up Aelfric's cloak, she laid it over his shoulders and dared to smooth her hands over the contours of his back. The scent of wood smoke and fritter lard drifted from his clothes, and she smiled. Fortunately, Aelfric was too busy consoling Godwin with a fritter to notice.

Both boys had patched a wound in her heart she couldn't afford to have opened again. Aliwyn prayed for their safety. If she could do anything to protect her little flock, she would.

Aelfric

THE FIRST RAINDROPS LANDED on Aelfric's nose and made him bristle. Bad weather couldn't have waited for another day? He adjusted his hood over his head and hurried along the dirt path, pausing beside salt pools for Aliwyn to catch up. The light drizzle didn't stop the merchants from driving their wagons laden with crates of salt. Gaggles of geese waddled past them with their goslings peeping.

Aliwyn tiptoed around every rock. Aelfric struggled to be patient with how slow she was. He'd pull her by the arm if he didn't have to keep his knapsack from slipping off his shoulders.

The rain intensified into a sweeping downpour when they were a stone's throw away from the ships.

"Blast it!" Aelfric threw the edge of his cloak over Godwin and bolted for the closest salt house.

The boy bounced and giggled against his chest. Merchants scrambled to drive their carts toward sheltered areas, and women rallied each other as they packed up their baskets of eggs and herbs. Aelfric turned the corner and narrowly dodged a careening wagon. He pressed himself against a salt house and wiped water from his face.

Looking beside him, he gulped. Aliwyn was missing.

"Esla!" Aelfric peered over the edge of the building.

Aliwyn staggered in the rain. Her shoes slipped along the welling puddles, and her cloak threatened to trip her. She kept looking to one side until her footsteps ground to a stop. Why was she stalling? The rain could worsen her illness.

Aelfric lowered Godwin to the ground and tossed down his knapsack.

"Stay here, wee'un," he said hoarsely.

Godwin babbled under the overhang of the thatched roof, and Aelfric darted into the rain toward Aliwyn.

Her gaze snapped to him. "Look over there."

She pointed left. In the distance, downhill from where they stood, three wagons had lined up before the gates to the convent. Two horses—a gray and a brown one—pulled the first covered wagon. Although the drivers had taken shelter within their wagons, Aelfric recognized the leading one with its two horses as the wagon Wulfstan had driven yesterday. What was the constable doing at the convent?

Aliwyn gripped Aelfric's arm and pulled him toward the docks. "I just saw blue scarves in one of the wagons."

The militiamen had followed him here. A chill ran through Aelfric. He tore free of Aliwyn's grasp, then swerved back around to grab her by the wrist. Why would Wulfstan lead militiamen to the convent? He led Aliwyn onward until they were both huddled under the overhang of the salt house roof.

Aelfric wiped his wet brow. "What happened to Wulfstan? Why would he betray us?"

"He wouldn't. I think the Staddons paid the militia to come here. Wulfstan only came because it was his duty."

Aelfric hardened his jaw and shook his head. The Staddons couldn't accept that their days of abusing thralls were over. Aliwyn's teeth chattered softly, and she sneezed. He scowled and shook his head. It was somewhat his fault she was in trouble.

"Now, you can't go back to the convent," he said. "I have to bring you and Grafton with me."

She gave him a pained look, and his mind spun for a way to convince any captain to take her and a toddler on board. He had to strike a deal, fast.

Aliwyn gasped. "Where's Grafton?"

"He was just—" Aelfric's eyes widened. The boy had disappeared.

Aliwyn began circling the building, and Aelfric followed. To his relief, the sound of the boy babbling came from around the next corner.

They followed his voice to find him standing under the overhang with his hand extended to catch the raindrops.

"You little rascal." Aliwyn squatted and gathered him back into her arms. "I've told you many times it's not funny to hide. One day, you'll get lost."

She turned and glared at Aelfric. Godwin only giggled.

"You can't let him wander," she said.

Aelfric rubbed the back of his hood. "Yes. Sorry."

Godwin squealed and pointed at something that was entertaining him down by the waterfront.

CHAPTER 12

Both Aelfric and Aliwyn looked in the direction of his hand. In front of the moored ships bearing yellow sailcloth, one horse-drawn cart had toppled over on its way to the quays. Crates had tumbled onto the ground, split open, and spilled salt everywhere. The mounds of sparkling white were all turning brown as they soaked up muddy water. Aelfric pursed his lips and whistled. All that expensive salt—lost in a flash.

The driver of the unfortunate cart struggled to push his cart upright. His horse shuffled and whinnied in distress. Other carts sped past the accident, desperate to reach the ships. With no one to help him, the bearded driver swore in a booming voice and shook his fist at the sky.

Meanwhile, nearly a dozen men had disembarked from one of the ships in the background. Their pale goatskin capes flapping behind them, they hurried for the fallen cart with boots splashing in the puddles. One man amongst them wore an elaborately embroidered cape—the captain, perhaps?

This was Providence. Aelfric snapped his fingers as an idea came to mind.

"Both of you stay here. I'm going to help clean up that mess." He pointed at the cart crash. "I'll show the crew I'm worth hiring, and I'll get us all on board."

Aliwyn only squinted at him. "Those men just lost a small fortune. They won't want to hire anyone."

"Well." He threw up a hand. "Thanks for the encouragement!"

"Just be careful. This isn't a game."

"I know, I know."

Aelfric sped toward the scene with rain blowing over his hood and his heart pulsing in his throat. As Wulfstan had said, these ships had arrived just this morning. None of the crew would have heard about a runaway thrall. At least, Aelfric hoped not.

Aliwyn had told him this wasn't a game, but he could pretend it was.

Throwing back his shoulders, he strode toward the men who were hoisting the cart upright. All of them towered over him and had chests twice the width of his.

"Can I help you?" Aelfric called out over the horse's whinnies.

One man with a braided beard glared at him. "You, little boy? There's nothing you can do."

Aelfric's upper lip twitched. It wasn't as though the man's bulging biceps could save the spilled salt, either. The other men cursed as they leaned over a cracked wagon wheel, which rendered the whole cart useless. Crates littered the ground, and rain seeped in through their cracked edges.

"Carry 'em all on board!" ordered the man with the embroidered cloak. A hood hid his face.

One sailor lifted a crate with a grunt, and a second did the same. They marched off toward their ship, and Aelfric glanced behind him to where Aliwyn and Godwin were still huddled under the roof of the salt house. Lightning cracked the gray sky, and thunder rumbled overhead.

Aelfric gathered his resolve. Maybe he couldn't lug heavy objects, but he must be helpful in some other way. Running alongside the men, he pointed out rocks and other obstacles in their path.

The probable captain peered at Aelfric from under the shadow of his hood. Amidst the splashing and thunder, he called out, "Who are you?"

"I'm a cabin boy for hire! Name's Blane!"

"Blane! How good are you with hammers?"

Aelfric grinned. "Very good! How can I help you?"

The man introduced himself as Captain Lars and asked Aelfric to hammer his crates shut. Aelfric readily agreed. He could've done two somersaults before they raced up the ramp of the ship. The vessel featured two platforms, one at the bow and one at the stern. For the first time, Aelfric set foot on the slippery deck of a ship after constructing countless ladders for such vessels. The rocking motion made him teeter. Lars passed him a hammer and a bag of nails to repair the crates. They'd worry about inspecting the salt after the storm.

Aelfric approached the back platform, where the men placed their crates amongst a pile of salvaged wooden planks. Squeezing in between the boxes, Aelfric tossed aside his knapsack. He pushed several nails in between his teeth to hold them and began a rhythmic hammering that made him quiver with its familiarity.

CHAPTER 12

Every strike was perfectly angled to drive the nail. The damp wood under his left hand vibrated up his forearms. The endless thumping and body odor of Cuthbert's workshop seemed to envelop him again, but the sea wind howling past his ears heralded a new reality. Shivering, Aelfric smiled with the tang of metal on his tongue.

He had only come this far because Aliwyn had remained loyal to his cause. The thought made his chest swell. Aelfric pulled another nail from between his teeth and continued his work.

Lars was watching when he finished repairing the last crate.

"Who taught you carpentry?" He crossed his arms, his face unreadable.

It wasn't just Lars, but many other sailors who stared at him. Aelfric's stomach dropped. Surely no one had heard of the thralls who had burned down a furniture workshop in Hull? "My... uh... father taught me."

"Hmph. He's the carpenter of which town?"

"He was killed in the rebellion, and I want to go to Scotland. If you hire me, I'll help you fix anything on this ship."

Lars barked a laugh. He shouted orders to the men behind him, and they stopped climbing up the rope ladder along the mast. A yellow sail overhead curled under a massive crossbeam, and water dripped from the many ropes binding the sail in a giant roll.

"No sailing until the waves settle down," Lars muttered. Turning back to Aelfric, he pulled back his hood, revealing shaggy blond hair and a diagonal scar crossing half his face. "As for cabin boys, I don't hire children."

Aelfric kept his gaze steady. "I'm almost fifteen. I work just as hard as anyone." He raised the hammer as a reminder. "And I come with advantages. I eat less than the big ones, take up less space, and stink less."

The captain chuckled, a grumbling sound that could've indicated pleasure or simmering wrath. Aelfric held his breath. Maybe he shouldn't try to jest. His sister had often told him to shut his mouth because he wasn't funny.

"The seas will be rough," Lars said. "Where are your parents? Do you have their permission to travel?"

"My parents are dead." Aelfric suppressed a sneeze. "But I have...uh...a sister and brother I need to care for."

Aliwyn and Godwin weren't his siblings, but Aelfric needed a compelling reason to bring them on board. When what looked like sympathy shone in the captain's eyes, Aelfric seized the opportunity.

"My sister and brother want to attend Easter Sunday service at Beverley Minster," he said. "Captain Lars, you must be stopping close to a big town like Beverley?"

"Hmm, so your siblings are pilgrims to the sacred Minster." The captain rubbed his stubbly chin, his fingers laden with jeweled rings. "The closest stop I make is at Hornsea. I do take pilgrims from time to time, but for a fee."

Aelfric squeezed the hammer's handle. "How much?"

"Let me see your siblings first."

Chapter 13

Aelfric

Just below the ship's ramp, Aliwyn stood in the rain with Godwin huddled by her legs and under her cloak. Her face was frozen with fear, and Aelfric shook his head. He should've told her what he was doing before he'd disappeared on board.

"What's happening?" she called out. "Why were you gone for so long?"

He scampered down the ship's ramp.

"I was negotiating," he said. "Come with me. Captain Lars wants to meet you."

Aelfric picked up Godwin, wrapped his cloak around the boy, and took Aliwyn's arm. Pulling her up the ramp, he avoided the disgruntled stares from the crew. The sailors crowded under the front platform and pushed biscuits into their mouths, grumbling amongst themselves. Aelfric glared back at them. If only Aliwyn's face and hands weren't covered in purple blotches.

Bloodrot, the sailors seemed to mutter. What was that?

Lars sat on a crate with his eyes narrowed and his leg folded over the other knee. His opened cloak revealed both a crucifix and a dagger hanging from his neck, and the combination made Aelfric raise an eyebrow.

"This is your sister?" Lars asked.

Aliwyn's forearm was cold and trembling within Aelfric's hold. She shot him a puzzled frown, and he gave her arm a squeeze.

"Yes, my sister." He winked at her. "Her name is Esla."

"Is your brother ill as well?"

"No. Grafton is fine." Aelfric lifted his cloak from the boy's head. Godwin pulled his thumb from his mouth and grinned, but Aelfric's pulse raced. What if no captain wanted Aliwyn on board because she looked so unwell?

Lars cocked his head. "Esla, do your gums bleed from time to time? And does your hair come out in clumps?"

"Yes, Captain." Aliwyn's voice was tiny.

So Aelfric had not imagined the bright red gums he'd seen in her mouth yesterday. He shuddered despite himself.

The captain narrowed his eyes. "You have the bloodrot of sailors. If you board my ship, you'll only get worse. Soon, your teeth will fall out."

Aliwyn gasped, and the ominous words punched Aelfric in the guts. "Her teeth are not going to fall out! And what the Devil is bloodrot?"

"A fatal ailment that strikes sailors who have been at sea too long. The only cure is to step onto land."

"But I've had this illness before I ever sailed anywhere," Aliwyn said. "And I was only on a ship for three days, with other people escaping the Normans. A few people who embarked with me also had my kind of rash, and they'd never sailed before."

"Hmph, how curious. I cannot explain why." Lars lowered his eyes. "But you most certainly have bloodrot, given what I see. It almost claimed my life, and I lost many a fellow Norsemen when we began new livelihoods..." He grunted and thumped on the crate of salt he sat upon. "The only merciful thing about bloodrot, if one can call it mercy, is that it appears not to be contagious."

Aliwyn grabbed Aelfric's arm and leaned close to his ear.

"He just admitted he's a Norseman!" she whispered. "A bloody raider!"

Any louder, and she'd tear up the deal he was about to make. "But Lars is a merchant now. Many Norsemen are."

He distanced himself from Aliwyn. "Captain Lars, you still haven't told me how much you'd charge for Esla's fare. And for my brother's."

For the first time, Lars smiled. "If you insist, I'll take her on board. It's only profit for me, after all. But I will increase the price to dissuade you...fifteen pennies for her and one penny for your brother."

CHAPTER 13

Aelfric tilted back from where he stood, and Aliwyn shook her head. "That's ridiculous! That's the fare all the way to Scotland!" She stepped before Aelfric. "Captain Lars, can you please be more reasonable? The cost for such a trip shouldn't be more than—"

"A reasonable person with bloodrot wouldn't set sail." Lars shook his head slowly. "Pay me sixteen pennies, or get off."

Aliwyn gave Aelfric a frightened look, and he struggled to appear calm. Sixteen pennies was an extravagant price, but with the militia at their heels, he couldn't bear to leave Aliwyn and Godwin behind. One more glance at her shivering frame convinced him he was making the right choice.

"Esla, I'll pay."

Just a day ago, he wouldn't have believed what he'd just said. Her chapped lips parted in surprise, and he grimaced at her blood-smeared teeth. Blast it. What if she fled the militia only to have this trip kill her?

"But...but what if you do have bloodrot?" he asked.

"I don't have bloodrot. I'm unwell because of what I told you about yesterday, so sailing won't hurt me." Aliwyn suppressed a sneeze. She pulled on his cloak so that he leaned toward her again. "Blane, I can't pay you back for this. Are you sure?"

She stepped back, her eyes moist, and a knot formed his throat. Now that he was finally willing to pay for her, she should just be thankful, not question whether her safety was worth the price.

"Do you even have sixteen pennies, boy?" Lars uncorked the costrel strapped over his shoulder and took a sip.

"I do."

Aelfric eased himself free from Aliwyn's grip and set Godwin onto the floorboards. The boy began banging on the crates with gleeful squealing, and Aelfric smiled. He tugged open his drawstring pouch, but Aliwyn only watched him with a stricken face.

"You've lost your mind," she said.

"I know. Losing my mind has been quite an adventure. So, want to sail with me?"

"I do, but I don't understand..."

"We can talk later."

"Thank you, Blane."

Grinning, he reached into his pocket and fished out a mound of money. The sailors nearby gasped, but Aelfric ignored them.

Lars grinned, displaying a few missing front teeth. He picked up the coins one by one, counting in what sounded like Danish.

"Impressive. I won't ask where you procured all these." He slipped all the coins into his belt pouch. "Welcome aboard my beautiful hulk ship, the *Trana*."

Aelfric

WHEN THE RAIN DIED, the crew unfurled the ship's square sail, and the *Trana* parted ways with the shore. Aelfric followed the captain's orders to help the crew pull the ropes and adjust the sail's angle to the wind. Afterward, he hurried back to Aliwyn and Godwin as they sat under the flat platform. The crew had given her extra blankets, but she was still pale and shivering. Godwin had fallen asleep on her lap.

"Still cold?" He squatted by her side. Working on deck had kept him warm.

"I'll warm up eventually." She smiled, then dropped her voice to a whisper. "I hope we lost them."

"Me too."

"He's so persistent, it's incredible. Is it because you..." Her voice trailed off with a tremor.

She looked down to where Aelfric hid his eating knife in his cloak's pocket. He frowned at her and drew back.

"I'm not a thief or a murderer," he said. "I only...only ran."

Without warning, Royd's cries from down the well pierced his thoughts. Aelfric jolted in his seat. It struck him that Cuthbert Staddon was not only tracking down his thralls and lost possessions; he was out to avenge his best friend. Royd may indeed have drowned. Anyone who saw Aelfric the night of his escape, staring down that well, could've told Cuthbert Aelfric was especially to blame. Maybe this was why Cuthbert wouldn't stop his pursuit.

"Blane?" Aliwyn whispered.

"Nothing. I'd better get back to work."

Aelfric scrambled to his feet and trudged back to the crew. He had never seen Cuthbert as more than a demon with a whip. Certainly not someone who cared about friends. But now that Aelfric had found Aliwyn and Godwin, he could only imagine what it would feel like if someone hurt or killed them. It was a wrath that burned in his bones and went deeper than losing any object he owned.

Aelfric shivered for the first time since boarding the ship. Someone out there downright hated him, and what would Aliwyn think if he ever told her about Royd? Unable to look back at her, he grabbed a rag from a sack and joined other sailors in drying up standing water on the deck.

He wouldn't tell her. Maybe she still admired him for being a hardworking musician, and he wasn't about to change that.

Aliwyn

ALIWYN FAKED A SMILE at the sailors as she nursed her bandaged hand. They were sympathetic when she accidentally nicked herself while peeling turnips, but the way they encircled her made her sweaty and faint. She had fought off similar men in the church sanctuaries she had sheltered in while escaping her razed village. Every throng Aliwyn encountered still made her feel trapped.

"Delicious pottage!" A voice behind her shouted.

Aliwyn yelped. She veered away from the man who spoke and hurried for the stairwell. Never before had she been surrounded by so many Norsemen, even retired Norsemen. The hull downstairs had been her only place of relative peace.

"You all right?" Aelfric called out. He looked up from hammering a worn-out plank under the back platform. Godwin and Captain Lars stood beside him, staring at her.

"I'm going to sleep," Aliwyn managed to say. It was hard to see Aelfric's face in the shadow of the afternoon sun. The ship crested a wave, and her stomach heaved.

Neither Aelfric nor Godwin had appeared seasick since they boarded yesterday. They were lucky.

She staggered down the creaky staircase and tried not to bump her wounded hand on either side. It wouldn't stop bleeding, but it was just a small cut. Aelfric had paid dearly for her fare, and there was nothing to complain about.

The hull of the ship was dark. Shadows gathered in the crevices where beams of wood met in sharp angles along the ceiling. Creaks echoed from all sides, broken and eerie in the confined space. Aliwyn placed her good hand on one post after another for support as she made her way to her hammock.

She crawled onto two layers of fraying linens and lay down. The hammock's rope rose on either side of her like the bars of a cage. In the enveloping darkness, she pressed on her bandages and felt the fabric soak through. Tears stung her eyes. Her fingers had been so weak when she peeled those turnips. Was this also a part of the strange illness? If she lost the dexterity of her hands, she'd be useless.

Footsteps thumped toward the stairwell.

"Esla?" Aelfric called out. "I didn't see you eat!"

He descended the staircase, illuminated by a column of light. The scent of salt and seaweed blew in after him. Aliwyn was too nauseous to eat, and everything tasted foul when her gums bled. When she tried to answer, her voice was too hoarse to be heard.

CHAPTER 13

Lars's cry sounded soon enough. "Blane! We need you to turn the capstan!"

The capstan was a vertical axle that reeled in the ship's anchor. Several sailors had to push the wooden spokes for it to turn. The *Trana* was setting sail after a stop to deliver cargo, and soon, waves would rock the ship again. Aliwyn curled her toes within her tattered shoes.

Aelfric squinted up at the sunlight and sighed. "Grafton's been good, by the way. Don't worry."

His feet pounded back up the stairs.

She picked at her bandages. Aelfric had been forced to work almost incessantly, and he never complained. She would've liked to fetch him water or to help him scrub the deck. At least she had assisted the ship's cook on Aelfric's behalf so he could rest awhile, but now her hands...

The hammock swayed back and forth with the ship's movements. Sleep failed to come, and the raw ache in the back of her throat intensified. She couldn't stop shivering. The last time she had felt this way, she had come down with a fever and cough.

What if she never became healthy? Aliwyn struggled to quell the storm within. By tomorrow, she needed to regain her strength and travel with Godwin to Beverley. Even if she felt unwell, she mustn't hold Aelfric back again.

She fumbled one of his seashells out of her belt pouch. The cool contours comforted her aching hand, but the pain expanded within her chest.

She'd never see him again, and she didn't know how to let him go.

THE SHIP'S HULL GROANED with the waves, and voices from above broke through the din. Sailors had congregated below the front platform, probably during their time off duty. Aliwyn caught Aelfric's name in their conversation. She frowned and lifted her head.

"I sweat like a pig on this ship for two pennies a day...that boy half my size..."

More grumbling followed. Some men spoke perfect English, while others spoke with a foreign accent. Aliwyn rubbed her bleary eyes. The sunshine streaming down the stairwell had darkened with the bronze hues of evening, and Aelfric had stopped hammering. Her temples pulsed as she swung her legs over the side of the hammock and stood. What else were they saying about Aelfric?

The men continued. "Sixteen pennies without blinking an eye..."

"Just look at Lars. He's entranced by that..."

She forced herself to move toward the conversation as she steadied herself along the wooden posts. So, these Norsemen were jealous of Aelfric. How noble of them.

"The boy's a thief, certainly."

"He must've robbed his master carpenter."

Aliwyn looked up at the floorboards above and clenched her fists. She was the thief, not Aelfric. He was a talented piper.

"So a thief, a tot, and a girl with bloodrot?"

There was a yawn. "I wouldn't have let them on."

"For sixteen pennies? Yes, you would've."

A man chuckled. His voice was low and menacing. "How much money do you think the boy still has?"

Their footsteps creaked all over deck. "We'll find out tonight."

"Tie him up until the next port? Or throw..."

"What about the other two?"

Aliwyn's mouth fell open. The voices continued, drowned out by the sound of constant footsteps, and her nostrils flared.

She shouldn't have made pottage for these men. They were heartless, like the people who crowded in churches up north, beating up children and expectant mothers to grab their blankets and food.

Aelfric shouldn't have dealt with men who once pillaged English villages for glory and gain. Where was he? The three of them had to disembark before nightfall.

CHAPTER 13

Her head spun as she staggered toward the stairwell. Were Aelfric and Godwin all right upstairs?

The setting sun warmed her face, but she shook with chills. Her hands were too weak to grip the rail, and she began crawling up the steps instead. The ship rocked and threw her against the side of the staircase with a thump. She sucked in her breath and got back up on all fours. Her arms wobbled, but she kept crawling.

Rapid footfalls thudded above her.

"Esla?"

Aelfric's slim shadow blocked the sunlight before he flew down the stairs. Aliwyn had time to sit back before he landed across from her. Sweat gleamed on his face, but he had not removed his scarf or hat.

"Were you...crying?" he asked, his brows drawn.

She ignored the twinge of her bruises. "Where's God—I mean, Grafton?"

"Asleep under the stern's platform. Everything's fine."

"No, it isn't." She reached for his arm. "I need to talk to you."

Other shadows drifted over the two of them—Captain Lars and other sailors.

Aliwyn held her breath. Her time alone with Aelfric was limited. She pushed herself to stand in the stairwell, and Aelfric shot to his feet to steady her.

"What's wrong?" He helped her walk to the bottom of the steps.

With all her might, she pulled him toward the hammocks at the stern of the ship. "The sailors are..."

Boots stomped down the stairs, and she snapped her mouth shut. Captain Lars and several sailors descended, their brows weary and greasy. The crew walked for their hammocks, their footsteps vibrating the floorboards beneath her, while Captain Lars approached Aliwyn with a sullen gaze.

"Complaints about your voyage?" he asked. "Then tell me directly."

Aliwyn's heart thrummed. On either side of her, sailors sat on their hammocks and began pulling off their shoes. She winced at the stench.

"I'm..." she glanced at Aelfric's deepening scowl. "My condition is getting worse. I think you're right after all, Captain Lars. I do have bloodrot. I need to get off this ship, and so do my brothers."

Aelfric's eyes rounded, and the way his mouth fell open made her tremble.

"How are you worse?" he cried. "You look the same as—"

"I have a fever, and my throat hurts."

She gasped when Aelfric unceremoniously slapped his palm over her forehead. His clammy skin cooled the heat of her fever.

"Captain Lars, she's burning hot." Aelfric grimaced. "Does...does bloodrot do this?"

Aliwyn shivered when he lifted his hand. Despite everything, she resisted grasping his hand and intertwining her fingers with his.

Behind Aelfric, the Captain sank into a hammock and rested his elbows on his knees. "Bloodrot does many things. Fever, trouble walking, bleeding..." He shrugged. "It all ends in death."

"But it's not too late for me," Aliwyn said. "Where can I get off? The sooner, the better. Please, Captain Lars. We're in the Holy Week before Easter."

What sounded like a growl rumbled in Lars' throat. "If you get off, no refunds on your fare."

"You don't have to refund me." Aelfric turned back to the captain. "My sister is more important."

Aliwyn's chin quivered. Sixteen pennies could buy him sixteen pairs of new shoes.

"Who exactly is getting off?" Captain Lars asked. "Only her, or all three of you?"

Aelfric scowled at the floorboards, his posture straight and stiff, and Aliwyn struggled to appear calm. Aelfric needed to board a different ship to reach Scotland. Even if Lars had shown no menace thus far, his crew might kill Aelfric overnight.

Aelfric, get off with me! She tapped his toe with her own and tried to catch his eye, imitating how he had winked at her earlier that day. It was a failure; she didn't know how to wink, and Aelfric raised an eyebrow at her attempts. The bridge of his nose twitched. She finally squeezed his hand, and what looked like understanding eased the lines on his face.

"I'll also get off," he muttered, his eyes fixed on Aliwyn.

Lars grunted. "I suppose I could moor at Kilnsea. They have several shipyards, and I could use more tar for my rigging. It's the only stop I'm willing to make. Do you accept?"

Something about the mention of Kilnsea made Aelfric's hands claw over her own. Was there something wrong with the place? Aliwyn studied Aelfric's expression for a hint, but he only turned back to the captain with his head held high. "I accept."

The sailors sat on their hammocks, chewing their biscuits, and frowned at him.

"Thank you for making the stop, Captain Lars," Aliwyn stammered.

Lars stood again and strode for the stairs. Aliwyn felt the stare of the sailors bore into her back. Stepping after the captain, she pulled Aelfric along.

"I'll stay with you and Grafton upstairs," she said.

Aelfric followed her, his expression bleak. Once they were at the foot of the stairs, he narrowed his eyes. "What's going on?"

"I'll tell you later." She cast a wary glance behind him. The crew sipped on their costrels and muttered amongst themselves. "Please trust me, Blane."

She spread her hand over the sleeve of his forearm as he held onto the rail. If he changed his mind about disembarking or lost his temper before they arrived in Kilnsea, she didn't know what she'd do.

Aelfric held her gaze for a moment before stepping onto the stairs. When Aliwyn struggled to grab onto the rail, he turned around and offered his hand. He appeared calm, and Aliwyn released a long-held breath. Somewhere along their whirlwind journey, he had come to trust her.

She smiled and took his hand.

Chapter 14

Aelfric

The ground felt as though it was rocking when Aelfric stepped off the ramp of the *Trana*. He hugged a drowsy Godwin against his shoulder and waited for Aliwyn to catch up. The scent of conifers and smoke drifted in the air, a welcome change from the stink of the ship's privy pot. Few people walked the ports this late in the afternoon, and the merchant booths were deserted.

Aelfric kept a stoic face as Aliwyn pressed her shoulder against his. Cuthbert regularly shipped benches and chests along the Humber River to Kilnsea, where the products were sorted for delivery to various buyers. Once emptied of furniture, the ships would return to Hull filled with English oak and other raw materials for the thralls to use.

The lumbermen delivering wood to Hull didn't stay long enough to recognize Aelfric among the workshop's several dozen thralls. Nonetheless, Aelfric pulled his scarf higher along his neck as he walked.

Aliwyn had been desperate for him to get off the ship. He had seen the panic in her eyes, even if he didn't understand it. The three walked in silence until the dark outline of the *Trana* was far behind them.

Aliwyn spoke first. "I don't have bloodrot. It was an excuse to get us off."

"I thought so," he muttered. Her attempts to wink had been almost comical. "But what was wrong with staying onboard the *Trana*?"

"The crew thinks you stole the money you own. I overheard them when I was downstairs. They wanted to attack you and take whatever you had left."

A shiver ran through him.

"The sailors did grumble a lot about not being paid enough." He tried to scratch beneath his scarf. "But I never suspected...what you just said."

Despite escaping the danger, Aclfric still ached over giving up his sixteen pennies. The only solution was not to think about it. Aliwyn's look of sympathy helped a little.

"You're not angry?" she whispered. "You believe what I said about the sailors?"

"Yea. I mean...you don't have a reason to lie about it."

She nibbled on her lip. "I'm sorry. You lost a lot of money."

"Don't mention it. It's not only the money. Kilnsea is..." he looked warily around him, but the only living thing within earshot was a donkey chewing hay outside a wheelwright's workshop.

Aelfric leaned close to Aliwyn's ear. "Kilnsea trades often with Hull. Everyone here probably knows about Cuthbert's workshop burning down and all the thralls escaping."

Aliwyn frowned at him. "Then you must leave this place. Find another ship to hire you as a cabin boy."

"I know, but I can't find work this late. The ships won't sail again until tomorrow, and no wagon will take you to Beverley either. We need a place to sleep tonight."

The thought of leaving her and Godwin tomorrow almost made his knees buckle, but he kept a blank face.

"But where is a safe place to sleep?" she whispered.

Leaving the town at night would attract the militia's attention, and Aelfric didn't want to run into wolves outside the town walls.

"I've heard a thing or two about Kilnsea," he said. "There's a hospital somewhere in town. Let's look for it. You'll find a bed overnight to share with Godwin. I'll just sleep on the ground."

The lumbermen visiting Hull had once told tales of patients screaming from within the hospital walls. Delirious women would roll out the doors while frothing at the mouth. How much of that was true, Aelfric didn't know, but the thought of staying with such people made his scarf even itchier. At least the Staddons and the able-bodied lumbermen would stay away from places like the hospital.

"I'll miss you," Aliwyn said. Her voice drew him back to the present.

Aelfric adjusted his knapsack over his shoulder. He kept his hand on her back as they walked, and no words came to mind.

"Do you think Grafton's parents would keep you as a servant, too?" she asked.

"Even if they did, people will start asking questions whenever I take this off." He gestured at his scarf.

"I think some of your scars can still heal…"

"Not fast enough."

Aelfric had heard of other masters freeing their thralls and throwing a freedom feast to elevate the status of the freed thrall before the whole village. The freeman would even receive a silver pendant to wear to symbolize his freedom, as the scars and brands on his body might never fade.

The Staddons never freed their thralls. They simply sold the extras. Aelfric had been such a small boy that no one had wanted to buy him.

He swallowed and refocused on the present. Godwin slumped against his shoulder and jerked his leg once in his sleep. An evening breeze chilled Aelfric's hairline as he and Aliwyn walked on, their twin shadows stretching before them on the pebbly path.

Hospitals were usually rectangular buildings next to a church, but they passed no such structure.

Kilnsea didn't appear to be as wealthy as Mablethorpe. A man and a boy sat on the thatched rooftop of their wattle and daub home, hunched over in the golden sunset as they unpacked bundles of straw to repair a rotten area. Smoke drifted from the corners of windowless homes. Children laughed from within, and the voices of their mothers followed.

Aelfric shuddered. He wanted to throw open the door of the closest house and find his parents, grandmother, and sister sitting around their dining table, alive and well. Never before had he felt such a longing.

He shifted Godwin's weight in his arms. The boy's hair was warm with the lingering scent of fritters. Back onboard the *Trana*, Aelfric had lied that Aliwyn and Godwin were his siblings. It no longer felt like a lie.

For the first time since he had darted out of Cuthbert's workshop, Aelfric ached over the thought of having to leave England. He had reasons to stay now. He prayed for a way to stay without getting caught, but it was only a matter of time before someone recognized him. His prayer flickered like a lamp in the blackness of a stormy night. Aelfric wiped his eyes and hoped Aliwyn didn't notice.

It was unfair. Why had he met her and Godwin, only to have to leave them again?

Aliwyn

THE SUN SANK BEHIND the horizon, and they still couldn't find the hospital. They neared a shipyard along the beach, where the framework of an unfinished ship loomed above the workers' cabin nearby. Several people still moved about.

Aelfric moved quickly despite all he carried, but Aliwyn fought to keep up. The rush lamps dotting the shipyard and the smell of campfires intensified her longing for a hearth and a bed. She passed a girl her age sweeping outside a worker cabin. Her black cloak swayed about the black linen strips gartering her stockings.

It was the typical attire for someone who had lost a loved one, and Aliwyn felt a tug of sympathy. Perhaps she would give them directions to the hospital. Aliwyn stepped toward the stranger, but Aelfric jerked her back with a scowl.

She frowned back but didn't protest. They kept walking, and she caught sight of Captain Lars standing beside a blazing campfire. His crew sat around the orange flame with bowls in their hands, and they looked up with shadows dancing over their scarred faces. Aliwyn looked away and quickened her pace.

"Are you's lost?" a voice shouted from behind. "I be watching you circle the shipyard three times now!"

Aliwyn turned around at the man's strange accent. The speaker was portly and appeared several decades older than herself. Smiling, he sat on the side of a well with two donkeys drinking from buckets nearby.

Aelfric stopped beside her, but he only glared at the man.

"We should ask for directions," she whispered. When Aelfric remained silent, she spoke instead. "Sir, can you tell us where the hospital is?"

"You passed it." He jerked his thumb back toward the harbor. "That old Roman bathhouse by the water is the hospital. Didn't expect that, did ya? What brings you all to Kilnsea, if I may ask?"

Without a word, Aelfric marched in the direction the man pointed to. Aliwyn watched his back with her lips pressed together. Even if he was nervous about staying in Kilnsea, acting like this would probably draw attention.

"Thank you for the directions, sir," she said, hurrying after Aelfric.

THEY RETURNED TO THE waterfront, where a building decorated with faded mosaic tiles rose above the mud and straw huts surrounding it. Such ruins were not rare, and Aliwyn had seen one in her village. Wooden scaffolding and a timber roof replaced the section where the marble pillars had collapsed.

When they knocked, a lay brother dressed in a long brown robe opened the door. Aelfric asked him for a place to stay, and the man hesitated. To Aliwyn's relief, he stepped aside and allowed them to enter.

The hospital was a spacious building with whitewashed walls that remained chilly despite the bins of heated rocks between patient beds. Throughout the night, wind blew through the gaps between the old and new ceiling. The smell of mold mingled with medicines and incense.

CHAPTER 14

Aliwyn was given a mattress big enough for her and Godwin, while Aelfric had to sleep on the floor. He lay with his back turned on a layer of blankets, his dark hair blending into the shadows along the wall.

Only Godwin slept soundly in the hospital. Aliwyn tossed for hours and coughed into her pillow. Finally, Aelfric rolled onto his back with his eyes open and sighed. He kicked off his blanket and sat up. The rush lamps illuminated the marble arches overhead and flickered over his tired squint.

"I'm sorry for waking you up," Aliwyn croaked.

"I wasn't sleeping." He held out his hand. "Give me your costrel. I'll fill it up."

As Aelfric pulled on his shoes, Aliwyn lifted her pillow and pulled out her flattened water pouch from underneath. She had sucked it dry already but had been too tired to refill it, even if the well was just outside.

Aelfric took her costrel, his eyes downcast. He had been nothing but frowns since they arrived in Kilnsea. Could she help cheer him up?

"Thank you, Aelfric," she whispered.

His scowl deepened. "Blane."

"B-Blane." She crumpled the linens by her chin. An elderly lay sister had changed the bandages around Aliwyn's injured hand, but her wound still stung.

Aelfric stood. He stirred up the scent of vinegar and thyme as he shuffled in between the rows of hospital beds for the exit. The lay sisters and brothers tending to the patients had retired, and peasants young and old slept on hay mattresses several paces away. Some coughed into the night, others snored, but few patients remained. Aliwyn had heard that most patients had traveled to Beverley in hopes of a miraculous cure on Easter Day.

Feverish heat pulsed at Aliwyn's temples. Aelfric had to endure this terrible night because of her, and she had just let his name slip. Everyone she saw appeared asleep, but her heart raced nonetheless.

Aelfric returned with his face flushed down to the scarf he never took off. Her water pouch remained flattened and rolled up in his fist.

Aliwyn stared at him. "Was the well empty?"

"Just take mine."

He tossed her wrinkled pouch onto her pillow and unclasped his own from his belt. Setting it on her mattress, he sat on his woolen blanket on the ground and turned his back.

Aliwyn frowned. She tucked Godwin's blankets snugly around the boy and pushed herself up to sit.

"Blane?" she whispered.

Something told her Aelfric wasn't still sulking over sixteen wasted pennies. When he didn't answer, she slid off her mattress. Her legs felt as stiff as wood, but she managed to crawl and sit beside him. Back in Mablethorpe, he had also avoided the well outside the smokehouse, but why? She placed a hand on his shoulder.

"What's wrong?"

Aelfric rubbed one eye, then the other. Aliwyn kept her hand on his shoulder and tried to memorize his profile—the slightly upturned nose and still boyish jaw. Ten years from now, would she still remember how he looked?

"I'm here if you want to talk," she said softly.

He glanced at her a few times. Finally, he sighed. "I once left an old man to drown in a well. It was the night I had to run..."

Aliwyn could guess the rest of that sentence, and she tightened her hold on his shoulder.

Aelfric continued. "Today, while we were walking to this hospital, I saw that man's two sons at the shipyard. They were negotiating the price for a new ship. Both sons wore black gowns."

Just like the girl who had been sweeping her doorstep. Aliwyn bit her lip. "How did that man fall into a well?"

Aelfric leaned over and whispered, "Cuthbert's other thralls threw him in after they broke his arm. This was in Hull, the night I escaped."

His warmth and closeness made her scalp tingle. She struggled to keep a calm composure as he continued. "I could've thrown him a bucket to turn upside down and float with, but I didn't. His family is mourning. He must be dead now."

"I'm sorry," she said. "What was his name?"

"Royd. He wasn't a good person. A black-hearted thrall master and Cuthbert's best friend, in fact. But I should've done something. All his friends were getting beaten. I just watched him while he screamed my name for help...he was still alive when I ran away."

His voice cracked. Royd's death had probably contributed to Cuthbert's drive to recapture his thralls and take revenge. Aliwyn sighed.

"Could you have pulled Royd out by yourself?" she whispered. "Or stayed long enough to find a bucket? Cuthbert would've arrived to kill you. He must've been furious."

"But I...just left someone to die."

He rubbed his eyes, and she dared to slip her arm around his. She treasured the heat of his clothes, and the heaviness of his arm relaxed within her hold. Nonetheless, his story made her throat pulse. There had been no easy or good choice for Aelfric to make. The result would've been dismal whether he'd stayed or left.

Could it be Providence that a cruel man should die like this? Aliwyn didn't know, but someone else might have felt no guilt in leaving Royd to die. Aelfric had a tender heart.

"You didn't run away back in Mablethorpe," she whispered.

"What?"

"Well, you did run at first, but then you came back to me and Grafton, remember? In the burned section of town."

"I suppose I did."

"Thanks for coming back."

He looked at her, his scowl fading, and Aliwyn smiled.

"You don't think I'm a bad person?" he asked. "A coward?"

"No, you're not a bad person or a coward for trying to survive."

Aelfric gave a pained smile. She had to share something with him, and she forced herself to speak.

"When I escaped my village up north, I saw many people who needed help, but I had to keep all my food and clothing for myself. My best friend Brona was limping beside me, and I was carrying my little brother. We kept walking. The rest of my family had already died. I felt horrible for leaving others in the snow, but I tell myself now it doesn't make me a bad person. Sometimes you have to... to keep walking."

She coughed and barely finished her sentence. Aelfric uncorked his costrel and handed it to her, and she poured some water into her mouth.

"I'm glad you made it out," he said.

The sympathy in his deep-set eyes made her shiver. Aliwyn thanked him for the water. Corking his costrel, she handed it back to him.

"Where is your little brother now?" he asked. "And Brona?"

She glanced at the ceiling, a missing square revealing the heavens above. Sobs shook her frame.

"I'm sorry." Aelfric bowed his head. "How did you finally cross that river?"

"A Norman priest arrived on a ship just two days too late. My brother and Brona would've lived if we hadn't been stranded beside a river. We couldn't cross because the Vasfians had burned the bridge down."

Aelfric's eyes widened. "What? Why would they do that?"

"Because they're despicable. They killed our priest, so the lord of our manor burned their sacred groves."

There was silence for a while, then Aelfric's voice took on a strange lilt. "So you see, they did it for a reason."

Aliwyn almost dug her fingers into his arm. He had been such a good listener up to that point. Why would he defend the Vasfians?

"How is burning a few trees the same as starving dozens of people to death?" she demanded. "I'll never forgive the redheads for what they did."

"I'm just saying there was a reason."

Aelfric shook his arm loose of her hold. He left his costrel on her mattress, crawled back to his blanket, and lay down with his back turned.

Aliwyn's chest heaved. What had just happened? She had only wanted him to stop berating himself for choosing self-preservation over sacrifice.

Her eyes throbbing, she crawled back onto her mattress. Godwin had rolled onto her side of the bed, and she lay beside him and cuddled him. On the other side of Godwin, on the ground, Aelfric's body rose and fell with erratic breaths. What was it about his life as a thrall that would endear the Vasfians to him? Everyone in Aliwyn's community had felt the same about

CHAPTER 14

the redheads prowling in the forests, ready to harvest their next human skull.

Embracing Godwin only deepened Aliwyn's yearning for her brother. Of all the crimes the Vasfians had committed against her family—stealing her father's chickens, snatching fishing spears, and shooting her uncle while he cut firewood—the deaths of her six-year-old sibling and best friend had shattered her heart. She didn't know how she could move on.

A long time passed. Aliwyn sipped from Aelfric's water pouch, but the pain in her throat remained.

Aelfric shuffled underneath his linens, then turned to frown at the ceiling. Aliwyn's heart sank. If he had looked gloomy earlier that day, now he appeared even worse.

"Blane," she whispered.

When his dour face turned toward her, she continued. "Let's not talk about the Vasfians anymore. They're making us miserable, and they're not even here."

His eyebrows jerked up. Was it sorrow or surprise? It was too dim to tell.

"Fine," he grumbled, then rolled away from her again. "Good night."

"Good night..."

She coughed into her pillow until her temples throbbed.

"Wake me up if you're out of water," Aelfric said.

His back was still turned, but his voice had softened.

Aliwyn smiled. Her lips trembled against Godwin's warm little forehead. Tomorrow, Aelfric would be gone, and she hadn't intended for their last night together to end this way. Wouldn't it be wonderful to embrace him from behind and pretend they had never argued? Heat flushed her cheeks. She was in no position to crawl up behind him and snuggle.

Back in her village, she had been infatuated with someone else a few years older, but it hadn't felt like this. That young man had never given her a second glance anyway, preferring to dance with the bustier girls at every marketplace festival.

Aelfric was different.

She picked up his water pouch and laid it above her head. The scent of wood from his hands drifted over her, and she prayed for Aelfric's happiness once he arrived in Scotland. He'd have no trouble finding work. Once again, he'd be ruddy-faced, playing music with the ocean waves lapping behind him. His talent would attract many young women, and she was confident he'd grow up to be a handsome man.

One day, he would fall in love with a lady in Scotland and marry her. Who would she be? Tears flowed from the corners of Aliwyn's eyes. It wouldn't be her.

Aelfric had told her beauty on the inside mattered most, but she struggled to believe it when she looked the way she did. The fear she'd never recover rattled her once more. She was also losing the dexterity of her hands. What would she still be worth if she looked like a mess and couldn't sew or cook?

Chapter 15

Aelfric

The next morning, the back of Aelfric's head ached from sleeping face-up on the ground. At least the aroma of fatty food filled the hospital. The free mutton stew and an endless supply of fritters for patients—in the middle of Lent—almost made up for the awful night.

Almost.

Aelfric had faked a few coughs to appear ill. Once a lay sister served him stew, he ate like a ravenous wolf.

Whenever he remembered how Aliwyn would never forgive the Vasfians, he'd ask for another bowl to wash down the hurt. It didn't help. He stared at this last bowl of bumpy stew and wanted to throw up, but he shouldn't waste food.

It seemed like Aliwyn hated the Vasfians more than the Normans. That was a scary thing, because the Normans were monsters who leveled entire villages. Those invaders had taken English widows as their wives after slaughtering their husbands. Wasn't this worse than the Vasfians burning one bridge? Maybe the local tribe didn't know what a tragedy a single lost bridge would cause. Even if the priest who'd saved Aliwyn was Norman, she should resent those conquerors more.

Aelfric's ribs ached as he breathed. Deep down, he knew why Aliwyn despised the Vasfians; the tribes were heathen and looked different. The Normans killed and pillaged, but they also went to church on Sundays. A Norman man who grew his hair out would look just like an Englishman, and so he'd be easier to tolerate.

Thank goodness Aelfric hadn't been born with red hair and freckles. Yet, it didn't feel right to be grateful for that. He wanted to punch a wall.

Glancing at Aliwyn, he sipped his fifth bowl. She was still working on her first, and her glum silence kept him on edge. Godwin, thank God, was the only one who appeared in good spirits. They exited the hospital with Aliwyn holding the boy's hand as he chewed on a fritter, his eyes bright and alert.

Aelfric walked ahead of them and shook out his arm, still sore from the hammering he'd done yesterday.

The sunshine warmed his face, and the golden morning sky lifted his spirits. He adjusted his knapsack over his shoulder and inhaled deeply, only to regret it when the pangs of his overly full stomach restarted. Aliwyn didn't want to talk about the Vasfians anymore? Fine, neither did he. Aelfric shoved all the thoughts from that morning out of his head.

They walked toward the church's stables, where swallows swooped through the air after insects. A queue of wagons and drivers waited for their next customer along the dusty roads.

Today was a day of goodbyes. After Aelfric sent Godwin and Aliwyn off on their journey, he'd have to find another ship to board. He could imagine the harbor front teeming again with ships and red ribbons tied to the quays.

The day felt unreal.

They approached a series of three drivers. The first two claimed they didn't travel to Beverley. The way their eyes roved over Aliwyn's bruised face and hands made Aelfric believe otherwise. When the third driver rejected them, prickly heat began crawling up his neck.

"She's not contagious." He raised his voice.

The driver only turned his back to pet his donkey, and Aelfric clenched his fists. Beside him, Aliwyn suppressed a cough. Her slender fingers folded around his forearm, and he blew out his anger. In a strange way, he was glad the drivers didn't want to take her. Now, he had an excuse to stay longer.

They waited for another driver to arrive. Godwin waddled for a black kitten that darted between the carriages, and Aelfric lunged to hold the boy back.

CHAPTER 15

"Kitty!" Godwin whined.

The thought of never hearing the boy's voice again made Aelfric's throat clog. Despite his aching arms, Aelfric picked up Godwin and hugged him. The boy stopped squealing and settled against his chest.

Aliwyn pressed her shoulders against his. He tried not to look at her, but it was too late. The tears welling in his eyes were obvious.

"Can you come over here?" she asked. "I want to talk to you."

They walked to the nearby village green, where many women had set up drying racks for laundry. Between the flapping sheets, children rolled red-dyed eggs, and geese pulled up blades of grass between their bills. From there, the line of carriages was still visible. Aliwyn sat on one of the logs provided for passersby to rest on. She lowered her head, and a breeze sifted through her light brown hair. Aelfric looked around for anyone who might overhear them, but the closest children and their mothers were out of earshot.

"What did you want to tell me?" he asked.

She was silent for a long time.

"I wanted to say I'm sorry," she said. "I never properly apologized for making you miss your ship on Monday. I ruined all of your plans."

She sniffed and stroked her bandaged hand. Aelfric shuffled his feet in a patch of weeds. The stitches of his shoe held.

"I'd almost forgotten about what happened on Monday," he murmured.

"Really? You'd be on your way to Scotland by now if I didn't steal…"

"I'd be on my way, sure. But I'd be feeling mighty empty about it."

He sighed and sat on the log beside her. Godwin crawled out of his lap and onto hers, and she welcomed him with a smile.

"Why would you feel empty?" she asked.

Aelfric scratched the back of his hood. Despite all their arguing over Vasfians, he'd still miss this girl. "I think you know why. I didn't have friends before I met you. Thanks for watching my back. That more than makes up for taking my recorder."

"I can never repay you for the money you spent on me."

"You don't need to. I'll make money again." He turned to face her fully. "And about my recorder, I forgive you because I want to. You can't buy something like that."

The tension lifted from her face. He smiled at the way the sunlight gave a golden hue to her skin. Once she entered Godwin's household, the purple blotches would disappear, and her cheeks would fill out. He wanted to believe it would happen even if he wouldn't be there to see it.

Aliwyn leaned close and whispered, "Thank you, Aelfie."

"What did you call me?"

"Aelfie. Is that all right with you?"

"Sure. No one's called me that before."

She pulled back and smiled. "What did your loved ones call you, then?"

They could talk for days, and Aelfric jolted back to his senses. It would be easier to let her go now before he got to know her any better. Mum had once commented on how the crickets chirped most fervently before the frost set in because they knew their time was coming.

He remembered her words, but he wished he didn't.

Aliwyn's expression fell from his abrupt silence. Another cart pulled onto the outskirts of the village green, joining the three who had refused to let Aliwyn board. This new driver, the short and stout man who had given Aelfric directions last night, jumped off and helped six bouncy children and their parents off his cart.

The man put his hands on his hips and announced he would take other passengers for a good price.

Aelfric stood, his gaze on his feet. "You should go now."

THE THREE OF THEM stopped before the driver, and Aelfric gestured at Aliwyn. "She's not contagious. A ship captain told us she has bloodrot."

"Oh, hello again!" The man studied Aliwyn up and down. "I agree with the captain's assessment. What was his name?"

CHAPTER 15

"Lars."

"Ah, Lars. That old scoundrel. Tell him he still owes Olaf two swigs of fine Normandy poiré!"

Aelfric thinned his lips. How many people in Kilnsea were acquainted with that unsavory Norseman?

"Well, we're not seeing him again." Aliwyn scowled. "My younger brother and I want to go to Beverley. How much do you charge?"

"Beverley, eh." Olaf scratched his thinning gray hair. "That be very far. I can only take you as far as Hull, and then you be needing to change carriages—"

"Hull?" Aelfric cut in. "Please take her elsewhere. Somewhere further north."

"Eh? What have you got against Hull?"

Because the Staddons might have returned to their workshop in Hull by now. Aelfric blurted out the first village he could think of. "What about Swine? It's also halfway to Beverley."

Olaf shrugged. "Hull has a very nice market. Most clients go there, but I can take this maiden and the young'un to Swine. It'll cost you three quarter pennies."

He extended a hand for payment.

Aliwyn fumbled with the flap of her belt pouch, and Aelfric closed his eyes. He hugged Godwin so tightly his cheek itched against the boy's skin. All the drool Godwin smeared over his ear felt like a parting gift.

What happened next was a blur. Aliwyn paid the fare and said something in her sweet voice that Aelfric couldn't register. He said nothing in return, his face steamy and his body stiff. Aliwyn climbed on board the back of the covered carriage and raised her arms for Godwin.

Aelfric peeled the boy off his chest. He'd never know how the tot sensed something was awry. Godwin shrieked and grabbed Aelfric's scarf, yanking it until Aelfric couldn't breathe. Wheezing, Aelfric tore the boy's hands off his scarf and staggered backward.

Godwin burst into tears. "Daaa!"

Aliwyn pulled back the writhing boy, and the two of them melted into the shadows of the carriage. Olaf climbed onto the driver's seat and set the donkey cart into motion. Godwin's screams echoed in Aelfric's ears, fading into the cries of gulls and the voices of haggling merchants in the town. Pain tore down his ribs.

Cuthbert Staddon could feed himself to the Devil.

Aelfric bolted after the carriage. "Wait!"

If Aliwyn and Godwin disappeared now, he'd wonder for the rest of his life if they managed to find the boy's family, and if Aliwyn found the miraculous cure she so needed.

The cart turned a corner. Aelfric swerved around the buildings to follow, still shouting at the top of his lungs. Finally, the carriage wheels ground to a halt. Aliwyn peered out the rear while holding a fussy Godwin back with one arm. "Did you forget something?"

"I didn't forget," he panted, his vision tunneling. "Olaf, how much for three people?"

Olaf leaned outward from the driver's seat. "Another halfpenny for you, young man!"

Aelfric ignored how spacious his coin pouch felt when he reached in. He slapped the required amount onto Olaf's hand. With pins and needles shooting through his limbs, he climbed onto the dim carriage and threw himself on the hay pallet beside Aliwyn. She gawked at him. Godwin squeezed himself between the two of them and grinned at Aelfric.

"Ada, Da!"

The carriage jolted back into movement.

"You..." Aliwyn's nostrils flared. "You're not thinking."

"That's not true." Aelfric wiped his sweaty forehead. "In fact, I've been thinking a lot. I need to know if you'll get better. And I don't want to leave you with this fever."

The sound of his panting filled the carriage. He placed his hand over her forehead, careful not to make her head snap back like he did the last time.

"I've had many fevers before." She frowned at him. "I'll get better, but you keep putting yourself in danger. I didn't make you a hat and a scarf so you could become reckless."

CHAPTER 15

Aelfric pulled back his hand. The two of them glared at each other as the carriage passed a lumber yard, where the sound of wood splitting overtook the carriage's jostling for a moment.

"I have to leave eventually, after I help you get to Beverley," he said. "I don't have much time left. Stop being angry with me, please."

"Beverley's a busy place. You shouldn't come."

"I'll just blend into the crowd."

"I'm..." Her expression crumpled. "I'm not...worth staying for."

"Yes, you are."

She might be confident that she'd reach Beverley, but Aelfric had seen her stumble and fall more and more often. If Godwin scurried after another cat, she wouldn't be able to catch him.

So many families had been torn apart because of the rebellion. So many children had lost their parents, and the people who survived were busy putting their lives back together. If no one else would escort her and Godwin to the Minster, he'd do it.

Aliwyn's face flushed. She turned away and locked her arms across her waist.

He couldn't imagine what scorn she had endured in the last few weeks. Had he not crawled into the smokehouse last Sunday, he would've avoided her, too. The thought worsened the heaviness of his shoulders.

"Remember what I told you about the seashells." He spoke also to remind himself.

Aelfric reached behind her and rubbed her back until the stiffness of her spine relaxed. Godwin, squished in between them, wiggled himself free and crawled onto Aelfric's lap. He babbled in an endearing young voice, and Aelfric grinned. He embraced the boy with his other arm. Scooting against Aliwyn, he rested her head on his shoulder the way his parents had once done to comfort him.

It was the first time he had comforted someone else like this. Being close to her felt good in a way he couldn't express.

Aliwyn had lived through things he never had, and he shouldn't have yelled at her for disliking the Vasfians. Her forehead warmed his chin, and her bony frame shook under his arm. Aelfric smoothed her shoulder with his thumb.

He decided on two things. One, that he would never shout at her again when she complained about Vasfians. And two, that he'd always keep his Vasfian heritage a secret from her.

The last decision didn't sit well with him. Aelfric scowled at the floorboards, but no better solution came to mind.

Godwin grasped his scarf again to chew on it, and Aelfric chuckled. He might as well enjoy the present.

"So," he said softly. "You want to know what my family used to call me? They called me Ick-boy."

He was delighted to hear her giggle.

"Ick-boy! But why?"

'Cause I used to do this when my mouth was dirty." He pulled back and wiped his mouth on his free shoulder. "All my tunics were stained on both shoulders. It made Mum so mad. I don't do that anymore, but the nickname stuck."

The two of them sniggered.

"Do you want me to call you Ick-boy?" she asked.

"Oh, definitely not. Aelfie is much better."

At that moment, smiling at her, Aelfric forgot where he was. The carriage could have been a canoe sinking in the ocean, and he wouldn't have noticed.

"What about you?" he asked. "What did people use to call you?"

"Just Ali."

"I like that. It's sweet and simple. I'll call you Ali from now on."

Her smile trembled. "It's been a long time since I heard my nickname."

Aelfric pulled her close again. The roughness of her scabbed forehead rubbed his ear, and she suppressed a cough.

"Try to sleep some more," he said. "We'll be on this carriage all morning."

He laid his knapsack on a hay pallet to serve as her pillow. Aliwyn curled up on the makeshift mattress and closed her eyes.

Godwin began walking away along the carriage's edge, and Aelfric scooped up the boy and brought him back to his side.

"Be good now, wee'un."

He gave Godwin several seashells to clink together and spin on the floorboards. Every time the carriage hit a bump, the boy would bounce on his seat and squeal. The entertainment never seemed to wear off. Thankfully, Aliwyn seemed to sleep through the noise.

With time, the scent of blood wafted from her body. Aelfric tensed. He squinted in the tangential sunlight, partly blocked by the driver's body. A patch of bright red had seeped through the bandages of her hands as they rested by her chin.

She bled easily and didn't stop.

The bruises from Cwenhild's beating probably weren't healing, either. What kind of wicked ailment was this?

Aelfric struggled to calm himself, but doubt spread like wildfire in his mind. Aliwyn might be convinced that finding a loving home would cure her, but maybe it wouldn't.

He needed to find her another option in case one 'treatment' failed. Aliwyn had not yet visited the healer in Brocklesby, but she had called the woman's Vasfian medicine 'demonic.' Aelfric rubbed his eyes until they burned. Maybe the local healer in Swine could help her?

Aliwyn tapped his knee, and he flinched.

"Why don't you take a nap as well?" she murmured.

"One of us needs to stay awake in case something happens."

"You look awfully tired."

He grinned. "I'm fine. Don't worry about me."

"You're a good friend, Aelfie." She smiled, her eyes rolling back before closing. "Thank you..."

She needed to call him by his fake name, but Aelfric didn't scold her. He shifted back in his seat with the scent of her blood hanging over his head. They had been fixated on his escape from Cuthbert, but time had been running out for her since the beginning.

It would take a miracle to fix whatever was wrong with her, but he'd never witnessed a miracle. Even if his father told him stories about miracles, no one in his family or in the thrall compound had seen any, either. What if they never even found Godwin's parents? He'd have to depart England while she remained gravely ill.

Aelfric steeled himself. All this doubt took him nowhere. His mind scrambled for something he could do.

When Godwin crawled away again, he reached out and drew the boy onto his lap. Godwin's parents must've had great faith to give their child the name he had. Aelfric struggled to have any. He resisted crushing the tot against him in a tight embrace.

For a long time, Godwin sucked on a seashell while sitting on his lap. Aelfric stared at the back of Olaf's head and the passing scenery. How had his father taught him to pray again?

God, you're my Father in Heaven. Please make Ali better. Even if you didn't save my parents and sister, save her. I'm warning you. I can't take another death.

Once he got off the carriage, he'd look for the local healer.

Chapter 16

Aliwyn

Aliwyn scowled at Olaf as he untethered his donkeys.

"Can't help you," he said, shuffling his feet. "I told you I be taking you only halfway. My wife's a-waiting me in Kilnsea. I needs be getting back."

Aelfric jutted his chin. "You can't take us even one town further?"

"No, sorry. You's can take your chances walking through them woods, but it be a bad idea."

With that, Olaf led his two donkeys toward a well. Aelfric bounced a whiny and hungry Godwin against his shoulder. They had arrived in Swine, a hamlet of less than ten households in the middle of nowhere, only to learn no wagons departed for Beverley until Easter Sunday.

"Drat it all," Aelfric grumbled. "I shouldn't have picked this pig pen to travel to."

Aliwyn's throat ached as she swallowed. Now, they'd lose their chance to find Godwin's parents on Good Friday and Holy Saturday, but being annoyed at Aelfric's poor decision wouldn't help.

"We'll wait," she said. "Going to Beverley on Easter Sunday isn't too late."

Aelfric's frown didn't ease.

The three of them spent the night in the barn adjacent to the village chapel. Aliwyn coughed so much the priest wouldn't let her enter the sanctuary where vagabonds took shelter.

The following day, she was flustered to see Aelfric rushing to leave the barn. She coughed for several hours on her mattress while Godwin fussed out of boredom. Aelfric only returned at noon with a bowl of what looked like sludge. He shut the door behind him with a queasy twist of his mouth.

"What is this?" Aliwyn sat up and stared at the bowl.

"Pork liver boiled in soured wine. For you."

"For me?" Aliwyn coughed into her sleeve. "But I never asked for it."

"I know, but apparently, this gunk is good for bloodrot and coughs."

She glared at him. "I don't have bloodrot. And I already told you what would make me better."

"B-but what if going to Beverley doesn't cure you?"

Aliwyn inhaled slowly and held her breath. What had gotten into Aelfric?

He scratched between his eyebrows. "I'm just saying it's a good idea to keep trying other things in the meantime, right?"

"I've already tried this pork liver remedy back in Mablethorpe, and it didn't work."

"Oh..." The area between his brows reddened from the scratching. "That apothecary lady was so convincing."

"You should've asked if I wanted medicine," she said. "I'm not eating this foul slop."

Aliwyn lay on her mattress and turned away. Flurries of grief swelled in her chest. Aelfric had meant well, but she couldn't bring herself to talk to him again. Of course she had doubts she would get better. The least he could do was to pretend he believed her confident façade.

At the sound of loud slurping, Aliwyn turned onto her back and peered at him. Every muscle of his face contorted with disgust as he sipped the pork liver slurry, and Godwin giggled at his expression. She chewed on her lip. At least this young man didn't waste anything that was marginally edible.

Godwin thumped Aelfric's back, and a mischievous grin spread across Aelfric's face.

"Too good not to share, wee'un." He dipped his finger into the brown liquid, turned around, and stuck it into Godwin's mouth.

The tot fell silent. He whimpered and raised his fist to his mouth.

CHAPTER 16

Aelfric burst out laughing. His voice echoed in the barn, and Aliwyn giggled despite herself. Her temples ached, and the rooftop spun.

She called his name, and Aelfric stopped laughing. Setting down his bowl, he took Godwin by the hand and walked to her side. He squatted with the boy standing by his knee, and Aliwyn smiled at the two boys who had stolen her heart. Aelfric's face blurred in and out of focus, his expression grim.

"I know you wanted to help me," she wheezed, then cleared her throat. "Thank you, but I need you to believe in what I'm doing. Please."

Aelfric lowered his eyes. His grimace made her want to sit up and throw her arms around his neck.

"Sometimes I have a hard time believing things I can't see," he said.

"Sometimes I do, too. But I still want to believe. I don't want to give up."

She extended her unbandaged hand toward him along the mattress's edge, and Aelfric took it. His fingers were calloused and warm, and Aliwyn smiled.

"Don't give up," he said. "I'll get you to Beverley. And I've been praying for you, too."

She squeezed his hand. "Thank you."

For the rest of the day, Aelfric fetched her everything she needed and helped the local peasants clean the stable. He took fragments of firewood and carved animal miniatures for Godwin to play with.

Night came. As Aliwyn's fever spiked and chills racked her body, she held onto the sound of Aelfric and Godwin laughing. Nothing could steal that memory from her. Her two friends remained by her side, and their presence kept fears at bay like two rushlights chasing away the darkness. As long as she had their support, she'd press on with her quest.

What would Godwin's parents be like? She hoped they were the loving people she had always imagined them to be.

Aelfric

By Easter Sunday at dawn, Aliwyn appeared gray. Aelfric had to pull her to her feet. Her legs wobbled, and panic flashed in her eyes. Worry also flooded his mind, but he didn't let it show.

Carts traveling to Beverly rolled into the village market. Aelfric paid for everyone to ride on one meant for transporting pigs, and piglets oinked from within their wicker baskets. Aelfric kept Godwin and Aliwyn close to him during the bumpy journey. The voyage lasted all morning through a fog that condensed on his cheeks and made him shiver. At least the fare was cheap. Aelfric had bought honey for Aliwyn's cough and was down to his last penny.

She slept against his shoulder. Her forehead heated his chin, and Aelfric struggled to appear cheerful before Godwin. The boy was content to peer at the pigs within their baskets.

The bells of Beverley Minster echoed in Aelfric's ears as the cart trundled through the farm fields surrounding the town walls. Other carts and wagons joined them as they neared the moat and imposing town gates. The sound of clattering hooves and the occasional jingling of harnesses filled the air. A piper in the marketplace up ahead played a cheerful tune, and Aelfric's ribs ached with longing. It had been days since he'd even looked at his recorder.

The cart they rode upon halted at the end of a line to cross the town's drawbridge.

Norman knights with conical helmets hiding their faces sat on warhorses near the gate to preside over the gathering. Each wore a red surcoat with a golden lion embroidered over the torso. The foot soldiers and squires beside them held spears whose sharp tips rose above the throng.

Only one brown-haired knight didn't wear a helmet, and he smiled at the crowd.

Aelfric scowled at the soldier's bizarre haircut, typical of Norman men—hair long on top but closely shaved around the sides. This knight should've kept his helmet on. Didn't he know most people in the crowd were English, and they wanted to throw rocks at him?

Wulfstan had said the Truce of God meant no fighting on Easter, but that sounded too good to be true. The Normans had crushed the rebellion only weeks ago. Tensions were still high. Aelfric glared at the knight, whose face beamed in the sunlight.

Pompous scoundrel. Had he smiled like this while killing entire English families? He deserved a rock to the face.

When the pig cart rolled onto the drawbridge, the knight's gaze seemed to fall on Aelfric. The man's smile vanished. He moved his horse toward the pig cart, and Aelfric gulped as the clopping hoofbeats approached. The Normans had better not be mind-readers!

"Greetings." The knight's shadow rose above the cart. "Has the maiden in the back been seen by a priest?"

Aelfric had never heard a Norman knight speak English this well. And they didn't usually converse with peasants; they only ordered common folk around and punished those who didn't obey. Aelfric stared, but Godwin babbled on his lap as though nothing was amiss.

The pig cart's driver shuffled in his seat. "I don't know these young'uns, sir. They only paid me for a ride. I know one of 'em is doin' poorly, but I put her with my pigs, not people. Supposed it was all right."

The knight looked at the driver, then at Aelfric again. "She cannot enter town. She needs a priest to evaluate her for leprosy."

Leprosy!

Aelfric grabbed Aliwyn by the shoulder. If she were thrown into a leper colony, she'd never get out.

"She doesn't have leprosy," he stammered. "She has bloodrot." He shook Aliwyn until she whimpered. "Esla, wake up. Show that man your gums."

Aliwyn's eyelids peeled apart. She looked up at the Norman and warhorse looming above her and shrieked. Her blood-streaked teeth flashed in the daylight, and the knight flinched in his seat. His horse snorted and shuffled back.

Aliwyn flailed her arms, and Aelfric withdrew his hold with a lump in his throat. He hadn't meant to scare her like this, but what else could he do? He caught one of her hands and displayed her pinpoint red rash and bruises to the knight.

"She has all her fingers, see? This isn't leprosy. A ship's captain told us she has bloodrot, and she's not contagious."

The cart driver spat on the ground. "Disgusting!"

Aelfric had kept Aliwyn as hidden as possible for a reason. He held his breath as the knight averted his eyes, frowning. Aliwyn pressed her shoulder against the railing, her face flushed. Strands of her fallen hair clung to the cloak Wulfstan had given her. The tightness in Aelfric's chest worsened.

Captain Lars had said all these signs were part of bloodrot, but Aliwyn still refused to believe she had it.

Finally, the knight said, "I know of this illness. Now I know the English call it 'bloodrot.' You may pass."

With that, he turned his horse around and joined the other knights along the town wall.

The cart lurched forward, and Aelfric ran a hand over his face. His heart was still pounding.

"I didn't mean to upset you." He looked at Aliwyn.

A scowl darkened her face, and she turned away until all he saw was her cloak and the bony knob at the back of her neck. Aelfric scratched his forehead under his hat and faked a grin at Godwin. If she wanted to be mad, there was nothing he could do.

What felt like forever passed. Aelfric's cart of pigs and people rolled within the town walls.

Beverley had as many tall buildings as Mablethorpe, but the streets were wider. Colorful flags fluttered from ropes that extended from one inn to another, and merchants announced their wares from booths along either side of the road. Godwin crawled back onto Aelfric's lap, and the two stared at the flower wreaths hanging on every door and the colorful tapestries on display at market booths. The scent of hot cross buns made Aelfric's mouth water. Had he been free, he'd have run to every stall to smell the spices, admire the textiles, and chase the baker selling those buns.

"I'm not upset at you," Aliwyn said beside him.

"Really?"

"Yes, really." She wiped her eyes. "I know I look horrendous. And I hate crowds and festivals."

"Even festivals? Why?"

"I've seen crowds like this turn from happy to murderous overnight once food became scarce. It happened in my village after the Normans came."

Aelfric frowned. "But the people here aren't from your village."

"They're all the same."

Her words drained the excitement out of him. He'd not lived through her experiences, and he counted himself lucky.

The cart stopped beside carriages in the market square. A main street extending from the market led up an incline to the impressively tall Beverley Minster with its sloping timber roofs. It was bigger than any church Aelfric had seen, and a stone bell tower stood at one end. A second stone tower was being built on the opposite end of the nave. The wooden scaffolding surrounding it rose as an intricate lattice toward the sky.

Pilgrims donning vibrant headwear packed the streets. Men in beige cloaks stood on stools, holding up bone relics and crosses for sale amidst eager worshippers.

Aelfric scratched his head. They'd have to find Godwin's parents—in this busy place?

The cart rolled to a stop.

"Now get off," the driver muttered. "I'm not driving you again."

Aelfric glared at him. He lifted Godwin off his lap, stood, and extended his hand to help Aliwyn.

Aliwyn

ALIWYN COULD SCARCELY MOVE her stiff limbs. The rattling floorboards had made her body ache, and her elbows twinged when she tried to sit. Facing Aelfric's scowl made her heart race. He braced her arm and helped her stand on the cart's bed, but her head spun, and she sagged against him. Godwin tottered past their legs for the cart's edge.

Aelfric jumped onto the dirt and helped Aliwyn step down. He let her go to lift Godwin from the cart bed. As he lowered the tot onto the ground, Aliwyn reached for the little boy's hand. Her right leg wouldn't flex. She lost balance and fell onto her side.

"Esla!" Aelfric cried.

The impact sent pain shooting up Aliwyn's hip. She wrapped her arm around her left knee, but her right knee was too painful to bend. Aelfric knelt beside her and pulled her back up to a sitting position. His presence kept sobs from rising in her chest.

"What happened to your leg?" He cupped her right knee between his hands, and Aliwyn winced.

"This knee feels bigger," she whispered. "It's happened to me before and goes away after a week or two."

"I'm going to look, all right?"

His lips pressed together, Aelfric began unwinding the linen strip gartering her stockings and keeping them in place. Aliwyn almost grabbed his hand to stop him. The rash was even more pronounced on her shins, and her knee was horribly bruised. What would he think? What would this crowd think?

The cart behind them rolled away. So many people milled around them—merchants hollering about their wares, children running between legs, old women begging for alms. She was trapped within a sea of bodies.

Aelfric rolled her stocking down over her swollen kneecap and the red dots covering her shins. He cursed under his breath, and Aliwyn pulled her stocking back up with shaking hands. There was no wound for him to clean or patch. All the bleeding happened beneath her skin, and now, behind her kneecap.

"Can you stand at all?" he asked.

CHAPTER 16

"I can. I'm just stiff from sitting too long, but moving helps the stiffness go—"

Before Aliwyn could finish, an oxen cart turned the corner and sped toward them. Aelfric grabbed her from behind and dragged her aside. The muddy wheels rolled over her discarded linen strips, and the driver turned with his whipstick waving in the air. "Get off the road!"

Aliwyn squeezed Aelfric's hand. Beverley was even more suffocating and congested than she'd feared. They had better enter the Minster before another cart ran over children like—

She gasped. "Where's Grafton?"

Aelfric let her go and darted across the road. He called the boy's fake name into the edge of the gathering, but Godwin was nowhere to be seen. Aelfric spun around. His wide eyes deepened the dread roiling within her. How could this happen to them—in Beverley?

"He can't be far," she stammered. "But he won't answer to Grafton."

Aelfric turned in a circle, his hands at his hips. "Stay here. I'll find him."

He shoved his way into the crowd. "Godwin!"

Aliwyn's hair stood on end. How many people did he want staring at him? A moment later, Aelfric was out of sight, and many bodies closed in around her.

Aliwyn couldn't run with him to help him search. The most she could do was pull herself onto the marketplace platform and hope to find Godwin from there. She crawled toward the wooden structure, eliciting yelps as she brushed past skirts and new shoes. The stench of manure and rotten onion peels crept up her nose. With muddied hands, she grabbed the platform's edge and pulled herself to her feet.

Horse hooves approached her from the town gates. Aliwyn clung to the platform and looked behind. The knight who had nearly stopped her outside Beverley rode into the marketplace with his head turned in the direction of Aelfric's cries. Two foot soldiers strode alongside.

Heaven forbid. Aelfric's screaming had attracted the Norman knights. If they chased Aelfric down and identified him as a runaway, how would they punish him?

The helmetless knight directed his horse to trot toward Aliwyn, and her vision went white. Memories of Norman knights storming into her village at night and throwing torches on every rooftop flashed in her mind. She nearly screamed when the knight came within speaking distance.

"Who is Godwin?" he called out. "Was he the toddler sitting beside you?"

A hush came over the crowd. A Norman speaking to a scrawny peasant could only mean trouble. The eyes of many peasants skimmed over her as though she had been caught stealing again, and Aliwyn could scarcely breathe. Finally, one of the foot soldiers beside the knight stepped forward.

"Sir Marcotte and his men can help you find the lost boy." He had a perfect English accent. "Are you the child's sister?"

This Norman, Sir Marcotte, had recruited an Englishman as his foot soldier. At the familiar accent of her countrymen, Aliwyn stuttered, "I'm Godwin's nurse. He just ran away."

"Fourth child gone missing since Good Friday," said a second foot soldier, also in perfect English. He turned to Aliwyn. "Stay here, and we'll help you find him."

Aliwyn's teeth chattered. She envisioned the knight grabbing her by her hair and throwing her to the ground, but Sir Marcotte only tugged on the reins of his brown steed and rode away. The crowd readily parted before him. He hollered in French at the other knights and foot soldiers stationed at various crossroads, and several moved to join him.

Aliwyn wrung her hands. A Norman bailiff had once visited her village to recruit servants and foot soldiers, but no one had wanted to work for him. Sir Marcotte's English soldiers must've sided with him for the money. Had she done the right thing by speaking to them?

No. She should've kept her mouth shut or lied and said Godwin was a runaway cat. Instinct screamed that something terrible would now happen. The soldiers would probably find Aelfric racing through the streets before they spotted Godwin. What if they got too close and saw Aelfric's scars?

Godwin was her responsibility, not Aelfric's. He needed to leave this chaotic place. Where was he?

CHAPTER 16

Unable to straighten one leg, Aliwyn hobbled to the platform steps and staggered her way up. People were whipped for all to see upon this platform, and the town's pillory and stocks came into view. Despite the multitude spilling into every street, no one came up here.

Her throat burned. Against her will, she imagined Aelfric's neck and arms locked in the pillory while a thickset constable whipped him from behind. She stumbled past old blood stains on the wooden planks and braced herself on the pillory for support. Aelfric was still screaming Godwin's name somewhere in the crowd, or so she thought.

She called for both boys, but the throng drowned out her voice.

Through the chaos in her mind, she prayed for Godwin to be protected from any thrall traders in the crowd. She pleaded for Aelfric to come back safe and sound. She'd say goodbye to him for the last time and tell him to leave.

Disgruntled faces stared back at this unsightly girl with a half-fallen stocking. Aliwyn squinted in the morning sun with tears welling in her eyes. Aelfric had told her to wait here. If she limped into the multitude to look for him now, they'd lose track of each other.

The river flowing toward the Minster glittered in the sunlight. In the distance, the gates of the Minster opened to cheering and fanfare. Worshippers poured out following the first Easter service. Aelfric didn't return, but the sight struck a moment of clarity in her mind. Godwin's parents had to be within the Minster by the baptismal font. They could help her find their son, if only she could hobble inside and alert them.

"Blane!" she screamed again, her voice raw.

Once she sent him away, she'd make her way to the Minster.

A passing soldier pointed his spear at her. "You. Get off the platform."

Aliwyn chewed on her lip. Limping to the steps, she sat to scoot down one step at a time.

Many carriages had parked for their passengers to disembark. Her eyes fell on the back of the short and grey-haired Olaf. He stood by his carriage, petting his donkeys and gazing at the Minster.

What was he doing here after claiming Beverley was too far for his cart to travel?

She couldn't believe her ears when Aelfric's voice shot through the crowd, shouting her fake name. All her thoughts regarding Olaf vanished. Aelfric's sweaty face appeared behind the back of a man he struggled to get past.

"Did you find him?" Aliwyn croaked.

Her eyes widened when Aelfric pushed a wheelbarrow into view. His knapsack was already inside, and the wheelbarrow's dirty and creaky wheel left a trail in the mud. Panting, Aelfric ran to where she sat on the platform steps.

"I didn't find him, but I got a bargain on this." He thumped the wheelbarrow with his fist. "Get on. I didn't feel good about leaving you here."

He reached for her forearms and pulled her to her feet. Aliwyn stumbled, but his firm hands supported her like they had many times before. On a whim, she wrapped her arms around him. Aelfric squirmed.

"What are you doing?" he wheezed. "Godwin's still out there!"

She pressed her cheek against his scarf. "Listen to me. That Norman knight who thought I had leprosy heard you yelling about Godwin. He took his soldiers to look for him."

Aelfric's chest heaved against hers.

"He what?" he whispered in her ear. "That's bad! Godwin's father is an English thegn!"

Aliwyn gasped. Aelfric had made a connection she had failed to see. The nobles in England were a small group who constantly backstabbed one another for more power. There weren't many thegns left in England. Would the knight recognize Godwin as a thegn's heir? The boy had an English haircut and an English name more common amongst the upper class.

Norman knights had executed the thegn of her village and his sons. They had submitted to every Norman rule to survive; their only offense had been living where rebels hid. The Normans might tolerate the English peasants needed to plow their farmlands, but they wouldn't spare the aristocracy.

Aliwyn pulled back, shaking with chills.

"This is my fault," she said. "I have to find Godwin, and you need to leave Beverley. That knight and his soldiers will want to question you. One of them could recognize you."

Aelfric looked aside and swore under his breath.

"You have to go," she pleaded. "I'll find Godwin's parents so they can help me search. They'll stand up to that Norman knight."

He turned back to her, his brows knit into a single line.

"I already ran away once from that well," he said. "And I…I didn't come all the way to Beverley just to lose Godwin. I can't leave with him still missing."

She squeezed her eyes shut. "But the knight's coming back."

"Well, we're not waiting here." He gripped her shoulders. "You want to find Godwin's parents? The doors are still open before the second service." He pointed at Beverley Minster. "I'll push you there."

"I…" Aliwyn's head gave a dizzying spin, and the onlookers swerved from one side to the other.

Aelfric caught her and lowered her onto the wheelbarrow so that his knapsack cushioned her back. He picked up her legs and tucked them into the compartment.

She tried to pull off his hands. "You need to go."

"I like your idea. Let's find his parents first."

Aelfric tugged his hat over his eyebrows. His face hovered close to hers, his dark eyes unwavering. "You forget that this is all supposed to make you better. And I want to see that happen."

The determination and sympathy in his gaze made her eyes blur. Aliwyn curled against his knapsack as Aelfric ran to the back of the wheelbarrow.

"Hold on, Esla."

With a grunt, he lifted the handles and pushed it into the crowd.

Chapter 17

Aelfric

The two of them sped through the cluttered streets. Yes, Aelfric had to leave Beverley. If his older sister were alive, she'd smack him upside the head for having stayed this long, and his parents would be aghast at his recklessness.

But before spending his last penny on this wheelbarrow, Aelfric had sworn to himself that he wouldn't run away again when the situation became heated.

Between gasps for air, he shouted at the back of Aliwyn's head, "What do Godwin's parents look like? His nurse must've told you?"

"His mother is blonde." Aliwyn tried to turn around, but a bump in the road made her slide back down. "His father has black hair, like you."

Was that why Godwin kept calling him Da? The boy's voice echoed in Aelfric's head, and his eyes smarted. He never knew it could hurt this much to lose a child, even for a while. Hopefully, not for long.

The squeaky wheelbarrow wheel warned the crowd to part on either side of them. They had almost reached the clearing outside Beverley Minster when horse hooves began closing in from behind. Panic flared within Aelfric's chest, but he couldn't let go of the wheelbarrow's handles.

Aliwyn twisted around, her bloodshot eyes wide. "Blane, get out of here!"

Before Aelfric could respond, a man's voice shouted, "Wait! You're the ones looking for Godwin? A little boy?"

Familiar babbling echoed to Aelfric's ears, and his heart thudded. He slowed the wheelbarrow to a stop, his back aching from the effort, and released the handles from his sweaty hands.

Aliwyn had frozen in place.

"Godwin," she whispered.

Aelfric spun around, his damp tunic plastered to his chest. As though out of a dream, Godwin appeared within the arms of the helmetless knight on horseback. The boy grinned and squealed. He kicked his legs and tugged on the reins within the man's hand.

Aelfric blinked several times at the imposing brown warhorse. The knight who held Godwin was neither smiling nor talking. Did he know Godwin's father? Had he driven the poor thegn out of his territory?

Aelfric's knees wobbled, but he rolled back his shoulders. "Give the boy back to us!"

"Not so fast," the knight said. "I found him just as another party was taking him. They claimed they had been looking for the same boy. What is your name and relationship to this child?"

Another party? But Godwin was theirs! Aelfric opened his mouth to speak, but Aliwyn's cool fingers slid over his wrist. He swallowed his crass words just in time.

"My name is Aliwyn," she said. "I'm his nurse, like I said. And my friend here is...Blane. We wanted to bring Godwin back to his parents in Beverley. Who is in the other party?"

Unexpectedly, the man's expression softened.

"I see," he said. "Then everything makes sense. The other party is a family of three, a couple and a grandfather. They say they had lost a boy of eighteen months named Godwin. He was last seen with his nurse."

Tears welled in Aliwyn's eyes. "Those people must be Godwin's family."

Aelfric swallowed several times. After everything he had been through with her and Godwin, this was how their journey would end? He felt cheated, somehow. He wasn't ready to leave.

"Sir Marcotte," Aliwyn said. "I'm not the nurse Godwin once had, but please, let me bring Godwin back to his family."

Sir Marcotte had a thoroughly French Norman name. Aelfric hung his head. Godwin's cheerful and nonsensical words washed him in a wave of grief.

"Ada! Da!"

Aelfric looked up as Sir Marcotte jumped off his warhorse with Godwin held in one arm. The boy wiggled to turn around and extend both arms toward Aelfric and Aliwyn.

"I had to be cautious." Sir Marcotte approached the wheelbarrow. "Many children have gone missing since the uprising."

He set Godwin on the ground as Aliwyn levered herself out of the wheelbarrow. The boy pattered toward them with a big smile, and Aelfric rushed to see him. Aliwyn limped after him.

She threw her arms around Godwin and kissed him all over his head, but Aelfric only stiffened at being this close to a Norman man. The knight towered above him in height, and Aelfric was too nervous to look up past his chin. Sir Marcotte smelled very clean—or rather, he didn't smell at all—and he had no beard. Everything about him was foreign.

Behind Aelfric, men speaking French called out to Sir Marcotte. Aelfric turned around just as one of these men, another knight on horseback, put his hand to his heart and dipped his chin in reverence. Aelfric narrowed his eyes. What was so special about this knight who had found Godwin?

"Thank you, Sir Marcotte," Aliwyn said. "Please tell me where Godwin's family is."

"I told them to wait by the well outside the Minster while I determined who should take custody of this boy." Sir Marcotte gestured down the street. Beyond the bustling marketplace, a sizeable hill led to the Minster behind it.

"Head straight down this way," the man said. "You'll see the well once you get closer. I have to return to my post now."

Aliwyn thanked him again, and the knight mounted his steed. Aelfric didn't watch him go. He squatted by Godwin and placed his hand on the boy's shoulder. Godwin smiled, and Aelfric held his breath to shut in the turmoil. He suddenly didn't want Godwin to go home. Why couldn't his parents be alive instead of Godwin's? It was an inappropriate question. Heartless.

"Blane," Aliwyn said, "I know where to go. I can still walk. Thank you for everything."

She pushed to stand next to Aelfric, and his face burned. All around them, soldiers in conical helmets stood between the market booths with their spears held upright. The longer Aelfric looked, the more soldiers he saw. He needed to leave.

Where would he stay tonight, and what would he eat? Unless he resold the wheelbarrow, he had not a penny left, but it wasn't his empty pocket tearing him apart.

Aliwyn stepped into his field of view, but he couldn't look up at her face. The bandage covering her hand was bloody again.

"I wish you could come with me," she said. "Enter Godwin's household with me..."

"I wasn't born free like you were." Aelfric caught a glance of her glistening blue eyes. He'd never forget that shade of blue.

She reached for his hand. Her fingers were as rough as his own.

"I'll always remember you, my dear friend," she said. "Godspeed."

Aliwyn pushed something frigid against his palm, and Aelfric flinched. His hand closed around several coins. "You're giving me—"

"Please keep everything and take care of yourself."

He opened his hand and stared at the sparkly silver. "Isn't this all you have left from Wulfstan?"

"Yes, but it's all right. You need money to travel. I hope you find everything you've ever wanted in Scotland."

Tears clouded his vision. How the winds of fortune had changed.

Aelfric tried for a smile. Whatever came out of that attempt didn't feel like a smile.

"Goodbye," he whispered.

He ducked his head and turned away. The edges of the penny pieces dug into his palm as he clenched his fist. Looking back, he wanted to thank Aliwyn and wish her and Godwin well, but only chattering and smiling peasants milled past. His only friends were gone.

Heat flashed down his chest. Standing amidst a sea of people, he had never felt more alone. Everywhere he looked, happy people wished each other a blessed Easter. Parents carried their little ones and laughed. He knew he should be overjoyed for Aliwyn and Godwin, but he wasn't.

Aelfric dropped his sweaty pennies into his pocket. He picked up the wheelbarrow's handles but wanted to bash his head against its edge instead. No matter how fast he walked, he couldn't escape the joyful crowd he didn't want to see.

Memories with Aliwyn and Godwin glimmered in the blackness of his mind. Back in Swine, he'd found snails for Godwin to play with and had thumped Aliwyn's back at night when she coughed. He'd shared a roof with donkeys and mice and had almost no money left, but he'd felt fulfilled. Dare he say it—happy.

A cart bustled through the busy street. He let go of the wheelbarrow to reach for Aliwyn and pull her aside, but she wasn't there.

It was too late to tell her and Godwin what they meant to him. Aelfric's knapsack cut into the side of his neck, but he ignored the pain and kept walking.

Two figures seemed to pass him in his peripheral view. He spun to see merchants carrying bags of spices to replenish their displays. The scent of thyme reminded him of Aliwyn's stew, and his stomach growled. As soon as he paused, soldiers appeared from behind the colorful booths, and Aelfric turned away again.

He roamed without direction. The creaky wheelbarrow wheel made him want to kick it off, and Beverley never seemed to end.

Finally, his throbbing foot and a foul smell drew his attention. His shoe had split open again. It was full of pebbles, and he had stepped on animal feces. Rolling his eyes, Aelfric looked around for a place he could scrape it off without offending all these beautifully dressed people.

Down a side street, a group of beggars watched him as they sat by the lord's oven. A crowd of merchants walked past. The vagabonds extended their hands for money, but no one looked at them.

CHAPTER 17

Aelfric blinked several times, his mouth dry. Some of those beggars had lost a foot, maybe due to frostbite. They were the few people not so merry this Easter, and he knew what it felt like to beg and feel invisible.

Unlike them, he still could work. Aelfric could spare them a quarter penny.

He mustered a smile and approached them. "I'll give you something," he said. "I just want to clean my shoe first."

The beggars grinned. Some with teeth, many without.

Aelfric set down his wheelbarrow. He stopped by a building and extended his foot to scrape it against the bottom corner. Aliwyn's final words to him echoed in his mind. She had given him her goodbye blessings and memories he'd never forget. He should stop moping and live the life she hoped he'd have. Adventures awaited him in Scotland.

The ache in his throat remained, nonetheless. It would have to pass, somehow.

Aelfric had just taken off his shoe to shake out the rocks when a shadow pounced from his left.

His ribs seized. He dove and hit the ground chest-first. Two arms clad in black swung over his head to grab him. Aelfric rolled onto his back and narrowly missed a shovel smashing down on his stomach.

Two attackers! Aelfric recognized their stench—Cuthbert and Edgar Staddon.

Still on the ground, Aelfric kicked Cuthbert on the side of his bowlegged knee. The man howled and staggered. When Edgar swung his shovel down again, Aelfric rolled aside, grabbed it by its pole, and yanked. Edgar stumbled forward. Aelfric flung his feces-caked shoe onto the man's face. There was an earsplitting scream.

The beggars cheered and raised their fists in the air.

Aelfric scrambled to his feet and ran toward them. He scooped out his money and tossed the coins at their feet.

"Go get'em!" he shouted.

The ragged men rushed to grab the money, and their crouching bodies forced the Staddons to lurch to a halt. Aelfric swerved around the next building and onto a new street. If he had a chance, he'd slap Cuthbert with his other shoe! How did they track him down in this sprawling town?

"Stop that boy!" Edgar shouted from behind. "He's a runaway thrall!"

Aelfric gritted his teeth and shoved past startled peasants. No one grabbed him—for now. Scenes of his narrow escape in Mablethorpe come crashing back. Exactly one week later, he was fleeing yet again, but Beverley harbored no ships for him to escape onto. Could he make it to the town exit?

"Halt!" Numerous foot soldiers crossed spears a few paces ahead.

Aelfric skidded to a stop on his sore foot. The soldiers charged to trap him between their weapons, and Aelfric grabbed the first thing to his right—a scoop of spices. He flung the powdery stuff with a sweep of his arm, and the spices burst into clouds upon hitting the soldiers' faces. They yelped and covered their eyes. The spears they held clattered left and right.

"My pepper!" a woman screamed.

Aelfric flung the empty scoop at the sputtering soldiers, and it struck one man's helmet with a clang. Diving below the spice display, Aelfric crawled between the crates and sacks below. His breath scorched his windpipe. When he stood again, he overturned the whole table.

French expletives rang in the air, followed by the whinnying of horses.

Now he'd done it—destroyed someone's market stall *and* angered the Norman knights. Aelfric had no plan except to run, but run to where? The town gates were too far behind.

With chaos erupting behind him, he jumped onto a stack of chicken cages, clambered up the pile, and leaped off the other side. Careening left, he darted into the cool alleyway behind the fuller's cabin.

Vats of urine and soaking wool lay ahead in the shadows. In the distance, the sloping timber roof of Beverley Minster seemed to glow in the sun. Aelfric couldn't rush back into the mayhem he had caused. He'd have to jump into the river curving behind the Minster. The only way out would be to swim through the wall's watergate, where the river also flowed.

Aelfric wove in between the urine basins toward the Minster. His shoeless foot pounded on the ground, and his calves burned from the strain.

He had wholeheartedly wanted to help Aliwyn and Godwin. How could this happen to him in return?

He couldn't get caught. Must not get caught. Where was Aliwyn? The Staddons would want to nab her, too, for being his accomplice.

By the Devil's tail, Ali! Find Godwin's parents and get out of here!

Aliwyn

ALIWYN HELD GODWIN'S HAND as they walked up the incline toward the well. Although she should have been excited to meet the boy's family, she trembled all over.

She turned around, imagining Aelfric running back toward her, saying he "forgot" something, but only the narrow and crowded streets lay behind her.

Aliwyn blinked back her tears and squeezed Godwin's hand. "Godwin, are you excited to see your parents?"

"Da." The boy frowned at her.

"Do you miss him already? He had to leave…"

They continued uphill. Aliwyn hastily combed her hair and wiped her cheeks. She could only hope she looked passable as a nurse. The well came into view at the top of the slope, and beside it stood a woman in a brown cloak. She gazed into the distance at the marketplace.

How strange. Weren't there supposed to be three people at the well?

The woman's eyes were dark and scornful beneath her hood, not the look of one longing for a child. Aliwyn stroked Godwin's hand with her thumb. It was not the appearance she had imagined his mother to have, but perhaps the woman was tired from her journey.

Trying for a smile, Aliwyn knelt by Godwin and pointed at the well. "That's your mum there, isn't it?"

The boy stared back at Aliwyn and sucked his fist.

Aliwyn's smile faded. She rubbed her swollen knee and squinted at the woman. Her features were familiar, but why?

Screams burst forth from the marketplace, and Aliwyn pulled Godwin to her chest.

"Stop that runaway!" came a hoarse cry.

She gasped. Aelfric bolted from the market's edge with chickens squawking and flapping feathers everywhere. Two men barreled out of the crowd in hot pursuit with their black cloaks fluttering. A prickling sensation shot up her spine when she saw their faces—the Staddons.

"Hildred!" Edgar cried. "Fetch the manor lord!"

"And you run that thrall into a dead end!" shouted the woman by the well.

Now Aliwyn remembered why this woman, Hildred, looked familiar—she had been standing behind Edgar in the inn back in Mablethorpe. She must've been Edgar's wife.

The meeting at the well had been a lie. Godwin's parents were not here.

Hildred pulled up her gown and ran downhill toward the market. Peasants on the dirt road scattered before her. Aliwyn struggled to stand again. With the woman's pounding feet about to strike her, Aliwyn grabbed Godwin's hand and pulled him into the noisy throng off the road. No one seemed willing to chase Aelfric in their impeccable clothing and clean boots.

Bodies crushed against her, but it was the understanding of what had happened that devastated Aliwyn. Cuthbert and his household must've overheard Aelfric yelling Godwin's name all around Beverley. When they couldn't track down Aelfric, the Staddons must've chanced upon Godwin instead. Sir Marcotte intercepted them to ask about the child, and they lied about being Godwin's relatives instead of admitting they were kidnapping the boy.

Perhaps they had been watching from the hilltop, just waiting to grab Aelfric. Once Sir Marcotte departed, Edgar and Cuthbert had gone on the hunt.

What could she do to help Aelfric now?

Foot soldiers shouted behind her. They shoved through the crowd to pursue Aelfric and the Staddons, and the throng surged to get out of the way. Aliwyn stumbled and fought to hold onto Godwin's hand. Behind the marketplace buildings, horses whinnied, and men yelled in French.

She pulled herself and Godwin out of the crowd in time to see Aelfric dart around the corner of the Minster and out of sight. The peasants in the vicinity erupted in mixed shouts of fright and glee as soldiers followed.

"Da!" Godwin clapped his hands.

Aliwyn mustered all her strength to pick up the boy. Godwin's real parents had to be at the baptismal font, and she must find them now. How they'd help Aelfric, she didn't know, but something told her they were his only hope.

Relic peddlers stood on their toes outside the Minster gates to watch the chase. Pilgrims began streaming out of the Minster to investigate the noise.

Against Aliwyn's will, the memory of Cwenhild thrashing her resurfaced in her mind. Her legs wobbled, but embracing Godwin steeled her resolve. She ducked her head and pushed against the flow of worshippers exiting the Minster.

Aelfric

AELFRIC SHOT PAST THE horses and carts parked behind the Minster. There was a sizeable cemetery, and beyond that lay a muddy riverbank covered in gulls. A river of murky water coursed in the distance.

His chest heaving, Aelfric darted toward the riverbank. He was scaring away the first gulls when a rock sailed past his head. Edgar's voice rang out behind him.

The Staddons were slinging stones.

Aelfric ducked to miss a second one. He had scarcely caught his breath when another rock struck his left shoulder blade. His upper back burst in pain.

Aelfric yelped and gripped his shoulder. He stumbled forward but caught himself in time. The pain tore down to his bone, and he couldn't lift his left arm. Swimming as fast as possible was now out of the question. With a glance behind, Aelfric pivoted from his trajectory and bolted back toward the Minster.

His sudden change in direction threw his pursuers off guard. Foot soldiers bumped into each other as the Staddons doubled back to scramble after Aelfric. The wooden scaffolding of the incomplete tower loomed before Aelfric, and its narrow windows stared back like two black eyes.

He marshaled the last of his stamina. Tearing through the grassy plain, he approached the wall and spun his body sideways. A moment later, he shoved himself through a tower window.

Chapter 18

Aelfric

AELFRIC'S NOSE SCRAPED ON the rough stone, and he landed on his back. The impact punched the air from his lungs. He staggered onto his feet, but his knees gave out, and he collapsed back against the wall. The frigid stone behind him sent shivers through his body.

He dared to let go of his injured left side. Nothing was broken, it seemed. Ignoring the pain, he rotated his shoulder a few times.

The tower lacked a roof. Shafts of tangential sunlight shone from a blue sky above, and a chilly breeze sliced through him. The circular walls were just like the ones in the Mablethorpe smokehouse. Aelfric could almost see Aliwyn and Godwin appearing from the shadows, and his teeth chattered.

But they were not here. This was now his battle and his alone. Aelfric muttered a prayer that they were long gone with Godwin's parents.

Angry yelling reverberated from outside and echoed within the tower. The Staddons could scream and curse all they wanted, but they couldn't enter. Aelfric was in a church tower and had the right to sanctuary for forty days. Although he was safe for now, there was a problem—he had to exit eventually.

Aelfric stared at the walls around him with sweat trickling down his back. No roof, no bed, no firewood. There wasn't even a door installed yet—only a wooden plank leaning against the exterior of the wall where the hole was.

A fine place to stay for forty days.

He jolted when a meaty hand reached into one of the slit-like windows. The sound of a man straining rang forth, and an arm clothed in black writhed itself in. Aelfric bared his teeth and pushed to his feet. When would these fools give up?

He withdrew his eating knife from his cloak. His left shoulder still throbbing, Aelfric skirted along the shadowy walls. His mind flooded with a sickening fantasy that Cuthbert and Edgar were dead instead of his family. The dark images spiraled out of control, and Aelfric almost dropped his weapon.

Cuthbert shoved his shoulder and balding head through the opening, but he couldn't see Aelfric behind him.

Veins bulged on the man's neck. Aelfric adjusted his grip on his knife and approached on his toes. His right arm twitched to make that stab through the neck of a demon.

I'm not a thief or a murderer. I only...only ran.

Those had been his words to Aliwyn. Her pale blue eyes and frightened face passed through his memory, and Aelfric quivered. He staggered to a stop. His arm wouldn't move, and his eyes filled. He couldn't do it; he couldn't kill a man he wished had never been born.

Cuthbert twisted his head around. With his eyes bulging and his face warped, he finally pulled himself back out.

"You're trapped!" he shouted. "Come out here this instant!"

"I have the right to a sanctuary for forty days!" Aelfric yelled back.

He wiped his eyes and put his knife away. Sliding down the wall, he sat with his legs sprawled out. He shed his cloak and used it to rub his face until the salty tears burned. Forty days it was. Would the priest send him food? Have pity and give him a privy pot? He'd rather die than come out.

Aelfric unclasped his water costrel and raised it to his lips with shaking hands. More spilled down his chin than made it into his mouth.

The yelling outside wouldn't stop. Aelfric couldn't comprehend everything, but he recognized French words amongst the garbled voices. The Normans didn't have the right to drag him out either, but after forty days, the Staddons would still be waiting.

CHAPTER 18

Aelfric tilted back his head. The view of a circular sky above resembled what a man would see at the bottom of a well.

The irony.

A flock of doves glided past, so graceful and free. Maybe this was Providence. Aelfric had done his share of bad and selfish things. He tipped his head back against the stone wall, his throat tight.

There was nothing here, not even a thief and her stash of stolen goods. Aliwyn seemed to walk into view, brandishing her scissors, then disappear. Her voice and Godwin's emerged from the shadows cast by the wooden scaffolding overhead.

But he wasn't just imagining her voice. Aelfric's eyes widened. Through the turmoil outside, a woman who sounded like Aliwyn spoke again. Something was wrong. She was sobbing on the other side of the wall, within the Minster proper.

Only a few words came through.

"Please! Please let me stay with him—"

The woman's voice faded as though she had exited the Minster gates.

Aelfric pushed to his feet with a fresh wave of dread. Was this really Aliwyn? Why had she not left the pandemonium with Godwin's family?

He stumbled up the incomplete steps of the tower that spiraled alongside the walls. Maybe he could peer outside and see what had happened to Aliwyn. Before he'd walked far, a knocking sound came from below. Someone was outside the wooden plank barring the tower's opening.

"Aelfric," came Sir Marcotte's voice. "I am the lord of Beverley. You've made quite the mess of my town."

Aelfric gulped, and the world seemed to tilt to one side. The sound of a woman crying echoed forth again. Now, he was sure it was Aliwyn, and his heart sank to the pit of his stomach. Judging by the direction of her voice, she was standing beside Sir Marcotte on the other side of the makeshift door.

Aelfric hurried downstairs, his knees almost buckling.

"Ali?" he croaked.

Sir Marcotte answered instead. "I have her in custody. Surrender yourself now, and I will release your friend without punishment."

"We never agreed to that!" hissed an older woman. "This skinny wench lied about Aelfric's identity back in Mablethorpe. She helped him get away!"

Aelfric recognized the woman's voice as Hildred, Edgar's wife. *By the Devil's tail.* How many Staddons were outside?

"You lied to me about being the relatives of a lost boy," Sir Marcotte said. "Keep your mouth shut before I penalize you also."

Low bickering ensued between people whose voices he recognized as members of the Staddon household. Aelfric walked beside the temporary door and pressed his forehead against the stone wall. The pieces began to fit together. The couple and a grandfather by the well had not been Godwin's relatives. They were Cuthbert, Edgar, and his wife, who must've heard from the Mablethorpe priest that Aliwyn wanted to reunite Godwin with his family in Beverley. They had used Godwin as bait to catch Aelfric.

Fire shot through his veins. He could only guess who had alerted the Staddons that he had indeed followed Aliwyn to Beverley. Now, she was neck-deep in trouble because of him.

"Aelfie," she called out, "don't come out for another week. The Staddons will be exiled in a few days—"

"Shut your mouth!" Edgar yelled.

"I will not!" Aliwyn shouted. "I heard you speaking to your wife, and I will repeat everything! By next week, your entire household will be evicted from England, and you deserve it!"

Aelfric's mouth hung open. The Normans had finally evicted the tax-evading Staddons. They were about to lose everything they couldn't carry. A rush of satisfaction coursed through him, but a crippling pain soon followed. Even if the Staddons departed next week, Aliwyn would still be punished today.

"Stay in there, Aelfie," Aliwyn said firmly. "They can't pull you out of a sanctuary. Don't worry about me."

A fist pounded on the wooden plank barring the door.

"Come out now, or I'm dragging this hag to the whipping post!" Cuthbert yelled.

CHAPTER 18

"Aelfric, you're a fugitive and you've wrecked my marketplace," Sir Marcotte said. "I am being lenient on your friend because she is ill. Exit now and face your punishment before I lose my patience."

Aelfric wiped his wet eyes. Aliwyn whimpered again on the other side, and he wanted to drive his head into the wall. She was going to be whipped. It was either her or him, but while he could withstand over a dozen lashes, the corporal punishment would kill her.

Out of nowhere, the sound of Aliwyn's singing and the taste of her turnip stew flooded his senses as if he were reliving everything. He felt the comfort of her arm around his. Saw her smile as she listened to him talk about things he'd never told anyone. An unexpected warmth stirred within him. In a few days, she had given him companionship and a sense of belonging he didn't know he craved. He had been free to leave her all along, but he hadn't wanted to.

Now that she was in danger, Aelfric felt as though he had returned to another well. This time, he wouldn't shy away again.

The perpetual weight lifted from his chest. He stepped back and balled his hands into fists.

"I'm coming out!" he shouted. "How do I move this plank?"

"No, Aelfie!" Aliwyn cried.

"You're small enough to squeeze through the sides," Sir Marcotte said. "The entrance isn't perfectly sealed."

Aelfric winced as the sound of an imaginary whip cracked in his ears, but he had been through that before.

As though floating across the floor, he walked toward the light streaming in beneath one edge of the wooden barricade. He saw his father's smiling face in his mind, and Aelfric looked up at the circle of blue. Would his father up there be proud or devastated?

Aelfric squeezed the tears from his eyes and pushed his shoulder through the gap.

HANDS GRABBED HIS UPPER arms and threw him face-first onto the ground. Aelfric was too startled to scream. He tried to cover his head, but someone wrenched his arms and pinned them behind his back.

"You killed my friend!" Cuthbert yelled.

Aelfric opened his mouth to protest, but mud coated his tongue instead. Someone yanked off his hat. He didn't know how many boots stepped on his back and legs to hold him down, and he fought to breathe.

The first kick to the ribs came, and he writhed. He gritted his teeth and refused to scream. It never helped anyway, and he wasn't going to give the Staddons any satisfaction.

Through his blurry vision, Aelfric struggled to see if Sir Marcotte had let Aliwyn go. Feet flew in all directions, and a shadow rose over his head—one boot raised to stomp on his face. He closed his eyes.

"Stop!" Aliwyn screamed.

The pummel to his head never came. Aelfric opened his eyes and gasped for air. Enough weight lifted from his back for him to turn his head. Black cloaks and feet whirled around him, and he caught sight of Aliwyn kicking Cuthbert's shin and swiping her scissors at Edgar.

"You monsters!" she yelled. "You pile of worms! You go to Easter service dressed like kings, and this is what you do! Inside, you're all stink and rot!"

Aelfric swallowed the blood from his cracked lip. No one was standing on him anymore, and he forced his aching body to roll onto one side. A wall of embroidered cloaks and soldiers' surcoats seemed to rotate and then stop. His eyesight refocused on the Staddons, who had backed away with a manic look in their eyes. Sir Marcotte gripped his sword hilt, but he hadn't withdrawn his blade.

Aliwyn shuffled back until she stood between them and Aelfric. She kept her scissors raised.

"Cuthbert Staddon!" she shouted. "Aelfric did not kill your friend! The other thralls threw him into a well. Stop blaming him for all the evil you've brought upon yourself!"

She staggered to one side. Her hand, brandishing the scissors, shook. Her weapon tumbled down, and Aliwyn's legs crumpled. Aelfric pushed himself to sitting and caught her before she slumped onto the ground.

She reached for him, her face drenched with tears. He pulled her shoulder against him and wrapped his arms around her.

It was only a matter of time before someone dragged him away. Aelfric struggled to swallow the lump in his throat. He rubbed Aliwyn's shoulders and tried to memorize how it felt to hold her. Her hood had fallen back, and her forehead and hair warmed his clammy neck. Sliding his hand over the bones of her frame made him shake. Maybe she wasn't strong, but he had never heard anyone speak so courageously.

He glared up at Cuthbert. The man stood his ground as if the stillness of the crowd had cast an invisible net over him. Not even Sir Marcotte or the soldiers moved.

"Royd died of a wet cough and fever after I pulled him out of the well," Cuthbert said hoarsely. "He kept mumbling Aelfric's name on his deathbed."

"I didn't hurt him, and I didn't throw him in." Aelfric wiped blood from his nose. "I only watched him flailing in the water. He saw me, but I couldn't pull him out by myself."

Cuthbert's cloudy eyes widened, and his ugly, leathery face wrinkled with agony. Aelfric stared with both revulsion and pity churning in his gut. He didn't know the man was capable of sorrow.

"Where are the other escapees?" Cuthbert demanded.

"Scotland. They stole all your belongings and sailed away. I didn't steal anything."

"Then how did you have sixteen pennies to pay Lars?" asked a familiar voice.

Aelfric's eyes darted to the crowd on his left. Olaf, the carriage driver, stepped into view from behind Edgar, and Aelfric hardened his jaw. He should've known that this gossiping driver had spoken with Captain Lars. Olaf frequented Hull, while Lars had seen Aelfric's skills with the hammer. Together, the two had likely figured out the mysterious boy on the Trana was a runaway thrall.

The air around Aelfric seemed to seethe with heat.

"I earned all sixteen pennies!" he yelled. "I never stole anything. I also—" his voice broke. "I also don't have any money left. You can't get anything out of me."

"Prove that you didn't steal anything," Cuthbert said through his teeth.

There was no way to prove it, and Aelfric shivered with cold sweat. Yet, the voice of an elderly woman soon spoke from within the crowd. "This young man was our piper in Mablethorpe. He slept in our church. I never saw him with more than a daypack with some old clothes and a blanket inside. Certainly nothing worth stealing."

"He's a gifted musician," said another woman. "I gave him money, and so did my mother. He made plenty every day."

"He didn't talk much, but he was always courteous."

Someone else Aelfric couldn't see spoke to confirm these statements, followed by another and another. His pulse roared in his ears. Members of his former audience had also traveled to the Minster for Easter. He'd never see these passing strangers the same way again. If he ever returned to their seaside town, he'd play even better for them, look them in the eyes, and thank them.

Turning back to Cuthbert, Aelfric called out, "You heard what everyone said. How can you prove that they're lying? Or that I'm lying?"

Cuthbert glowered back. Next to Cuthbert, Edgar sighed with his hands on his hips. Hildred leaned over and whispered something in Cuthbert's ear. Whatever she said seemed to make his snarling face screw into one of misery. Perhaps he finally accepted that his stolen goods and thralls were gone forever.

All gone except one thrall. There was no escaping Cuthbert now, with a knight and soldiers surrounding him. Aelfric rubbed Aliwyn's shoulders and cherished this last moment between them. He had no regrets for saving her, but the way she whimpered tore at his heart.

His mind flashed to an alarming thought. Aliwyn didn't have Godwin with her when she had charged with her scissors. Not a shadow of the boy remained.

"Ali," he said. "What happened to Godwin?"

CHAPTER 18

He tilted her back to see her face, and her expression contorted with a fresh surge of tears. "I brought him to his parents, but they didn't want me. They all left the Minster. No one wants me."

The news chilled Aelfric to the bone. He stared at the ground and saw nothing. When Aliwyn wiped her eyes, he pulled her close again.

"I want you," he whispered. "Don't cry."

"I'm so scared for you..."

By the Devil's tail. Everything she hoped for had dissipated like a frosty breath. All around him, a circle of faces bearing everything from bewilderment to sympathy stared back at him. Still, no one moved to pull him and Aliwyn apart.

To Aelfric's left, Olaf dipped his chin. He placed a hand on Cuthbert's shoulder.

"Let's get back on the carriage," he said. "Royd is not coming back."

"This thrall is still mine," Cuthbert growled.

The hefty man glanced at the crowd and at Sir Marcotte, who watched everything with a tight-lipped frown. A look of unease crossed his face.

Aelfric flinched when the gathering to his right shifted. Someone was moving through the crowd from the back. As bodies stepped aside, a small hand peeked from in between the colorful dresses. A familiar voice babbled, and Aelfric broke into a grin. He withdrew his arms so Aliwyn could turn toward the sound.

Godwin walked into view, tugging on the hand of a slender blonde woman. Both she and her son shared the same round eyes, and she smiled at Aelfric.

"My name is Kendra," she said. "I'm Godwin's mother."

Aelfric gawked. Had an angel descended from the sky and changed into a simple dress, she'd probably look like this.

Kendra beckoned to someone behind her. "Osbeorn, come here."

A man with wavy black hair stepped into the center of the gathering. With his thick beard and dark brows, he didn't resemble Godwin, but the boy immediately reached for him. Osbeorn picked up the smiling child and fixed his glare on Cuthbert, who stumbled to one side.

"Aliwyn told me about you, Aelfric," Kendra said. "Thank you both for taking care of my son." She turned to her husband and shook her head. "We cannot leave these two young ones like this."

Osbeorn's frown now shifted to Sir Marcotte, who took measured steps to approach the man. The two were of similar height and build, but the Englishman had grown his hair down to his shoulders, while the Norman had shaved half his scalp. The tension between them was almost palpable, and Aelfric stiffened.

Sir Marcotte spoke first. "You asked me for permission to worship at Beverley Minster, but you never told me you were searching for your son."

Osbeorn's scowl remained. "Why would you be concerned with such details?"

He passed Godwin to Kendra, and his gaze snapped back to Cuthbert. "Enough violence on Easter Sunday. I'm setting this thrall free. How much do you charge?"

Aelfric's jaw dropped.

"One pound," Cuthbert mumbled.

"I accept," Osbeorn said. "I'll pay you before I leave for Scotland. Now leave the Minster grounds and stop disgracing yourself and your household." He extended an upturned hand toward the crowd. "Everyone here is a witness that Aelfric is henceforth a free man."

One pound was equal to two hundred and forty pence! Aelfric's mind reeled from all that was happening. Cuthbert bowed his head, followed by Edgar and his wife. They only bowed to their wealthiest customers. Perhaps Osberon's household had purchased one of the dozens of stools Aelfric had made in the past.

The former thegn wore drab clothing, but his composure still held an air of authority. He glowered at all three Staddons as they scurried toward the edge of the crowd and out of sight.

Aelfric couldn't breathe, let alone thank Osbeorn for such a priceless gift. When Kendra set Godwin on the ground, the child ran toward Aelfric and Aliwyn with his arms outstretched. Aliwyn welcomed the child and wrapped her arms around him.

CHAPTER 18

Aelfric shifted his sore body and tried again to speak, but his voice was gone. His chin quivered. The shaking soon took over the rest of him.

Aliwyn released Godwin and turned to Aelfric with a tender smile. She reached for his face and stroked his forehead with a cool hand. Aelfric squeezed his eyes shut. Panic flared as the sobs within him surged beyond his control, but he felt Aliwyn's arms extend around him. Godwin's tiny hands patted his shoulders.

Aliwyn's hold was both steady and soothing. With time, the embarrassment of crying in public faded, and Aelfric relaxed into her embrace. With every breath, he had to remind himself he wasn't dreaming.

Godwin squealed and stopped tapping his shoulders. Aelfric forced his eyes open to see the boy's mother drawing him back into her arms. Osbeorn stood behind his wife and son.

"Thanks," Aelfric croaked. His face burned with tears.

"I wish you well." Osbeorn seemed to be smiling, but Aelfric's eyes were too blurry to see well.

Kendra kneeled and kissed her son. "Say goodbye, my love."

Godwin waved a small hand, but his grin had withered into a look of confusion. He whined in protest when his mother pulled him away from Aliwyn and Aelfric.

"My dear Aliwyn," Kendra said. "It's not that we don't want you, but the journey to Scotland may take several weeks. You're already ill with bloodrot and will surely perish on our ship. I'm deeply sorry."

She turned to Aelfric. "On the other hand, it would be our pleasure to take you with us. We can leave for Scotland right away."

Aelfric's eyes rounded. "I..."

Aliwyn tensed. She withdrew her arms from around him, and her hands trembled as she wrung them in her lap. "What...an opportunity, Aelfie. You should go."

Aelfric shook his head. His stomach knotted at the sight of her ashen face. He gathered Aliwyn back against him, but she was stiff and unyielding. When she tried to break out of his arms, he only tightened his hold. Unable to speak, he frowned at Kendra and shook his head again.

Her smile was warm, but a tinge of sorrow had entered her gaze. Godwin stood before his kneeling mother and sucked on his hand.

"I understand how you feel," she said. "Blessings be upon you both."

"Kendra," Osbeorn said. "We must go now."

The man kept his eyes on Sir Marcotte, who remained standing a short distance away. Kendra tried again to collect Godwin into her arms. This time, the boy didn't resist.

"Ada, Da," he said. He no longer smiled. Maybe he understood now what goodbye meant.

Kendra stood with her son in her arms, and Aelfric grinned through his tears. He'd go to the ends of the earth to have his parents back again, but at least he had helped return Godwin to his. They seemed to be good parents, as good as Aelfric's had been, and he silently wished them a lifetime of happiness.

The murmuring crowd began to scatter, and Kendra turned to leave. Godwin looked over her shoulder, still sucking on his hand, and Osbeorn put his arm around his wife. A moment later, the family stepped out of sight. The last thing to disappear into the crowd was Godwin's wavy blond hair.

Aelfric beamed. He wanted to jump up and run in circles. He was as free as a bird! Free! Free! He could play his recorder whenever he wanted and go wherever he wanted!

Aelfric's head buzzed with the possibilities, but Aliwyn whimpered within his arms. Her shaking rattled him, and his elation plummeted at the sight of her bandaged hand grasping his sleeve. Godwin was gone. So was her dream of entering his household and finding a cure.

Sir Marcotte and his soldiers ushered the crowd back into the Minster. Many people were smiling, including Sir Marcotte, but Aelfric watched the knight warily and rubbed Aliwyn's back. What had just become the best day of his life was probably just as dismal for her as it was joyous for him.

"Ali, I'm..."

She broke into sobs. "You should've gone with Godwin's parents. I'm never going to get better."

"D-don't say that."

"I must have bloodrot. You should leave. I'm holding you back."

A sour tang flooded his mouth. His first day of freedom wasn't turning out to be what he had expected, but he'd never leave Aliwyn in this state. How in the world could he help her recover now?

Sir Marcotte turned back toward him, and Aelfric froze. Numerous stoic foot soldiers stood behind the Norman. The pepper still clinging to the men's beards made Aelfric grow hot.

Sir Marcotte approached with his hands behind his back. He smiled, but a solemnness remained in his voice.

"Normally, a thrall master is to hold a freedom feast for his newly freed thrall," he said. "But since today was so unusual, you can both come with me."

"Go with you where?" Aelfric stared up at the man. "The pillory?"

"No. To my manor house."

"I destroyed your marketplace. Why would you want me in your manor house?"

To Aelfric's bewilderment, Sir Marcotte squatted so they could see each other at the same level.

"What I saw today was remarkable," the knight said. "I'd like to speak to you. Both of you can remain in Beverley as my servants if you wish."

Servants?

Aelfric almost screamed. Servants couldn't be sold or bought like property, but never in his wildest dreams did he imagine he'd attach himself to a lord. Certainly not a Norman! At the same time, he'd never expected to be freed on English soil. His thoughts tumbled into chaos. Freedom had to be a good thing, but he didn't know what to do with it.

The Norman man didn't move, as though waiting for a response. Try as he might, Aelfric couldn't find malice in the knight's brown eyes.

"We can't refuse him, Aelfie." Aliwyn squirmed against Aelfric. "He's the lord of Beverley."

Aelfric finally released her, and she gave a quivering smile. "Let's go."

She staggered to her feet, and Aelfric forced his stiff legs to straighten. He had just stood beside her when Aliwyn's eyes rolled back. She teetered, then collapsed.

Aelfric gasped. He caught her by her upper arms and lowered her to the ground. Blood rimmed her parted lips, and a wave of chills swept through him. He rested her head against his shoulder and called her name. Aliwyn's eyes opened only to close again. His pulse racing, Aelfric turned around as Sir Marcotte stood again and waved at his foot soldiers.

"Call a cart to carry her," he ordered.

Who knew how long that would take?

"Sir," Aelfric called out. "How far is your manor house? I'll carry her on my back."

"I don't live far, but are you sure you're strong enough?"

"Yes."

Aelfric patted Aliwyn's cheek until she opened her eyes again, but her gaze was distant. The quick-witted young woman who had repeatedly pulled him out of trouble was fading. He was too distraught to thank the foot soldier who supported Aliwyn as he turned and pulled her arms over his shoulders.

Sir Marcotte furrowed his brows as Aelfric stood.

"Her case of bloodrot is advanced." He turned to lead the way. "I'm not sure what my personal physician can still do for her."

Aelfric followed, his footsteps heavy. Aliwyn's limbs twitched as her head rested over his shoulder, and he shifted her higher against his back. This was not the end for her. It couldn't be. From the recesses of his mind, Reiya's voice spoke to him again. The healer in Brocklesby practiced Vasfian medicine, something Aliwyn had never tried.

Brocklesby might be Aliwyn's only hope now, but how could he convince her to go?

Chapter 19

Aelfric

"Bald boy! You're not allowed to leave!" The Marcotte's cook tried to grab Aelfric's arm.

No one was the master of him. Aelfric dodged the man's grasp, darted out of the kitchen, and slammed the door behind him. The sun was setting over the spacious manor courtyard, and Aelfric hobbled along the shadows of the buildings on his one shoe. The one he had smacked Edgar with wasn't worth finding.

But Aliwyn—he had to find her.

Earlier that day, the Marcotte manor's bailiff had ordered two female servants to take away Aliwyn for a bath and a change of clothes. Aliwyn had been barely conscious at the time. Aelfric had thought a bath would rejuvenate her and had grudgingly handed her over. He'd wiped himself down with a bucket of water, changed into servants' clothes, and waited in the kitchen for hours.

Aliwyn had never returned to him.

Behind him, the kitchen door flew open again. The annoying man who'd tried to order Aelfric around stood at the doorway with his crooked teeth bared.

"Get back here! Sir Marcotte ordered you to stay here!"

Just because he'd been forced to wear servants' clothes didn't mean he was anyone's servant. The cook had refused to feed Aelfric because of his surliness, but he didn't care.

Aelfric pushed his knapsack higher over his shoulder. He turned left at the dovecot and eyed the jabbering men and women who carried trays upon trays of dirty platters from the Easter banquet in the Great Hall. The celebration must be over.

The manor's laundress had taken Aelfric's scarf and hat for cleaning, and a breeze tickled the bare skin of his neck. Aelfric skirted the courtyard with his back against the wall of the stable. The men who piled hay for the Marcottes' horses eyed him with various degrees of curiosity, but no one grabbed him.

What had the Norman priests done to Aliwyn? He had to convince her that Brocklesby might be her only hope.

The chapel stood at the opposite end of the manor, and its timber roof jutted upward as a triangular shadow against the bronze sky. Next to a side wall stood Aelfric's wheelbarrow; at least it was still there for him to push Aliwyn on. He turned toward the chapel and limped across the courtyard, past carts of emptied mead barrels emanating their sickly sweet fragrance.

The ground sloped upward. Soon, he'd walked to an elevation where the cemetery behind Beverley Minster appeared. Wooden crosses stretched across the land, and their shadows mimicked open graves. Aelfric shuddered. Everyone ended up in one of those one day. His mind conjured up the image of Aliwyn being lowered into a pit, and he wanted to punch himself.

The sound of people crying in the cemetery echoed to his ears. Aelfric kept walking, but his throat swelled.

Against his will, he paused to look. Men and women wearing black cloaks clustered around a cross whose wood wasn't yet black with rot. Aelfric stumbled back. Cuthbert Staddon was on his knees before that cross. Many people around him also bowed their heads in mourning, and Aelfric could guess why.

According to Cuthbert, Royd had not drowned the same night he was thrown into the well. Perhaps he had only recently died of fever and had been buried at Beverley Minster because of his wealth. Well, he had taken none of that wealth with him. Aelfric counted the people below and wrestled with the knot in his stomach. Children half his height and women

CHAPTER 19

in dark head coverings stood in between the men, and everyone wore black. They were probably all of Royd's family and friends.

Unable to look away, Aelfric dragged his feet toward the Marcotte chapel. He saw himself digging a hole closer to the shadows of the Minster and burying his family's charred belongings. The evening sun added to the burn of his face. No one was spared the pain of losing a loved one.

A moment later, he walked into a stump. Whatever had been on top went flying, and Aelfric gasped. Black and red wooden pieces scattered onto the ground before him—a chess game. Thanks to his kick, a board of polished wood had flipped upside down. From off to one side came angry shouting in French.

Blast it, of all the things he could've stumbled into! Aelfric staggered back.

Two older boys—both bearing the Norman hairstyle—came running to assess their wrecked chess game. They had been playing multiple rounds at once, and other chess boards lay on crates and stumps across the clearing.

Aelfric put up his hands and stuttered an apology. The Normans carried swords with jeweled sheaths at their waist. Who could afford such things other than nobles?

"I'm sorry," Aelfric stammered. Both boys stood a head above him in height, and Aelfric expected a punch to his face.

The shorter one of the two Normans crossed his arms. With his dark brows furrowed, he said something in French.

"I don't understand you." Aelfric backed away some more, but running would only escalate the situation. "Again, I'm sorry. I'm looking for Sir Marcotte."

That wasn't true, but they should understand one word in that sentence. The same Norman who had spoken cocked his head. He raised a finger at Aelfric, his frown lifting.

"A-Fick?"

Chills washed down Aelfric's scalp. Had the whole manor heard about him tossing up Beverley's marketplace?

He reached to tug his hood over his head, but he had nothing to hide under. "It's pronounced Aelfric. But you can call me A-Fick."

The Norman pointed at himself. "Matthieu."

"Uh... Matthew?"

The boy shrugged. "A-Fick. Matthew."

Aelfric eyed the second Norman boy, whose upper lip twitched in a snarl. When Matthew beckoned Aelfric to follow, Aelfric readily obliged. He scurried after Matthew to a large rectangular building at the edge of the courtyard, the great hall. Sweat broke at his hairline. Lord Marcotte must've been attending to important matters, and Aelfric wasn't even supposed to be outside. He resisted bolting for the chapel.

Matthew knocked on the door of the building. He turned around and smirked at Aelfric, who stood like a stunned deer behind him.

"I losing game," he said. "You destroyed. Thank you."

Aelfric blinked several times. Matthew spoke English with a thick Norman accent, but he was understandable.

"You're welcome." Aelfric forced a smile back. At least he had flipped the right chessboard.

"You stay? My foot soldier?"

Aelfric sucked in his breath. "What? Your—no, sorry. I'm not becoming anyone's foot soldier."

Matthew's smile disappeared, and Aelfric pressed his lips together. Sir Marcotte and his bailiff shouldn't have given Matthew false hope.

The door to the great hall opened, and Matthew spoke to a male servant. Aelfric scrambled for words. Sir Marcotte appeared at the doorway, and Aelfric shook at the sight of the imposing knight. The words went flying from his mind.

"My nephew tells me you were looking for me," Sir Marcotte said.

The knight wore a dark red tunic and a black cape. Aelfric stared at him, then at Matthew, and the facial resemblance between the two became clear. The realization that he had been plunged into a family of Normans punched the air out of Aelfric.

"Where is Aliwyn?" he wheezed. "I need to get her out of—I mean, take her to Brocklesby."

CHAPTER 19

Sir Marcotte said something to Matthew, who nodded once, smiled at Aelfric wistfully, and turned to leave. Aelfric watched him go. For some reason, he'd hoped the boy would stay longer.

Sir Marcotte lowered his eyes. "I don't think you can take Aliwyn anywhere with you."

"Why?"

"My priest and personal physician have assessed her. She's been moved to the Minster...and they want to perform last rites."

Aelfric's face went numb. "She's not dying."

Sir Marcotte frowned, and what felt like a rock pummeled into Aelfric's chest. He balled his hands into fists.

"She's not going to die," he repeated. "I heard there's a good healer in Brocklesby who knows Vasfian medicine. I'm taking Aliwyn there, and I need to see her."

"Watch your tongue." The servant who had opened the door narrowed his eyes.

Aelfric dug his toes into the ground. He didn't know how servants usually spoke to their Norman overlords, but they probably weren't as bold. All the same, Aelfric would never get what he wanted if he didn't ask.

"You can see Aliwyn," Sir Marcotte said. "But first, did my bailiff talk to you about serving me?"

Yes, but I don't want to. Aelfric clomped his mouth shut just in time. "Thank you for the opportunity, but who would take Aliwyn to Brocklesby if I stayed?"

Sir Marcotte stepped outside. "I'll take you to see her, and you can decide if you still want to make the journey."

"Th-thank you."

Aelfric followed the knight, nearly tripping over his feet. Was a Norman noble really taking time just for him?

"I'm sorry for disturbing you," Aelfric stuttered. "And I'm sorry about the mess I made in your town."

"I visit Beverley Minster every Sunday evening. As for the marketplace, Osbeorn covered the costs of the damage. I've sent his household safely on their way."

Aelfric lowered his eyes. He hoped Osbeorn knew how grateful he was. "That was very kind of Osbeorn. And I'm... I'm glad you let them leave."

He didn't expect Sir Marcotte to sigh. "I used to hunt with Osbeorn before his son was born."

Was that how Sir Marcotte had learned to speak English so well? Aelfric stared at him, but the knight remained solemn and didn't elaborate.

"As for the healer in Brocklesby," he said, "I've heard of her. Her name is Miriam."

"You know her? She's famous?"

"She's an expert at wound care. I know of a squire whose broken arm she fixed perfectly."

"Oh! Then she must be able to help Aliwyn."

"I wouldn't be so certain. Bloodrot is not the same as a broken arm."

Aelfric kicked the pebbles in his path. Why would Sir Marcotte discourage him from going to Brocklesby? If the knight wanted servants, he could hire any other peasant.

Aelfric wasn't giving up on Aliwyn so easily. Nonetheless, as they passed the cemetery where Cuthbert and Royd's households still stood, the universality of death began to chill him from the inside out. Aelfric crossed his arms and bowed his head.

Many people watched them as they exited the manor walls and walked for the Minster. It probably looked odd, the lord of the manor leading an English boy with almost no hair. Aelfric hurried after the knight with his arms pressed against his sides. He still tensed as he passed under the shadows of the Minster, even if the Staddons were no longer a threat.

The Minster's wooden doors featured intricate carvings of saints and angels, all painted in vibrant colors. Yet, despite the pleasing exterior, the pungent smell of blood and vinegar wafted to Aelfric's nose when Sir Marcotte opened the doors a crack.

Aelfric's stomach twisted. "Your priests and physicians didn't do bloodletting on her?"

"They did. It's a standard procedure to balance the four humors."

Aelfric almost threw up his hands. Was this the best medicine the Normans could offer? They should've known bloodrot didn't get better with bloodletting! Sir Marcotte stepped inside first, and Aelfric rushed in after him.

The Minster was as large as it looked from the outside, and the wooden vaulted ceiling was the tallest Aelfric had ever seen. Beeswax candles flickered from their stands on either side of the pews, and a central pathway led to the elevated pulpit at the front.

Aliwyn lay on her side on a mattress to the right of the pulpit, facing the entrance with firelight dancing over her sunken cheeks. A large cross kept watch behind her on the wall. Aelfric's scalp prickled, and his feet slowed to a stop. She had been so full of life when she'd chased Cuthbert away with her scissors. Now she looked dead.

It was all because of bloodletting. Heat flooded Aelfric's face, but none of the priests or that blasted physician remained in sight for him to yell at. He shook with a strange urge to bolt out of the building and find the real Aliwyn. Yet, he stared at the girl on the bed, at the bowls of water and uneaten porridge near her pillow, and couldn't deny the truth. There was no other Aliwyn.

Sir Marcotte spoke to a few men who were sweeping the floors. They bowed to him and exited.

The knight then turned to Aelfric. "You displayed great courage in choosing to save your friend today. Unfortunately, my physician has informed me she has refused to eat and drink since then."

Aelfric's chest heaved. He walked to Aliwyn, tossed down his knapsack, and sat on a stone step leading up to her mattress. Her forearm was bandaged from the bloodletting. Taking her hand, he tried not to despair at how cold and stiff she felt. Aelfric squeezed her wrist, patted her back, and called her name. No response. She was still breathing beneath her blankets, but it seemed as though she had given up. Had her refusal to drink harmed her beyond repair?

Aliwyn had been so convinced she'd find a cure. Now, he was alone in believing she'd get better—or maybe he should no longer believe. Her giggles when he had donned a gown in Mablethorpe echoed in his mind. He hadn't known what loneliness was until he'd had companionship. Perhaps it wasn't worth knowing what companionship was. Aelfric's vision blackened at the edges.

"If you still want to take her to Brocklesby," Sir Marcotte said, "know that the journey takes a full day on foot. Vasfians live in the surrounding forests, and they're a temperamental lot."

Not more talk about the Vasfians. Aelfric wanted to crawl somewhere and sulk alone, but there was nowhere to hide.

The longer he stared at the ornate crucifix, the more fiery his angst became. He had already lost his family and was about to lose another person dear to him.

"Why did you let her fall ill?" he shouted.

"Pardon me?" Sir Marcotte asked.

Aelfric's breath hitched, and he shuffled on his knees. "S-sorry. I wasn't talking to you."

Sobs surged up his throat. Could there be a worse person to cry in front of? Sir Marcotte's footsteps approached, and goosebumps formed all over Aelfric's arms.

"Are you saying Aliwyn doesn't deserve to be ill?" The knight spoke so kindly that Aelfric mustered the courage to look up.

"She definitely doesn't deserve it," Aelfric croaked. "It's not fair."

"You don't want life to be fair."

"Why?"

"If everything were fair, we wouldn't have many of our blessings, either. We don't deserve them."

Aelfric rubbed his sweaty palms on his knees. Osbeorn had paid for his freedom that very day, and it was one expensive and life-changing blessing Aelfric wasn't sure he deserved. He hadn't even celebrated. By habit, he raised his hand over the belt pouch that hid his recorder. He had not dared to touch the instrument for days, but he'd always played music with his family when they celebrated special occasions.

Now, Aelfric struggled for the enthusiasm to play anything.

Sir Marcotte walked to the closest set of candles with his head bowed. He picked up a reed and lit its tip to light another four candles. Behind those four candles stood a large golden plate with words etched onto them. Aelfric couldn't read, but he guessed the plaque featured a few names.

"Did you also lose someone, sir?" he asked. How in the world had he started talking to a Norman about this?

"My wife and unborn child, and my parents," Sir Marcotte answered. "I light candles for them every Sunday evening."

"Oh...I'm sorry to hear that."

The knight turned around. "The longer we live, the more sorrows we'll face, but also the more blessings we'll have." He smiled at Aelfric. "How you experience life depends on which you focus on."

Sir Marcotte lowered his gaze back onto the four newly-lit candles, and Aelfric grasped the outline of his recorder within his belt pouch. The melodies his father had taught him came to life in his memories, and he blinked back his tears. His family would want him to be happy, not dwell on all he'd lost. Aliwyn, too, would want him to be celebrating his freedom. He studied her tranquil face and wanted to perform for her again, even if she couldn't hear it.

"Sir, can I play my recorder in Beverley Minster?" he asked.

"Of course. I'll stay and listen."

The knight walked to a pew, and Aelfric fished out his recorder. After so many days, its worn surface felt foreign in his hand. Aelfric could scarcely take a full breath to blow. After a few false starts, however, his fingers graced over the holes on their own. He played *Kyrie Eleison*, the song Aliwyn had said she loved.

The melody poured from his heart. Aelfric perfected the vibratos and inflections in tones that characterized his music. His spirits lifted, but he wrestled with guilt for feeling content when Aliwyn was still unwell. Yet, what Sir Marcotte had said made sense; even when everything seemed bleak, he'd only be as miserable as he chose to be.

He tried his favorite techniques—playing two tones at once and mimicking bird chirps. What sounded like a symphony soon filled the Minster and reverberated within the walls. A tingling sensation rained over Aelfric's scalp and continued down his neck and spine. His father seemed to be duetting with him again in the ethereal concert, and his mother and sister sang.

Aelfric had suppressed the memories of making music with his family, but now he realized he had also locked away much joy. These moments flickered like sunlight reflecting off the ocean, never to return, but each memory shimmered in the depths of who he was.

He'd see his loved ones again in the next life. Until then, they lived within him, and he wasn't alone.

Aelfric paused his playing to settle the swirl of elation and nostalgia inside. To his amazement, the music in the Minster didn't stop. He wiped his eyes and looked up. Aliwyn's eyes were still closed, but her lips moved. She was singing, and her voice was fragile but beautiful.

Aelfric almost dropped his recorder. He wanted to pull her upright, give her water and food, and talk about Brocklesby, but something compelled him to finish his song. Their song. He smiled and raised his recorder again.

By the time he finished three repeats of *Kyrie Eleison*, over a dozen people had gathered within the Minster. They approached and placed quarter pennies at his feet, and Aelfric nodded in appreciation. The money would pay for the food and blankets he wanted to buy before his journey.

Funny how he hadn't even thought about money until now.

The last person to donate alms approached the line, and Aelfric almost screamed. Olaf the carriage driver walked up the pulpit steps, his gaze downcast, and extended his hand. His stout fingers pinched a halfpenny.

"That was brilliant," he said, glancing at Aelfric. "Good luck."

Aelfric stared at him. The air he breathed seemed to thicken. Someone cleared his throat by the Minster's entrance, and Aelfric tensed some more.

Cuthbert stood in the doorway, his arms crossed and his eyes swollen from mourning. Silence descended as Aelfric's audience shuffled out of the building. What felt like an eternity passed, and Aelfric felt a tug in his chest.

"I'm sorry about your friend, Cuthbert," he said.

The man bared his teeth. "Go watch yours rot and die."

Aelfric flinched, then rubbed his nose to hide the grimace on his face.

Cuthbert pushed open the Minster's gates and stepped out. "I need that carriage, Olaf."

Olaf patted his bald spot and followed without looking behind. Aelfric swallowed the sourness flooding his mouth.

Only Sir Marcotte and a few people remained on the pews. The knight leaned forward, his expression sympathetic.

"Some people choose to dwell in misery," he said softly.

Aelfric mustered a grin. He had done his part, and how Cuthbert responded didn't matter. The man's final curse also meant nothing. Aliwyn wouldn't die because there was still hope for her.

Putting away his recorder, Aelfric crawled to her side. Her lips were parted now, but she remained motionless. He rolled her onto her back with a shaking hand and sat her upright against him. She was limp, but she drank half the bowl of water when he raised it to her lips.

"Aelfie?" she whispered.

Aelfric gave a shaky smile.

"It's me." He spilled water as he set the bowl down. "Ali, I have to take you to see the healer in Brocklesby." He shifted her to look at her face. She opened her eyes slightly, her long eyelashes wet, then closed them again. Aelfric held his breath. He brushed back her bangs and scowled at how her forehead heated his fingers. "Can you hear me?"

"Enjoy your visit," she murmured.

"But the visit's for you!"

Her head slumped against his shoulder, and she didn't speak again. The ache Aelfric was tired of feeling intensified at the back of his throat.

Maybe it was the fever or the bloodroot and fever combined, but Aliwyn wasn't well enough to make decisions. He'd have to bring her to Brocklesby without her permission. She'd be furious with him, but he had no choice. Aelfric held her tightly and prayed for her future self to forgive him.

Shiny coins glimmered at his feet. His audience had been generous, and Aelfric had enough again for new shoes. Sir Marcotte sat on the pew with two girls. Both were younger than Aelfric, and based on their facial resemblance, they were likely the knight's daughters. Women who were probably the girls' nurses sat behind them.

They all smiled, and Aelfric's lower lip quivered. To think that he had fantasized about a rock flying toward the man's face.

"Now that she's willing to drink, ensure she gets plenty," Sir Marcotte said. "Much of her deterioration could be due to dehydration."

Aelfric nodded. "I'll follow your advice. Thank you for supporting me, sir. I'll spend the night here with Ali, and tomorrow, I'll leave for Brocklesby."

Sir Marcotte seemed to contemplate this. "I would send you away on a cart, but most of my carts are already elsewhere for Easter Monday. I need to keep my two remaining ones. Would you like me to search for a driver amongst my merchants?"

Aelfric cradled Aliwyn's fragile warmth against his chest, and his fingers traced over the contour of ribs beneath her robe. His throat knotted. What if they found another unreliable driver like Olaf? Or one who'd insult her because of how she looked?

Sir Marcotte rubbed his clean-shaven chin. "I admit it would be difficult to convince any merchant to leave Beverly until the festivities are over."

"It's all right, sir," Aelfric said. "I can push Aliwyn on my wheelbarrow tomorrow."

"You are bold indeed." The man was silent for a moment. "I suppose there is no keeping you here. The journey to Brocklesby by foot is not impossible, but it's a tedious one. You'll also have to take a ferry to cross the River Humber. I can give you money for the fare."

"Oh, yes. Thank you, sir."

"Come find me tomorrow for directions." A faint smile appeared on Sir Marcotte's lips. "If you ever want to serve me, you are welcome to return. So is Aliwyn."

"Understood. But...why us?"

"What you did for each other outside the Minster astounded me. I can teach men how to fight, but I cannot teach them loyalty and courage."

Aelfric flushed. "Thank you."

"Matthieu saw you in the marketplace today and was particularly impressed by your...let's call it agility." Sir Marcotte chuckled. "He pushed your wheelbarrow into my manor shortly afterward."

CHAPTER 19

"Really? Thank him for me."

"I will. If you return, I will assign you to Matthieu."

But life in the military was not what Aelfric wanted, and he was afraid to ask Sir Marcotte if the man had been involved in the killing up north. Even if Aelfric's role as a foot soldier was to keep the peace, he couldn't forget what the Normans had done. He squirmed and hoped Sir Marcotte wouldn't notice.

"My three children and nephew will grow up in England." The knight put his arm around the brunette girl beside him. "I hope to show your people that some Normans are deserving of their respect."

The melancholy in Sir Marcotte's gaze made Aelfric suspect the man had indeed been up north. His heart thrummed. After what he'd seen of the knight, he doubted Sir Marcotte had gone willingly. He had to follow King William's orders, after all.

Aelfric looked away. "I appreciate your offer, sir, but I can't seem to fight people."

"I'll teach you how to protect your loved ones. If you change your mind one day, return to me."

They bid each other goodbye. Sir Marcotte and his daughters stood to leave. Although Aelfric doubted he'd ever return, he'd never forget Sir Marcotte.

The men who were sweeping the Minster grounds returned to lower another mattress next to Aliwyn's, and Aelfric thanked them. He nudged Aliwyn until she was conscious enough to eat and drink. She didn't open her eyes again but finished her bowls of porridge and water. Aelfric breathed a sigh of relief.

Long into the night, he played other songs for her and set cool handkerchiefs on her forehead.

Sir Marcotte remained on his mind. Aelfric and Aliwyn's journey to return Godwin would've been for naught had the knight not granted Godwin's parents safe passage in and out of Beverley. The knight hadn't worn a helmet outside Beverley so he could show the English a vulnerable, human face. He had faith in the locals to keep the Truce of God. For the sake of building trust, he had risked his life.

If there was one Norman Aelfric chose not to resent anymore, it was Sir Marcotte. God forbid if his goodwill ever got him killed.

Aelfric became so drowsy he couldn't stop yawning, and the candles flickering around him blurred in and out of focus. He lay beside Aliwyn on a straw pallet. Watching her sleep in the warm candlelight, he prayed that her fever would break in the morning. His pulse raced despite his exhaustion. Chances were that he'd need to depart Beverley before she could agree to go with him.

Aelfric woke up twice to give Aliwyn more water, but she remained drowsy.

If she woke up in Brocklesby, would she think he had been loyal and courageous or stubborn and reckless?

Chapter 20

Aliwyn

The earthy scent of evergreens and rain stirred Aliwyn from her sleep. Someone had laid her on her left side, and a light mist cooled her cheeks. She forced her eyes open. Chicken feathers protruded from the cushion she was curled upon, and beyond that, Aelfric sat on a gnarly tree root while wrapping linen strips around his hand.

What had happened to his hand? A brisk breeze shifted the boughs around them, scattering the haze shrouding her mind. She vaguely recalled Aelfric waking her to give her water, but she had been too tired to speak.

"Aelfie?" she whispered.

He looked up, and a smile softened his scowl. "I was hoping you'd wake up. How are you feeling?"

"I...where are we?"

Aelfric's smile vanished. The afternoon shadows accentuated his sunken eyes, and her dull headache intensified. Without his hat or scarf, Aelfric looked much thinner.

"Why don't you eat and drink something first?" Aelfric stood up and reached out to feel her forehead. "Good. Your fever is finally gone."

He pulled back, and Aliwyn tensed at the sight of blisters covering the palm of his unwrapped hand. She was back on the wheelbarrow, wrapped in his cloak in addition to her own. Aelfric's hat was now on her head, and his scarf around her neck to keep her warm. His blisters must've come from hours of gripping the handles and pushing her. A weight settled over her shoulders.

"Aelfie, the bailiff said Sir Marcotte would hire you. Why did you leave?"

"That blasted physician almost killed you with bloodletting." His frown deepened. "I won't let that happen again, so I took you out of there."

Aliwyn shuddered at the memory. She had been too weak to refuse the Marcottes' physician, an aggressive man who hardly spoke English and had circled her mattress like a vulture around a carcass. Aelfric's absence during that terrifying hour had convinced her he'd never return, but she'd been wrong.

Aelfric reached underneath her shoulder and lifted her against his chest. He offered her soothing honey water from her costrel. As he adjusted the blankets behind her, she snuggled against him and tried to find the warmth that had offered her comfort before.

Yet, wheezing from within his ribcage soon reached her ears. His breathing had become labored, the way hers had been.

Her mouth fell open. Aelfric propped her against the back edge of the wheelbarrow. He coughed into his sleeve.

"I made you ill," she whispered.

"Don't worry about that." He retrieved a loaf of rye bread from a bag on the wheelbarrow and gave it to her. "My sister used to make me ill all the time. What's worse is, I have—" A grimace contorted his face. "There's something I have to tell you."

"What?"

He sighed. "You're not going to like it. We just got off a ferry that crosses the River Humber. We're halfway to Brocklesby."

Aliwyn dropped the bread despite wanting to squeeze it. Brocklesby. Fear slithered into her mind before she remembered why the name was familiar—Aelfric had mentioned it in the convent. The dense woods surrounding them seemed to close in, and redheads appeared to move in shadows.

"You're taking me to see the Vasfian healer?" she stammered.

"She's not Vasfian. She's an English woman who knows Vasfian medicine, and her name is Miriam." Aelfric shifted her so she could see his face, and his bloodshot eyes made her breath hitch. All the bruises from the Staddons' beating were now swollen and purple.

CHAPTER 20

"Whatever she does can't be demonic," Aelfric continued. "Why would she be respected if she was doing something like that? Also, the Vasfians have families too. They won't make up medicine to hurt their loved ones."

Aliwyn picked at the bandages around her hand and arm. What he said made sense; the Brocklesby healer was an English woman living in an English community, after all. Aelfric kept talking as though he had spent hours rehearsing what he should say, but Aliwyn struggled to listen.

Wounds covered his palms and who knows where else. He was ill and exhausted, but he wouldn't let himself rest. She wasn't worth all this trouble.

Aelfric's eyes had trailed to his feet. "I wanted to talk to you about Brocklesby, but you weren't fully there... Please don't be mad at me."

"You left the Marcottes so you could take me to Brocklesby?"

"No, I would've left them anyway. I don't want to be a foot soldier."

"Then what about playing as a piper in Mablethorpe again? Wouldn't that make you happy?"

His frown relaxed, and he looked up with a grin. "Oh, that's a great idea. I haven't even thought that far."

She crossed her arms over her stomach. "You can go now."

"What?"

"Just take me to the closest hospital or church. Then go."

Aelfric rubbed his nose. "I don't understand. You're *not* mad at me for taking you to Brocklesby?"

"No. I've had enough bloodletting. It's what all the English and Norman healers do, and it doesn't work." Her arm still throbbed from the incision the Norman physician had performed. "Maybe the Brocklesby healer does something different, but I doubt it'll cure me. I'm...wasting your time."

Her voice broke, and Aelfric shifted in his seat. "You're not wasting my time."

"I've caused you a lot of trouble. I even made up a disease caused by loneliness. It doesn't matter if I believed it was real, because it wasn't." She wiped her eyes. "Please go on with your life. I'm sorry for being a burden."

Aelfric shook his head, opening his mouth but not speaking, and Aliwyn's eyes grew moist again. He couldn't argue because what she said was true. She had taken so much of his money, energy, and health, and her condition had only worsened.

Aelfric grew still, the muscles of his jaw tensed. He scooted to her side.

"You're not a burden." He put his hand on her shoulder. "Let me ask you this. Was Godwin ever a burden?"

She'd never see the boy again, and she sniffled. "Of course he wasn't."

"But you took care of him day and night. You fed him and bathed him and sang to him and carried him everywhere, and he never even said 'thank you.' But remember how he made you feel." Aelfric looked away, his eyes brightening, and Aliwyn held her breath.

He turned back and held her gaze. "How Godwin made you feel is how you make me feel, so stop calling yourself a burden. It hurts me when you do that."

He didn't hide his sorrow, and Aliwyn's heart quivered. She reached for the hand he had placed on her shoulder and grasped his fingers. Aelfric smiled. He extended his other arm behind her, gathering her up from the wheelbarrow and against him in a warm embrace. Aliwyn hugged him around the neck and breathed the scent of wood smoke from his tunic. The strength of his arms reassured her.

"And I don't think you made up a disease caused by loneliness," he whispered in her ear. "It's real. It was choking me from the inside out until I found you and Godwin. I'm glad I did."

It was wonderful to feel his chest rise and fall against her own. Aliwyn smiled through her tears. She'd lost everything that she thought made her worthy before experiencing the truth—she'd never had to prove her worth at all.

"I'm glad I met you, too," she said, sliding her hand over his shoulder blades.

"Maybe Miriam is just the person to help you. Don't give up, all right?"

"All right, Aelfie…"

They were both silent until Aelfric coughed again. Aliwyn let him go and thumped his breastbone.

"We should enter the closest village," she said. "You need a hot meal."

"The closest village is Brocklesby." Aelfric cleared his throat and smiled. "I overheard the bailiff talking about this special shortcut that the Norman troops use." He pointed at the closest tree trunk. "See the circle with the line through it? These trees mark the fastest way to Brocklesby."

Aliwyn hadn't noticed the round symbols on the birch nearby until Aelfric spoke. The sight of tree trunks with sap oozing from their marked sides sent chills down her scalp. Those marks represented the Vasfian's reverent gesture to their god, Lenus.

Her head spun. Aelfric had pushed her into the heart of the Vasfian forests.

She turned back to his merry face and grabbed his arm. "Aelfie, we can't take this route. We're not Norman soldiers, and we don't have an alliance with the redheads. They'll shoot us!"

He blinked several times. "I thought we were not fighting over the Vasfians anymore."

"I'm not fighting, but we must return to the main road. The Vasfians kill trespassers!"

"I don't know anything about the main road, but doesn't it circle the forest? It'll take us much longer to walk to Brocklesby."

"Please, Aelfie." She struggled to keep her voice down. "We can't stay in these woods."

Her pulse raced until she gasped for breath. Aelfric had been a thrall who'd never experienced the brutality of the Vasfians, but she knew better. She squeezed his arm until he jerked himself free.

"Fine," he muttered. "I hate arguing with you."

Aelfric shot to his feet and rounded to the back of the wheelbarrow. He hoisted it up, and Aliwyn fell back onto her cushion as he began pushing. They sped into the thicket. The trees whipped past in a blur of green and brown, and the wheelbarrow barreled over roots and rotting leaves from last year. He was angry, and she chewed on her lip until it tasted raw. Was he defending the Vasfians because he wanted to be fair to everyone, or was it something else?

"What did that Vasfian woman tell you?" she called out.

"Who? The one at the convent?"

"Yes. Did she try to trick you into visiting her tribe? They're headhunters, you know? Their doorways are covered with skulls from—"

"Enough, Aliwyn!"

He no longer called her by her nickname. Aliwyn sank back onto her cushion with angst swelling in her throat. A long time passed, and the wheelbarrow veered onward. She shivered with the air slicing through her clothes, and jealousy wormed into her mind. Back at the warming house, Aliwyn didn't have to look at that Vasfian girl for long to see that she was tall and beautiful.

Each flash of bronze sunlight through the branches increased her anxiety. The night was descending, and Aelfric had not found the main road. Reason told her they were lost, but she was afraid to speak.

They entered a small clearing with a stream, and Aelfric's footsteps slowed to a halt. He set down the wheelbarrow and coughed. Aliwyn strained to turn around. The longer he coughed into his sleeve, the redder his face and neck became. She was sorry they had argued, but everything she'd said about the Vasfians was true.

Aelfric drained the rest of his costrel. Panting, he slumped on the ground beside her.

"I don't know where we are." He clutched his hands in his lap. "I thought the main road was to the east, but it wasn't."

Aliwyn stared at his hands and the blisters he tried to hide. Her body was stiff with fear, but there was no use in showing it. She straightened her sore knees and hung her ankles over the side of the wheelbarrow.

"You didn't mean to get us lost," she said. "Can I bandage your hands for you?"

"Who cares about my hands?" he snapped. "We're lost, and it's getting dark. I can't even find the shortcut anymore." He turned on his seat with a sweep of his arm. "None of these trees have the symbol!"

His voice echoed through the woods, and Aliwyn shuddered. Yet, yelling at him to be quiet wouldn't make him quiet.

"We may have to spend the night outside, but so be it." She spoke as calmly as she could. "Whatever happens now happens. You and I can still refill our costrels and eat something. Maybe we'll think of a way out."

She fought against the dread roiling within. There was no way out unless a path to Brocklesby opened before them. They couldn't start a fire tonight for fear of alerting the tribes; without a fire, they'd freeze. Wolves might attack them in the pitch blackness.

Maybe she should've let him take the Norman shortcut, but it was too late now.

Aelfric hung his head and said nothing. The whip mark he bore curved down his neck like a pale serpent. Now that he was finally free, he had entered another predicament for her sake. She slid out of the wheelbarrow and wanted to walk to his side, but her legs folded beneath her.

Aelfric looked up, his face gloomy. "What are you doing? You can't walk."

His voice was hoarse but quiet. When he scooted closer, Aliwyn hooked her arm around his and silently prayed for their safety. Her mouth was too dry to shape the words. Aelfric's breathing grew even again, and he tilted his forehead against hers.

"I'll rinse my hand in the stream over there," he said. "Then you can bandage it. I think I can trace my way back to the shortcut if I focus."

He paused as though waiting for her to protest, but Aliwyn didn't have the energy anymore. She let go when he pulled back, and Aelfric rubbed her back for a moment.

His face was flushed. The bruises spreading over his nose and forehead were so ghastly she was afraid to look at him.

Aelfric walked to the edge of the clearing, where the creek trickled past stones covered in moss. A dimming sunset silhouetted the peaks of evergreens. Aliwyn shivered all over. She hated the sight of him departing into the shadows alone.

He squatted to dip his unwrapped hand into the water, and soft whistling stirred through the trees overhead. The whistling peaked in intensity like a chorus of birds, and a chill crawled up Aliwyn's spine. She recalled where she had heard it before—the day she and her mother had collided with Vasfians crouching around a corpse.

Her vision tunneled. "Aelfie, run!"

He had just stood again when an arrow flew toward his torso. Aelfric spun aside and landed on his hands and knees.

"Run!" she shrieked.

The Vasfians had found them. She'd die tonight. Aliwyn kept screaming for Aelfric to run, but he scrambled back to his feet and bolted toward her. More arrows whipped past his body, and a few soared in her direction to pierce the trees behind with a loud thwack. The forest spun and faded out of focus. Aliwyn squeezed her eyes shut. She slammed her hands over her ears.

A moment later, Aelfric's footsteps pounded next to her knees. He lifted the wheelbarrow and flipped it over her huddled body. Aliwyn gasped as blankets and the cushion tumbled over her.

"Apisai!" he shouted.

What was he doing? Aliwyn writhed within the stuffy confinement and pushed the cushion off her face.

She peered through the space between the wheelbarrow and the ground. Aelfric stood a short distance away with his hands up. Four Vasfians approached, each wearing a painted wooden mask with holes for eyes and antlers affixed to the upper corners. They aimed their crossbows at Aelfric but no longer fired. One flick of their finger, and he'd fall dead.

He needed to run! But he didn't run, and Aliwyn couldn't speak through the strangling sensation in her throat.

"Apisai," Aelfric repeated. With a shaking arm, he circled his hand around his forehead as though tracing a crown, then brought his hand over his chest.

He just did the Vasfian greeting. Aliwyn's heart lodged in her throat. Who had taught him this?

"I'm looking for Reiya of the Mehi tribe," he continued. "She told me about a healer in Brocklesby. I'm taking my friend to see her."

This Reiya must've taught him the greeting. The redheads made no reaction, and Aliwyn wanted to burst. Finally, one of them—a woman—spoke in the Vasfian tongue and pointed at the wheelbarrow. She gestured by lifting an upturned hand.

"You want to see my friend?" Aelfric asked.

Aliwyn stiffened all over. Goosebumps prickled her neck as Aelfric lifted the wheelbarrow. She was on her side with her legs gathered to her chest. When Aelfric pulled her to sit up, she almost screamed. He smelled of blood. Her vision refocused on the horizontal gash along his chest, splitting his brown tunic in half. The arrow had injured him, after all.

"I'm sorry," he mouthed, his expression stricken.

She covered her mouth with her hand. Now Aelfric knew she had been right all along. He'd learned his lesson about the Vasfians, but what was the point of condemning him now?

Aliwyn pressed her arm over his wound and clung to him. The memory of him spinning away from that arrow devastated her. Worse than death would be to watch Aelfric die. If the Vasfians killed them now, may it be a quick ending.

But they did not kill her. They each lit a torch and leaned menacingly close with their fiendish masks. Tears streamed down her face. Aelfric kept his arm around her shoulders, and the Vasfians paced and talked nonsensically. What felt like an eternity passed. The terror storming within gradually gave way to a numbness that drained the strength from her limbs.

One Vasfian lifted her mask. Aliwyn jolted to her senses. Half the woman's face was painted blood red, and the other half was smattered with freckles.

"Abithi." The woman placed a hand on her chest. "Mother of Reiya."

Few Vasfians spoke English. Aliwyn gawked at the frightening face, but Aelfric's posture softened as he supported her.

"Pleased to meet you." His chest rose and fell.

There was no pleasure in meeting any of them, and Aliwyn squirmed. Had Aelfric forgotten how they almost killed him?

"We take to Miriam." The woman, Abithi, pointed to a rocky outcrop rising to their right, somewhere the wheelbarrow had passed before but couldn't traverse.

One of the Vasfians retrieved a blanket from her knapsack. They were going to carry her. Aliwyn recoiled from their piercing green eyes and tried to hide her face, but Aelfric held down her arms.

"Thank you so much for your help," he said. "Again, I'm sorry for trespassing."

Anger surged within Aliwyn before she could understand it. She bristled when Aelfric lowered her onto the Vasfians' blanket. The redheads held onto one corner each, ready to carry her away. Aliwyn's body throbbed. She couldn't move despite screaming inside, and she lay gasping and sobbing.

"Ali, I'll walk right beside you," Aelfric said. "Don't be scared."

He reached down and brushed her hair with his hand. The metallic scent of blood wafted over her. Had it not been for the sight of his ripped tunic, she would've swatted his hand away.

Pleased to meet you? Thank you for your help? What was wrong with him, talking to his almost-murderers like this? The Vasfians pulled up the blanket's corners and engulfed her in darkness. Aliwyn locked her arms around her stomach and couldn't stop crying.

"I'm here, Ali," Aelfric said. What must've been his hand touched her back from outside the blanket.

But angst had overtaken her fear. Aelfric hadn't learned his lesson after all. His attitude toward the redheads remained the same. These Vasfians must have some agreement with Miriam and had spared them for her sake. Just because they didn't kill this time didn't mean they were to be thanked, trusted, or welcomed. Their true intention had been made clear by the first arrow they'd fired—they wanted Aelfric dead.

Aliwyn's dark confinement swayed back and forth as the four Vasfians walked. Aelfric was stubborn to a fault. Loud and quick-tempered. He rushed in recklessly to help others, including her. One day, he might leave for an impossible mission and abandon everyone who loved him.

Aliwyn turned onto her side and buried her face in the blanket. Her chest seized repeatedly at the memory of Aelfric's bloodied tunic. Losing someone she cared about was worse than dying, and she had lost so many already.

Maybe she had begun to love Aelfric, but she couldn't afford to be with someone who lacked prudence.

Still, when he coughed, her arms jerked with the yearning to embrace him again. The top of his head came in and out of view over the edge of the blanket. He remained nearby, as he'd promised.

When the Vasfians paused to readjust their grip, she felt Aelfric's hand move along the length of the blanket until it came across her writhing fingers. He pressed against her hand until the blanket moved again.

Aliwyn chewed on her lip. She had been wrong to be jealous of that other girl. Aelfric had made mistakes, but he had become the best friend she could've asked for.

Her mind drifted into a haze. She soon couldn't remember the name of the Vasfian girl, and neither did she want to.

Time would tell what had happened between her and Aelfric. If the Normans managed to uphold peace for a few years, he might grow out of his brashness without getting hurt. The knot in her throat began to loosen. She could keep him close to her so he wouldn't go charging out into the unknown. Growing up in a thrall's cabin hadn't taught him how to behave like a proper peasant, but she could guide him.

All this depended on if she survived. What would the woman in Brocklesby do to her? Aliwyn pressed her hand against the blanket in hopes she'd feel Aelfric's presence again. The blanket was smooth this time, but he had to be walking alongside her. That was enough. Aelfric wouldn't let the Brocklesby healer hurt her.

Memories from her time spent with Aelfric and Godwin resurfaced in her mind, followed by all the Christmas celebrations she had spent with her family. Aliwyn steadied herself. She had lived through moments of great joy, and physical death was not the worst thing that could happen to her.

But she wasn't ready to go yet. Closing her eyes, she could once again hear Godwin and Aelfric snickering in the barn in Swine. She smiled, and her anxieties lifted.

Please, Lord. Please give me more time with Aelfie.

With time, Aliwyn fell into a dreamless sleep.

Chapter 21

Aelfric

AELFRIC DRAGGED HIS FEET after the Vasfians as the sky darkened and a faint moon appeared behind the wispy clouds. Distant flute music, drums, and chanting echoed in his ears. He must've trespassed during one of the Vasfian festivals—another reason the tribe had wanted to kill him.

His chest wound had dried, but it stung without ceasing. He deserved it after almost getting himself and Aliwyn killed. Taking the Normans' shortcut had sounded like a great idea when he'd overheard the bailiff discussing it with the English foot soldiers. Now Aelfric understood why Sir Marcotte hadn't even mentioned it.

Abithi led the group to the outskirts of the forest, where a lake glistened under the moonlight. A vegetable garden dotted with seedlings stretched from its sodden banks, and Aelfric's boots sank into the mud with every step.

The Vasfian leader paused and brought her whistle to her mouth. Standing tall, she blew a call that sounded like twittering birds, and Aelfric and the others shuffled to a stop behind her.

Abithi turned to Aelfric, her expression calm.

"Call Miriam," she explained.

He nodded and mustered a smile. Abithi looked much like her daughter, Reiya, and seemed to be far less bloodthirsty than the Vasfians in Aliwyn's stories. Had she not been willing to give him and Aliwyn another chance, they'd both be dead.

Aelfric felt again for Aliwyn's hand through the blankets. He hadn't meant to put her through such a scare. She no longer writhed like before and was hopefully asleep.

Abithi gestured at Aelfric's chest and blistered hands. She said something he didn't understand, but the worry in her eyes said enough.

"Please worry about me later," Aelfric said. "I'm glad you understand English."

"Reiya talk of you," she said. "Blane?"

"Uh…"

He had lied about his name back in Saltfleet, and Aelfric's face grew heated. Abithi cocked her head but didn't press him for an answer. They began walking again past the garden.

"Amah! Blane!" A voice shouted from behind him.

Aelfric turned to see Reiya running toward him with her braid flying behind her back.

"Hello," he croaked.

"I heard a whistle that someone was hurt!"

She held her mask by her side. Half her face was painted red like the other Vasfians. Reiya stopped before her mother and performed the greeting gesture.

"Amah," she said, bowing slightly.

She and her mother exchanged a few sentences before Reiya turned to Aelfric with her brows knit.

"What were you thinking?" she hissed. "It's the Festival of Eostre. No villager enters our forest during our festivals! And my mother thought you were poisoning our sacred spring."

"No. Not at all. I wanted to wash…" Aelfric extended his blistered hands, his voice choking. "I'm sorry, I didn't know. I grew up with thralls, and my name isn't Blane."

That was probably more than he should say at once, but Aelfric couldn't think straight.

Reiya narrowed her eyes. "Your real name is Aelfric, isn't it?"

He almost toppled backward. "How do you know?"

"A group of men rushed into the Saltfleet convent right after you left. They were looking for a runaway thrall named Aelfric and his two companions, a girl, and a small boy." She grinned and arched a ginger eyebrow. "The Norman nuns couldn't understand anything the men said. So, I told them I never saw you and sent them all home."

Aelfric swallowed several times. It had been a close call. Reiya could've told them he and the others had just left for the quays. "Th-thank you, Reiya."

"You're welcome. My people don't keep thralls, and we disagree with..." Her voice trailed off as her eyes descended to his tunic. "Kaba Lenus! You were shot!"

This time, Aelfric lowered his gaze and remained silent. Reiya fingered the tear on his clothes, making it sting some more. A sob swelled behind his ribs. He had been shivering for a long time without a cloak, but he'd been afraid to say anything and even more afraid of how he and Aliwyn had almost died. Every flashback seemed more terrifying than the first.

What if Reiya had never taught him the Vasfian greeting? What if bandits had attacked them instead? Aelfric didn't know how to fight.

Reiya took off her fur cloak and wrapped it around Aelfric's shoulders. She began tying the laces to hold it in place.

"I'll have Miriam look at your wound," she said. "It seems to be a shallow one. You were lucky."

Her cloak warmed him and smelled of wild roses, but Aelfric was too choked to thank her. He tried not to sputter onto her face.

"What about Aliwyn?" he wheezed. "Is she going to get better?"

"Your friend? Let's catch up with the others. Miriam is very good at what she does." She turned to lead the way, then paused and frowned at him. "Are those men still after you?"

"No." Aelfric's new reality lifted his spirits, and he smiled despite everything. "Someone set me free."

As the two of them strode after Abithi, he told her what had happened on Easter Sunday.

CHAPTER 21

The sloping thatched roof of a watermill rose in the distance. Behind it, across a ravine, a village protected by wooden ramparts rose on a gentle hill. Columns of smoke drifted from the various homes surrounding a large manor house. That settlement must be Brocklesby, and Aelfric quickened his pace. Strangely enough, the mill stood outside the ramparts and was easily accessible to the Vasfians.

Abithi and the others had lowered the blanket before the watermill as though waiting for the door to open. To Aelfric's surprise, a slender woman approached quickly from the side of the building.

"I'm sorry to keep you all waiting. Twyla just gave birth to a beautiful girl!" Wiping her hands on her apron, she beamed at the gathering before her home and adjusted her headscarf. "I'm here now. How can I help?"

Aelfric walked the remaining distance to Aliwyn's blanket and pulled Reiya's cloak tighter around himself. After all the anxiety that had gripped him tonight, the woman's joy made no sense to him. Was she Miriam?

She looked at the bundle of blankets at her doorstep, then at Aelfric, and her smile grew sympathetic. The Vasfians withdrew, exposing Aliwyn's face, and he squatted by her side. Her eyes were closed, but she was beginning to stir.

The watermill woman kneeled by Aelfric. "My name is Miriam. And yours?"

"My friend has bloodrot," he said. "What do you give for bloodrot?"

"Nettle tea and rosehips mixed with honey."

"What?" Aelfric jerked back. "You just give tea and sweets?"

"Yes, my dear. It's so simple that many refuse to try it. And what's your name?"

Her gentle tone was in such contrast to his that Aelfric looked away, his face burning. He had been too fixated on helping Aliwyn. "My name's Aelfric and my friend's name is Aliwyn."

"Aelfie?" came a soft voice by his knee.

He turned toward Aliwyn and smiled. Her light blue eyes glistened, and she looked alert.

"Did you hear that?" Aelfric nudged her shoulder. "Miriam treats bloodrot with things that taste good."

He didn't expect Aliwyn to smile but was glad she did.

"No bloodletting, please?" Fear returned to her gaze, and she looked at Miriam for the first time.

"No, I never perform bloodletting." Fine lines formed around Miriam's eyes as she smiled, and strands of wavy blonde hair flowed from her head covering. She brushed Aliwyn's cheek with the back of her hand.

"I just need to examine you and ensure you don't have something else," she said. "I'll ask your friend to wait outside for a moment. Is that all right with you?"

Aliwyn gazed at Aelfric, who pressed his lips together. Finally, Aliwyn turned back to Miriam and nodded.

Abithi and her companions moved to pick up the blanket again, and Aelfric rolled back on the ground. Now warm thanks to Reiya's fur cloak, he wanted to sink into the earth; all of him felt so heavy. The watermill door opened and released the scent of lavender and thyme. A hearth glowed within, and the Vasfians carried the blanket into the watermill. A short while later, everyone except Aliwyn and Miriam exited, and the door shut again.

The river powering the mill trickled with an occasional groan of the waterwheel. Aelfric's eyes drooped shut, but a hand soon patted his back.

"Aelfric," Reiya said. "You didn't say anything about your wound."

"I want her to see Aliwyn first," he mumbled. *By the Devil's tail.* He shouldn't fall asleep yet.

Reiya circled until she faced him, and Aelfric struggled to keep his eyes open. She watched him with her lips pursed, a strange mix of frustration and pity. Unease crept into him. She was treating him like Aelfric's sister once had, but he barely knew her.

"Do you want your cloak back?" he whispered.

"No. But I can look at your wound if you want. I'll fetch some supplies from the watermill."

Her voice was kind. Aelfric decided against questioning her for ulterior motives or asking how he could repay her. He simply nodded.

Reiya knocked on the watermill door. "Miriam, can I fetch a few things for Aelfric?"

When Miriam agreed from within, Reiya opened the door a slit and slipped through. Too late, Aelfric remembered why this wasn't a good idea.

Screaming erupted within the watermill, and Miriam struggled to calm the terrified girl. Aelfric covered his face with his hands. Even after the Vasfians had carried Aliwyn all the way here, she still saw them the same way.

Reiya returned with a bucket hanging from one wrist and a jar clenched in her other hand. Scowling, she shut the door behind her.

Aelfric gazed at the torn blisters on his right palm. "Sorry about that, Reiya."

She squatted before him and sighed. "I'll just stay away from your friend from now on."

Reiya directed Aelfric to lean against the side of the watermill. Lifting aside the cloak he wore, she dabbed his wound with what smelled like soured wine from the bucket. Aelfric's eyes watered from the heightened burning. Yet, what pained him more was knowing Aliwyn still resolutely hated the Vasfians. She refused to see anything good about them.

"Reiya." His voice shook. "Why is Miriam...so nice to you all? She's English."

Reiya picked pine needles off his tunic. "Many years ago, Miriam ran into my mother's forests carrying a baby boy. It was during a winter storm, so my mother took them in."

"Oh, really?" Any distraction from the fire on his chest was welcome. "A baby...her baby? How old is he now?"

Reiya grew still, her expression somber. "Kaba. Forget what I said. I wasn't supposed to tell you that."

"Why?"

"It's something Miriam never wants to talk about. The boy's gone."

Aelfric's heart twinged. "Oh, I see. I'll...I'll be quiet about it."

"I'd appreciate that, Aelfric." She smiled and changed the subject. "Now that you're a freed thrall, where do you want to live? How about Brocklesby?"

"I don't know. I doubt Aliwyn would want to stay here..."

Because of your tribe, he thought. He held his breath when Reiya gave him a blank stare.

"She matters a lot to you, obviously," she murmured.

Aelfric swallowed until his mouth was dry. He'd better avoid mentioning Reiya's name to Aliwyn.

Reiya cleaned his blisters, dumped out the soured wine, and fetched water from the stream that powered the watermill. She dabbed his wounds again with fresh water. Aelfric could hardly keep his eyes open as she dressed his wounds with ointment from the jar.

By the time he came to his senses, Abithi and two Vasfian women had left. Two remained with a torch each, and both had removed their masks. Reiya sat beside him against the watermill, wiping her deer-head mask with a handkerchief.

Aelfric admired the red and green checkered pattern of her dress. All the Vasfian women wore leggings, boots, and a robe that ended at their knees. It gave them flexibility of movement, but the cut was much too short by village norms. Aelfric blushed without wanting to. For some reason, he had yet to meet a Vasfian man.

"Reiya," he said. "You don't have to stay. You can join your family for the festival of...uh..."

"Eostre." She smiled. "It's an ancient festival celebrating spring. Then the priests took the name of our goddess and came up with 'Easter.'" She shrugged, then lowered her voice. "Anyway, I want to stay. My people value loyalty, and you never abandoned your friend. You're still one of us, even if we keep it a secret."

Aelfric smiled, but his pulse quickened. The more time he spent with Aliwyn, the more likely she'd uncover his secret.

"If you leave Brocklesby, where will you go?" Reiya asked.

Before he could answer, the watermill door opened. The hearth within silhouetted Miriam's frame in gold.

"You can come in now, Aelfric. Your friend does have bloodrot, but you brought her here in time. She should recover."

Aelfric inhaled deeply at those words. "You...you're sure?"

"I can't promise anything in medicine, but I've helped other patients with worse cases of bloodrot recover."

"How long will it take?"

"A few weeks. I'll send her home with the treatment to take three times a day."

Neither he nor Aliwyn had a home, and Aelfric lowered his eyes. "Thank you, Miriam. How much will everything cost?"

"Pay what you want, dear."

"I don't have anything. We also don't have a home." His teeth chattered with the wind. "Aliwyn and I are both orphans. I was a thrall, and I was just freed yesterday."

"Oh, what a wonderful Easter gift." Miriam exited the doorstep of her home. Her brows knit, and she seemed to study the scar on his neck and the wet patch on his tunic.

"I cleaned his wounds," Reiya said. "Please give him some bandages, Miriam."

Miriam nodded, then placed her hand on Aelfric's shoulder. "You and Aliwyn can both stay with me while she recovers."

"Really?"

"Yes. The Brocklesby church is already full of orphans, and I know what it's like not to have a home."

Aelfric smiled, his chest tight. What would Aliwyn think of this? "Th-thanks. I promise to help you when I can."

He leaned toward Miriam, and she placed her hand on his back. They walked to the mill. She was a kind person and probably the age of Aelfric's mum. Was she widowed and had never remarried? Maybe one day he'd ask her.

Reiya had not asked for her cloak back. Before Aelfric reached the door, he turned to see her holding the mask with her eyes lowered. *See you tomorrow, Blane?* Her voice echoed in his mind. He remembered her disappointment when she heard he'd leave England. Well, he'd never left.

"Reiya," he said. "See you tomorrow?"

Her expression brightened. "Not tomorrow, but my mum trades with Miriam every Sunday by the lake. I can come next Sunday to meet you."

"Then I'll see you Sunday." Aelfric took off her cloak and offered it back. "Thank you for everything tonight."

Reiya's smile grew. She accepted the cloak, but Aelfric sighed as she departed with her two companions. Miriam and the Vasfians met on the outskirts of the forest, far from Brocklesby, for a reason. If he kept Aliwyn and Reiya as friends, he'd have to see them separately every time. It was more than he wanted to think about.

He expected Miriam to open the door, but her hand remained on his back.

"Thank you for your openness toward Reiya. She is trying so hard to change the way we perceive Vasfians."

"I know," he mumbled. "It must be discouraging."

"It's not easy, but change takes place one person at a time."

Aelfric turned her words over in his head as she opened the mill's door. Maybe Reiya hoped he'd stay in Brocklesby so she could have his support, even if he was only one person. He'd have to seriously consider staying here, but would Aliwyn agree to it? He'd have to talk to her once she felt better.

Aelfric followed Miriam into a warm, smoky mill. The aroma of salted cod, garlic, and leek pottage wafted around him. Bundles of herbs hung from the sturdy wooden beam of the corner kitchen, and the hearth washed the walls in amber. In his wildest fantasies, he had dreamed of entering a home like this without Cuthbert ready to whip him outside.

It was no longer a fantasy, and his throat swelled.

He was searching for Aliwyn when her voice came from above. "Miriam, Aelfric has a cough and maybe a fever. Please take care of him, too."

Aelfric looked up. The watermill featured a second floor that didn't completely cover the first. Aliwyn lay on a mattress on the second level, close to the railing, with her eyes shining in the firelight. She looked safe and comfortable up there, finally.

CHAPTER 21

A hand stroked his ear, and Aelfric turned to Miriam. She placed her hand over his forehead. "Indeed, you're starting something. Come and sit, Aelfric. Are you hungry?"

He nodded and smiled. She reminded him of his mum, who was of similar age and always worried he might be hungry.

"I thought you might have an appetite." She smiled back. "I've warmed up some leftovers. Let me tend to your wounds first, then I'll serve you."

Aelfric's mouth was already watering.

Miriam led him to the dining table, where she bandaged his hands. She took his dirty tunic and soaked it in a bucket. After she'd bandaged his chest, she passed him a clean tunic.

Aelfric pulled it over his head and tugged on the sleeves. The length was perfect, and the width had been tailored for a boy of his size.

"Who did this belong to?" he asked.

"Oh…I took care of a boy with a broken arm for many months. He outgrew these clothes before he left." Her voice wavered. "He played the recorder, like you."

Her eyes fell on his belt, which Aelfric had laid on the table. His recorder once again protruded from his drawstring pouch.

Maybe Aelfric could duet with the other piper boy. "Does he live in Brocklesby?"

"No. I wanted to keep him as my apprentice, but his father had other plans for him."

She picked at a dull stain on her sleeve, and Aelfric shifted in his seat. Miriam looked and sounded very different when she was sad.

"Does he come to visit sometimes?" Aelfric asked. "I'd like to meet him."

She sighed. "He must be busy training for knighthood now. It has been around three years, and he has never visited."

Aelfric scowled at the shadows behind her, a sudden resentment twisting his gut for this other boy. How could he ignore or forget someone as tender-hearted as Miriam? She must miss him if she'd kept his clothes for years. But maybe the other piper had his reasons. Aelfric didn't want to condemn someone he'd never met.

"I can play my recorder for you tomorrow," he offered.

"Thank you, dear, but only when you feel better."

At least he had made her smile again.

With her brown gown fluttering above the dirt floor, Miriam walked to the cauldron over the hearth and served him a bowl of pottage. Aelfric tried not to slurp his food too loudly, but the chunks of tender, salty cod mixed with herbs were irresistible. Miriam watched him eat and chuckled.

"Aliwyn already had a bowl to eat. The leftovers are all yours tonight."

"Thank you." He wiped his mouth, his cheeks flushing. She was kind *and* an excellent cook.

Aelfric had one more helping of pottage before they walked for the stairs together. Miriam carried a bowl of mint and ginger tea for his cough, and Aelfric glanced at her with his scalp tingling. She felt familiar and comforting, like someone he'd known for years.

"Do you live alone here?" he asked as they ascended. "It's a big place."

"As fate would have it, yes. I prefer not to marry."

His eyes rounded. "Really? But why? I'm sure many men would want to marry you."

Miriam laughed. Her merry voice filled the mill, and her blue eyes sparkled. "You have a lot of questions, don't you?" She gave Aelfric's ear a playful tug. "We'll have a few weeks together to talk."

She turned to lead the way, and Aelfric followed with a sheepish grin. Miriam seemed to support herself without a husband, but it was too bad she had no children of her own.

The air grew warmer as they reached the second floor, where Aliwyn lay on a mattress large enough for two people. A worn wooden chest stood in the corner, but the place was otherwise unfurnished. Aliwyn opened her eyes and rolled onto her back when Aelfric sat beside her. He reached for her hand, covering it with his own, and they smiled at each other. Miriam opened the chest's creaky lid and retrieved linens from inside.

"Where will you sleep?" Aelfric asked.

She placed folded linens on the mattress to serve as his pillow. "There's hay in my storage room. I can make do for tonight."

"What about tomorrow night?"

"We'll worry about tomorrow, tomorrow." She patted his forearm. "You can lie down now, Aelfric."

If he stayed and worked odd jobs, he could buy wood and make her a new bed frame. Aelfric lay down and suppressed a cough. Miriam placed the tea close to his head and pulled a blanket over him. Firelight danced on the thatched roof behind her, and his body sank into the fluffy chicken feather mattress.

"Thank you so much," he whispered.

Miriam beamed and tucked the blanket under his shoulders. "My pleasure. Good night, my two young ones."

She descended again, and Aelfric's heart raced. Was she still looking for an apprentice? He didn't know how good he'd be with herbs and medicine, but he wanted to stay.

Aliwyn snuggled against his shoulder. "I really like her."

"Me too. I heard she tried to keep an apprentice once, but the boy had to leave. So, maybe…"

Silence for a moment.

"You want to stay here?" Aliwyn whispered. Uncertainly had entered her gaze.

Aelfric understood her hesitation. In Brocklesby, the Vasfians would be their neighbors.

"I do want to," he said, "but we'll talk about it later. You need to sleep, and we haven't visited the village yet. Are you excited? I don't have to hide my face anymore."

Her face melted with a smile, and his chest fluttered. A wave of heat shimmered down his back. Was this the fever?

"If you go, I'll go," she said. "Thanks for staying by my side, Aelfie."

"You did the same for me." He grinned. He'd never forget her courage outside the Minster, when she'd faced the Staddons and silenced everyone who watched.

They bid each other goodnight, and Aliwyn closed her eyes. He once again tried to picture her without any bruises or scratches. She had an endearing, heart-shaped face. To think he had almost lost her because of his stupidity.

His mind raced on with flashes of his near death in the forest. He pledged to be more careful with his decisions and to learn how to use the sling or another weapon to protect himself and others. Someone in Brocklesby must be able to teach him.

Scenes of his last week seemed to appear in the moving shadows of the ceiling. Godwin's face came and went. So did the images of Godwin's parents, Wulfstan, Reiya, and Sir Marcotte. Aelfric had not met all of them willingly, but he was grateful now that he had.

What was Godwin doing right now? Could he be sitting on his mum's lap, listening to her sing as their ship sailed north? Was he grasping his father's finger and smiling into his eyes as rushlights illuminated their faces? Aelfric's vision blurred. He missed the boy. Godwin wouldn't remember him, but maybe one day, his parents would tell him about a certain Aelfric and Aliwyn. Aelfric closed his eyes and wished the family a safe journey to Scotland.

People said miracles happened at Beverley Minster. Wonderful things had happened to Aelfric there, although he recognized the good in them only in retrospect. They weren't the miracles he had expected; they were better.

He was safe now, next to his best friend, and free.

With Miriam humming downstairs, he watched Aliwyn sleep and prayed she'd recover quickly from bloodrot. This time, a soothing reassurance washed over him. Miriam knew what she was doing, and so did his Father in Heaven. He trusted them both. It mattered more whose hands guided him than what his troubles were, and whether he found them fair or unfair.

Adventures awaited him in England. He was thankful he'd never left.

Aelfric fell asleep with his face turned toward Aliwyn.

Epilogue
The First Dance

Aelfric

Three days after Aliwyn began Miriam's remedy, she could walk again with help. Aelfric's fever left him, and he couldn't stop looking at Aliwyn and how she was coming back to life.

The first time she stepped out into the sun, he picked her up and twirled her in a circle. Aliwyn laughed. Two weeks later, a brightness returned to her eyes, and all her wounds healed. It was a miracle.

Aelfric eagerly introduced himself and Aliwyn to the peasants who came to grind grain at the mill. Miriam took her two patients to visit the garden by the lake, where Aelfric played music for them both beneath the evening skies. Aliwyn talked little but told him she felt at home with Miriam. Aelfric felt the same.

Miriam accepted Aliwyn and Aelfric as apprentices three weeks after they'd met. The Brocklesby bailiff recorded their names in a registry, and Aelfric couldn't have been happier to have a home.

Identifying herbs and mushrooms was difficult, but he kept trying. He followed Miriam during all her patient visits except when she visited women—Aelfric practiced his new sling instead. He and Aliwyn also joined the farmers in the fields and adjusted gears within the watermill when not studying medicine. Aliwyn speared eels with great skill and supplemented their dinner table with much-needed food.

Spring passed into summer. Aelfric befriended the blacksmiths, the baker, the wheelwright, and the carpenter's families. He attended holy day feasts in the Brocklesby marketplace and played his recorder alongside the town bards. Watching the couples dance made him eager to try it himself, but there was a problem—Aliwyn never attended festivals, and Aelfric didn't feel like dancing with another girl.

One sunny afternoon, two weeks before his fifteenth birthday, Miriam left alone to visit an expectant mother. Aelfric mustered the courage to invite Aliwyn to an upcoming holy day as she rinsed her fishing spear in the stream beside the mill. She wore one of Miriam's beige headscarves, and her brown hair fell gracefully to frame her face.

"Aliwyn," he said, his hands behind his back. "The feast of Saint Barnabas is tomorrow. Want to visit the marketplace with me today?"

She looked up from her bare feet. "Why go today if the feast is tomorrow?"

"Because—" He tried to swallow the ball in his throat. "The musicians are practicing today, and the villagers are dancing already. So it's a good time to...to..."

"To what?"

"Can you teach me how to dance?" Warmth flooded his face. "You must know how, right?"

Aliwyn straightened and wiped her hand on her apron. He may as well have asked her to cross the ravine on a tightrope; her expression would've been the same.

"You want me to teach you?" She shook her head. "With all those strangers watching?"

"They're not strangers anymore, and today isn't the real festival. There won't be as many people."

"I thought Miriam asked you to prepare twelve poultices before dark."

Aelfric rubbed his eyes. He'd hoped she wouldn't remember. "I can do that later. The musicians are playing *now*."

Her scowl didn't change, and Aelfric's shoulders sagged.

"You know how I feel about festivals," she said softly. "The villagers aren't strangers to you anymore, but they are to me. And you need to start the poultices now, or you won't finish all twelve before dark."

Aliwyn jabbed her triple-pronged spear into the stream even though it was already clean, and Aelfric rolled his eyes.

"Why don't I take you to visit all the families in Brocklesby?" he asked. "Then they won't be strangers."

"Not today."

"There's been at least five feasts in Brocklesby, and you've been to none of them."

"I don't like festivals. You know that."

"Are you ever going to like them?"

Silence. She frowned at the bucket of dead eels by her feet, and a dull ache began pulsing at Aelfric's temples.

"You're going to live a terribly boring life, you know that?" He turned and trudged back to the mill.

The wheelwright's daughter had already asked him twice to dance. He had said no, but telling Aliwyn that wouldn't change anything.

Aelfric carried several bundles of dried plants outside to identify them under the sun. He yawned as he crumbled dried flowers and mushrooms onto linen squares. Medicine was becoming tedious, but he had already agreed to be Miriam's apprentice.

An hour later, he was lying on his back and staring at the clouds. Funny how a brief talk with Aliwyn had made him question whether settling in Brocklesby was a good idea. What if he never enjoyed medicine as much as carpentry? He missed using his hands and building things, but Brocklesby already had enough carpenters.

Maybe Reiya would help him feel better when he met her this Sunday.

Aelfric heard Aliwyn shuffling his way. A fishy odor often announced her arrival, and this time was no different. Eel guts now stained her apron.

"Do you need some help with the poultices?" she asked.

Aelfric frowned at her upside-down face as it hovered above him. "You're not supposed to help me. This is my assignment."

"Aelfie, I never said I wouldn't go with you to the marketplace, only that you should finish your poultice pouches first. How about we go when the bells strike Vespers?"

Vespers meant sunset, and Aelfric sighed. "The music would be over. And I'm not in the mood to go anymore."

He rolled back up and returned to the scattered plant bundles, hoping Aliwyn would leave him alone. She only stood there as he picked up two plant stalks, one with narrow leaves and the other with broad leaves. Which one was comfrey again? And would Aliwyn go away already? Sweat beaded at his hairline.

"The one in your left hand is—" she began.

"Don't tell me!" he shouted, spinning around.

Aliwyn turned on her heel and left. Aelfric scratched his eyebrows with both hands until they burned. He had struggled with recipes and made mistakes every week, whereas Aliwyn seemed to memorize everything with ease. She was talented at fishing, too, but he only astounded everyone with his appetite. Today, all the resentment and guilt he had tried to bury finally erupted.

He was the one who'd wanted to stay in Brocklesby. He should apologize.

Aelfric forced himself to finish tying up the poultices. Once done, he dragged his feet to the watermill door and pushed it open.

"Ali—"

"I'm changing!" she cried from upstairs. "Stay outside!"

Aelfric whirled around and almost tripped. No one bothered to knock in the thrall compound full of men. His face flushing, he sat beside the mill and hung his head between his knees. A bucket of water sloshed within the mill. Before long, Aliwyn's footsteps pattered down the stairs.

She stepped outside in a faded blue dress. Aelfric glanced at her, then did a double-take. She'd never worn that gown before, and the colorful woven belt around her waist accentuated her curves. After gutting eels all afternoon, her face was rosy and radiant.

Aliwyn giggled. "Why are you staring? This is just Miriam's old dress."

"Uh... I like your belt."

"Thanks. It's the one you saw me weaving last week. I wanted to wear it to the marketplace."

He blinked. "We're going?"

"Yes, it's almost Vespers. I told you we'd go."

She smiled, but redness rimmed her eyes. He'd probably made her cry, and Aelfric's stomach dropped. He stood up slowly.

"I'm sorry for yelling at you," he said. "I'm not good with herbs the way you are."

"You're doing your best, Aelfie." She patted his elbow. "You're already much better than two weeks ago."

A strange tingling sensation spread down his shoulders and back. Sometimes, the tingling also happened when he and Aliwyn sweated alongside each other on the fields. He was probably not drinking enough water.

Aelfric smiled and followed her lead.

The two of them crossed the stone bridge that led to the Brocklesby village. Water gushed in the gorge below them, but no music echoed from within the town walls anymore. The dancing was over, and Aelfric sighed. What could he do with Aliwyn now? Watch the manor lord's servants hang garlands from the rooftops? Still, he didn't want to discourage her now that she'd left the mill for once.

The church tower and the manor house rose above the timber ramparts, and the soldiers guarding the town gates nodded in greeting as they entered. Donkey carts milled past them along a dusty road that circled the town periphery. Ahead lay a grassy slope, dotted with sheep, that led to the market square.

To his surprise, Aliwyn grabbed his wrist and pulled him onto the road after a cart full of hay.

"What are you doing?" he asked. "The market isn't this way."

"Oh, but I enjoy taking this route."

Behind the rear of a donkey? Aelfric raised an eyebrow but decided against arguing.

Aliwyn hurried on, and Aelfric tried not to inhale the donkey's stench. She pulled him left at the blacksmith's workshop, where he frowned at the counters devoid of people and the neglected fireplace. All the smithy tools had disappeared, and the workshop's door was ajar. The entire scene made him nervous. Aelfric was just about to pull Aliwyn closer to him for safety when—

"Surprise!" a boy swung the door open.

"Happy birthday!" cried another voice to his right.

Aelfric staggered and spun in a circle, but Aliwyn only snickered. Behind the sooty counters, the blacksmith's children and the baker stuck out their heads and laughed, all wishing him a happy birthday. Aelfric beamed and ran to hug them one by one.

"Why the surprise today?" He clapped the baker on the back. "My birthday isn't for another two weeks!"

"Yes, but he won't be here in two weeks."

Aelfric turned toward Miriam's voice. She appeared from behind the smithy, and beside her walked a familiar man with a brown beard.

"Wulfstan!" Aelfric's chest heaved. "Is that really you? What are you doing here?"

He bolted toward the man to hug him, but Wulfstan's pristine, embroidered tunic made Aelfric conscious of his stained clothes. Aelfric wiped his hand on his thigh and offered a handshake instead. Wulfstan had a firm grip.

"Happy birthday, my lad," he said with a smile. "I'm Lord Benoit Seville's bailiff now. He sent me to Brocklesby, and Aliwyn recognized me right away."

"Really? Aliwyn doesn't leave the mill much." Aelfric searched for her, but she had disappeared from his side.

"She spotted Wulfstan during one of our midwifery house calls," Miriam explained. "This surprise was her idea."

Aelfric grew still. It made sense now, why she had tried to keep him home all afternoon. He would've visited the blacksmith and his other friends before the celebration was ready. Aelfric sighed. Where was Aliwyn now? He wanted to find her, but couldn't turn away from his guest.

"I'm so happy to see you, Wulfstan. You said you're a bailiff now?"

"Yes. I reported Mablethorpe for failing to meet certain obligations, and its town charter was revoked." He stroked his beard and lowered his gaze for a moment. "Lord Seville now governs the area. He kept me as the bailiff of Mablethorpe."

"Mablethorpe had its share of problems, all right. Do you like your work better now?"

"Yes, and I'm recruiting servants for Lord Seville." Wulfstan grinned. "You've earned yourself a good reputation, Aelfric. Sir Marcotte and Lord Seville are friends. I was told to visit Brocklesby first."

Aelfric's breath caught in his throat. "But I'm Miriam's apprentice already. I don't want to leave."

To his relief, Wulfstan placed his hand on his shoulder. "Then I'll recruit someone else. I'm overjoyed to see you free and doing well."

He explained how he'd had to follow the militia to the Saltfleet convent to avoid appearing suspicious. Thankfully, Aelfric had already left, and a redheaded woman had directed the militia elsewhere.

Reiya. Aelfric was silent for a moment. He was only free and doing well because many people cared about him. Unable to resist, he walked into Wulfstan's chest and wrapped his arms around the man's broad torso.

"Thanks, Wulfstan," he said.

The bailiff returned his embrace with a strong arm. "Blessings, my boy. And I should thank you, too. It may sound odd, but after I saw you defend Aliwyn with only a bucket, I found the courage to report the town's corruption."

They smiled at each other, but Aelfric felt Aliwyn's absence at that moment. This crowd must've overwhelmed her even though she had planned for it. He'd better find her.

He and Wulfstan parted so the bailiff could mingle with other guests. The baker's wife and sister spoke with Miriam; everyone was chatting and joking. Children were already serving themselves berry tarts displayed upon colorful linens. The town bard snapped his fingers in the air to catch Aelfric's attention—it was time to play some festive music. Aelfric held up a finger to give himself more time.

He excused himself from the gathering and retraced his steps along the dirt road. His lone shadow stretched across the ground. Outside his vibrant little celebration, the workshops were largely closed, and the streets deserted.

"Aelfie?" came Aliwyn's voice.

He found her pressed against the wheelwright's cabin with her arms around her stomach like she was in pain. Aelfric shook his head.

"Miriam said you planned the surprise. Thank you so much." He reached for her arm. It was hard to act cheerful when her face was gray.

"It wasn't hard to plan, but I had to make sure you stayed at the mill until Vespers." She gave a quivering smile. "I didn't mean to upset you."

"It's not your fault. I was being awful to you."

He gathered her into his arms and rocked her slightly from side to side, cherishing the warmth of her forehead and how her hair tickled his chin. She still smelled a bit like fish, but he didn't care.

"I want to enjoy the crowd." She breathed in jerks. "I just can't. I'm sorry."

"It's all right, Ali. I know you tried."

She snuggled against his neck. Every night, she'd massage ointment over the scar on his neck, which had become smoother and less visible each week. Thanks to all the eels she'd fed him, he had grown taller since he'd arrived in Brocklesby. Aliwyn had been a blessing to him every day.

Her heart raced against his own, and her slender body relaxed into his arms. The tingling started down his back again. He slipped his hands around her waist. And then it struck him—he wanted to stroke her soft cheeks and kiss her.

Aelfric's stomach flipped. He was taking things too far. Aliwyn still didn't know he was half Vasfian, and she'd be furious if she knew.

He pulled back and convinced her to at least watch him perform for the celebration. Leading her by the hand, he walked with her back to the gathering, where Aliwyn stood stiffly at the periphery. Aelfric played his recorder alongside a lutist and drummer, but his mind was elsewhere. The rest of the night was a blur. Everyone danced except for him and Aliwyn.

The feeling of being an imposter haunted him. He had only told one person who he really was, and she wasn't in attendance.

EPILOGUE

The following Sunday, Aelfric and Miriam met the Vasfians by the lake to trade flour and eggs for honey and dried mushrooms. Aliwyn, as usual, stayed home. Aelfric lingered after the bartering to spend time with Reiya. She had given him a sling and taught him how to use it. They usually competed to see who could strike a bean bag off the branches first—him with his sling or her with her crossbow.

Today, Aelfric could barely load a rock. Reiya beat him four times.

"Something's wrong." She cocked her eyebrows.

"Yea," he mumbled. "Really wrong."

"Something to do with Aliwyn?"

"How did you know?" Aelfric took a deep breath. "I... I want to court her."

Reiya laughed in his face, and his eyes rounded. "Why is it funny?"

"It took you this long to realize you liked her?"

"So it's funny now?"

"Fine, fine, not funny." She waved a hand. "But go on, why is it so bad that you want to court her?"

"Because. If I were to marry her, all our children would be part Vasfian. I can't..." His throat clogged. "I can't do that to her, but I'm also too scared to tell her the truth."

Reiya aimed her crossbow at the bean bag above them.

"It's that important to you that you tell her about your Vasfian ancestry?"

"Yes. I want my future wife to accept me for all of me."

"Well, then." Reiya let loose an arrow, and the bean bag dropped to the ground. "Why dwell on Aliwyn? Why not court someone else who won't care about the Vasfian blood in you?"

Aelfric's nostrils flared. She was so practical, so *right*, that he didn't want to hear it.

"There are plenty of other girls in Brocklesby and in England," Reiya continued.

"I don't want to be with other girls."

"How about treating Aliwyn like your sister? That way, you two could still be close."

Aelfric tilted back as though she had tried to slap him. "You're not helping. I can't marry my sister!"

"Well, you say you can't tell Aliwyn the truth without losing her. I agree. So what else can you do?"

He shuffled his feet. "I don't know."

"She can also choose to marry someone else," Reiya said. "Or reveal your secret to the world if you tell her."

"She wouldn't do that." He was shuddering in cold sweat now. "You know what? I'm leaving."

Reiya's expression fell, and Aelfric struggled to settle the anger surging within him. At least she was frank. She wasn't giving him any false hope.

"See you next Sunday," he forced himself to say.

"I'll be here as usual," Reiya said, smiling. "Aelfric, one last thing."

"What?"

"A bailiff paid my mother recently so that he could take the route through our forest. He's staying for two weeks in Brocklesby to recruit servants for a certain Lord Seville. Maybe you should talk to him."

Wulfstan. Aelfric felt no urge to tell her he had already met the bailiff.

"Why should I talk to him?" he asked. "I don't want to leave the mill."

"Two reasons." She held up her fingers as she counted. "One—you don't seem happy picking at plants."

Aelfric gritted his teeth.

"Two—if this situation continues between you and Aliwyn, I think you'll want to leave. She's extremely stubborn and will probably never change her mind about our people."

The last statement pierced Aelfric with grief. All the frustration drained out of him, and he had barely the energy to speak.

"Goodbye, Reiya."

He trudged back along the lake's muddy banks, and Reiya called after him.

"Good luck, Aelfric." She added in a softer tone, "You know I care about you."

EPILOGUE

Aelfric inhaled slowly. He turned around one last time and waved at her. Reiya smiled back as she sat on a stump with her red braid hanging over one shoulder and her crossbow at her side.

Recently, she had told him she was seventeen years old. Aelfric had begun to see her as an older sister, and one pretend sister was enough.

The two of them agreed to meet again the following Sunday after trading was over.

AELFRIC RETURNED TO THE watermill as the sun slid behind the rolling hillside. Aliwyn stood in the clearing before their home with hens and chicks pecking nearby. She once again wore Miriam's faded blue dress, and Aelfric averted his eyes. Maybe it was a good thing they'd never danced that night; he might have just lost control, kissed her before a quarter of the village, and thrown himself onto a path he wasn't prepared for.

She hurried toward him with the gown trailing over yellow buttercups. "Aelfie, are you all right? Did the Vasfians give you any trouble?"

"No, not at all."

"Why were you gone so long?"

"I practiced shooting my sling." He tried to wipe the sour look off his face. Yet, one thought remained on his mind. "Ali, can you please come with me and Miriam to meet the Vasfians next week?"

She stiffened, her footsteps coming to a halt, but he pressed on. "Maybe one day Miriam and I will both fall ill, and you'll have to trade with them."

Aliwyn hardened her lips. "If you're both unwell, I'll just buy from the market."

"Please. They...uh...have some mushrooms and herbs the markets never have."

Aelfric didn't know where to hide his flushing face. After a moment of silence, Aliwyn closed the distance between them, and her expression softened. She placed a hand on his upper arm.

"All right, Aelfie. For the sake of our patients, I'll go with you and Miriam next Sunday."

"Thanks," he croaked. He couldn't tell her how much that meant to him, and Aliwyn stared with her brows drawn in sympathy.

"But I have to add...I'll just trade and leave," she said.

He nodded. That would already be better than no interaction at all.

Aliwyn stroked his sleeve with her thumb. "Are you still sad about not dancing during your birthday celebration?"

He'd better give a reason for tearing up. "I guess I am."

"What if I taught you how to dance this evening? We don't need music."

He swallowed several times. "You mean it?"

"Yes." She smiled. "Happy fifteenth birthday to my best friend."

He wanted to be more than her best friend, but he'd have to settle for that for now. Aelfric managed a grin back at her glowing face. "Thanks. This has been my best birthday yet."

Aliwyn took his hands and counted in sets of four, showing him the steps she'd do and how he could match her. The chickens clucked and circled them. As hues of gold and pink brightened the edges of clouds overhead, Miriam came out to sing as Aliwyn continued to show him the movements of both her arms and feet.

Aelfric couldn't focus. He stumbled several times, but he didn't care. Aliwyn beamed and seemed entirely at ease. He began to see what kind of person she was before the rebellion, and he blushed. She never lost patience, no matter how badly he danced.

He'd do his best to be patient with her. Maybe in six months, she'd get over her resentment of the Vasfians, and he'd tell her the truth about himself. If she accepted him, he'd court her in hopes of marriage.

But what if three or five years passed, and she was still the same? Aelfric didn't know how long he could wait. He tried not to worry.

When a half-moon appeared in the darkening sky, Aelfric and Aliwyn called the chickens back into their coop behind the mill. A flock of wood pigeons flew overhead as they returned to the front door. Miriam had kindled the hearth inside, and smoke drifted from the corners of the roof. She stood smiling at the opened door of their home.

Aelfric took Aliwyn's hand and led her inside.

Reviews

Reviews are the lifeblood of indie authors. They encourage us to keep writing and help our books get discovered.

Your review is unique and so greatly appreciated!
Please consider writing one for *The Thief's Keeper* on Amazon, Goodreads, and/or Bookbub.

For a list of sites where you can leave reviews, please visit
KyrieWang.com/leavereviews
Thank you!

Aliwyn, Aelfric, Reiya, and Matthew return in *Healer's Blade (Enemy's Keeper Book 1)*.
All available books of the *Enemy's Keeper Series* can be found at
books.kyriewang.com

I'd love to keep in touch! Feel free to email me at Author@KyrieWang.com

Receive a free ebook of **The Thief's Keeper** *(An Enemy's Keeper Prequel)* when you subscribe to my newsletter!
KyrieWang.com/EK

****

Bonus: **A free medieval fantasy coloring book and a graphic novel, The First Dance (An Illustrated Epilogue of The Thief's Keeper)**
Once a month, I send a newsletter with book giveaways, raffle prizes, new character art, historical tidbits, and more!

Author's Note

I outlined *The Thief's Keeper* while mourning the loss of two friends whose funerals were on the same weekend. Aliwyn's story and happy ending were my way of imagining a different outcome for my friends. Of all the stories I've written since elementary school, *The Thief's Keeper* provides the most commentary on my struggles with my faith in God as I grappled with loss and the "unfairness" of it all.

The fragility of life and society's focus on the divine in the Middle Ages made it the perfect setting for my creative outlet. Other themes began to emerge—the fact that loneliness is a timeless plight we all face from time to time and how the most valuable things in life are not bought. I adored weaving together Aelfric and Aliwyn's story.

I hope their story inspires readers to be grateful for every blessing in life, great or small. Aelfric, Aliwyn, Reiya, and Matthew return in *Healer's Blade* (*Enemy's Keeper Book 1*).

Alternative History and the Vasfians

The Thief's Keeper takes place in a re-imagined, alternative medieval world where the Celts, the last Vikings, the Anglo-Saxons, and the Norman knights coexisted.

While many details of daily life in AD 1070 England are historically accurate, I created the Vasfians based on peoples such as the Celtic Britons, who inhabited England before the Anglo-Saxons arrived. I enjoyed incorporating elements of their culture, such as the Celtic god Lenus, into this story.

Beverley Minster

Beverley Minster was originally established during the 8th century. The present Minster, built of stone, was constructed in AD 1220-1425, and we do not know what it looked like during the time of my story. Most likely, it was made of wood.

The minster is named for Saint John of Beverley. Saint John's reputation and the reported miracles that happened after his death made the Minster a prestigious sanctuary as well as a prime destination for pilgrimages. In my story, even William the Conqueror spared the Minster during his murderous Harrying of the North. This is historically accurate.

The story goes like this: King William had sent Thustinus, one of his most ruthless men, to loot Beverley Minster in Yorkshire and drag out the people who had taken refuge in there. But, the moment Thustinus approached the altar, St John struck him off his horse with a blinding light. All his limbs swelled up, and the impact rotated his head in a full circle.

William the Conqueror decided that what happened to Thustinus was "celestial intimidation," and he wisely decided to leave Beverley's sanctuary alone.

Source:

Oliver, George. *The History and Antiquities of the Town and Minster of Beverley, in the County of York, from the Most Early Period: With Historical and Descriptive Sketches of the Abbeys of Watton and Meaux, the Convent of Haltemprise, the Villages of Cottingham, Leckonfield, Bishop and Cherry Burton, Walkington, Risby, Scorburgh, and the Hamlets Comprised Within the Liberties of Beverley*, pp. 65–67

Medical Notes

Bloodrot is a fictional name I've given to scurvy, an illness caused by a vitamin C deficiency. It's inspired by the Chinese term for scurvy, *huai xue bing*, which literally means "bad blood disease." Scurvy was not understood in the 11th century, and there is scant historical evidence of how English peasants referred to this illness.

Scurvy was particularly prevalent during the Age of Exploration when sailors were often unable to access fresh fruits and vegetables for months at a time. In my story, I hypothesize that scurvy would've affected English villages during the Harrying of the North—a widespread destruction of towns and villages perpetrated by William the Conqueror over the winter of AD 1069-70.

During winter, peasants such as Aliwyn would likely have been in a state of subclinical vitamin C deficiency while awaiting spring. Common medieval methods of conserving fresh fruits and vegetables for winter, such as boiling, would have largely destroyed the vitamin C content. The famine following the Harrying would only have worsened existing nutritional deficiencies. Aliwyn had subsisted on low levels of vitamin C in whatever foods she ate until she met Aelfric, but it wouldn't be until she took therapeutic doses that her illness could be reversed.

Unfortunately, the turnip and liver she ingested before meeting Miriam were boiled into stew and slurry, ensuring that most of their vitamin C content had been destroyed.

Miriam's remedies of sun-dried (not boiled) rosehips and nettle leaf tea are both cheap and accessible foods high in vitamin C. Through trial and error, she and the Vasfians would've concluded that these foods cured "bloodrot" despite not understanding disease pathogenesis.

As an author, I found it most fascinating that the symptoms of such a debilitating disease (extreme fatigue, for example) can improve in as little as 24 hours following vitamin C intake. Patients can experience dramatic reversals in their health in just two weeks. Such an improvement from eating simple foods would've been especially dramatic to people like Aelfric in the Middle Ages. It is the principal reason I wrote about scurvy in *The Thief's Keeper*.

Scurvy continues to afflict refugees, people on fad diets, and hospitalized patients. It is far from being a thing of the past and remains a diagnostic challenge for physicians today.

Sources:

The World Health Organization. *Scurvy*.

Stephen R, Utecht T. Scurvy identified in the emergency department: a case report. *J Emerg Med*. 2001 Oct;21(3):235-7.

The Thief's Keeper Audiobook

Relive the adventure with a 100% human-narrated audiobook!
Wishing Shelf Book Awards- Finalist (Best Young Adult Audiobook)

It's free on Hoopla and streams at no extra cost for Spotify Premium members.
For a complete list of retailers, including Audible and more:
Books2read.com/TheThiefsKeeper

About the Author

By day, Kyrie is a medical sleuth (also known as a pathologist, MD) in a small mining town in Quebec, Canada. By night, she scrawls story inspirations on various notebooks by her bed. These eventually become novels with medical intrigue sprinkled throughout!

She has been writing fiction since age nine and has always been fascinated by the tales of loyalty, redemption, and sacrifice from the Middle Ages. Few things excite her more than attending medieval fairs and cheering for jousting knights.

Her character-driven stories feature nuanced protagonists, riveting adventure, forbidden romance, and ordinary people who discover extraordinary courage from within. When she's not writing, she enjoys Zumba dancing and cycling with her husband and daughter.